A Sweetbrook Family

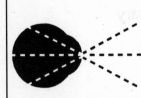

A SWEETBROOK FAMILY

ANNA DESTEFANO

THORNDIKE PRESS
A part of Gale, Cengage Learning

GALE
CENGAGE Learning·

Detroit • New York • San Francisco • New Haven, Conn • Waterville, Maine • London

GALE
CENGAGE Learning®

Copyright © 2012 by Anna DeStefano.
Originally published as A FAMILY FOR DANIEL
Copyright © 2005 by Anna DeStefano.
Thorndike Press, a part of Gale, Cengage Learning.

Thorndike Press® Large Print Clean Reads.
The text of this Large Print edition is unabridged.
Other aspects of the book may vary from the original edition.
Set in 16 pt. Plantin.

LIBRARY OF CONGRESS CATALOGING-IN-PUBLICATION DATA

DeStefano, Anna.
    [Family for Daniel]
    A Sweetbrook family / by Anna DeStefano. — Large Print edition.
        pages cm. — (Thorndike Press Large Print Clean Reads)
    "Originally published as A FAMILY FOR DANIEL"—T.p. verso.
    ISBN-13: 978-1-4104-5847-6 (hardcover)
    ISBN-10: 1-4104-5847-4 (hardcover)
    1. Families—Fiction. 2. Love stories. gsafd 3. Large type books. I. Title.
PS3604.E764S94 2013
813'.6—dc23   2013005566

Published in 2013 by arrangement with Harlequin Books S.A.

Printed in the United States of America
1 2 3 4 5 6 7 17 16 15 14 13

To the blessings of family.

To love's defiant victory over the toughest of life's challenges.

CHAPTER ONE

Life stinks sometimes.

That's what Daniel's psy . . . psychol . . . That's what the stupid doctor his uncle made him talk to said. Life could stink, for kids most of all. But when you get through the bad stuff, Dr. Steve said, there's a world of good things waiting on the other side.

Just wait and see.

Life will get better.

Trudging down the hallway of White Elementary School, headed for the principal's office for the second time that week, Daniel rolled his eyes. *Dr. Steve* didn't have a clue.

Daniel had to get out of this place. But where? Where did he have to go? Back to his uncle's home? There was only there or here, which left Daniel exactly where he'd been for the last four months.

Nowhere.

Forget Dr. Steve.

There was no bright side just around the corner.

Daniel's mother was dead. His chest heaved from the sharp pain that came, even as he shoved the memory aside. His dad had split years ago, never to be heard from again. Living in Sweetbrook, South Carolina, with his uncle wasn't working, no matter how hard Daniel tried.

Life stinks. Period.

He turned left at the end of the hall and shuffled into the bustling school office. His sneaker caught as he stepped from the tiled floor onto carpet. Arms and legs flailing, he managed not to fall on his face. Barely. But now every person in the room was staring at him, when what he really wanted was to be invisible.

"Have a seat." Mrs. Lyons pointed to the ugly couch the kids called death row. "Principal White's expecting you, but he's on the phone."

Mrs. Lyons had worked here for over forty years, he'd heard. She'd worked here when his uncle was in elementary school. Rumor had it his uncle had done his own time on death row. Maybe she'd pointed that same bony finger at him. Maybe she'd stared him down like he was trouble, too.

Probably not. What could his perfect, by-the-book uncle have done to match the mess Daniel made out of school every day?

He dropped onto the couch and gave Mrs. Lyons his best glare. He kept right on staring, until she looked away. He knew exactly what she was thinking. What they were all thinking — the teachers and everyone. He'd heard them talking when they didn't think he was listening. He'd seen the looks on their faces, just like the one on Mrs. Lyons's now. And he hated them all. Hated their nosey questions, the way they pretended to understand. . . .

He's always been such an angry little boy. . . . But he could be such a good student. Before his mother's accident, he was starting to settle in. . . . It's just so sad! And his poor uncle . . . can you imagine trying to deal with a troubled child he barely knows on top of everything else?

What did they know?

What did he care?

"Daniel." The door to the principal's office opened. As usual, the man was wearing freshly pressed dress clothes, plus the frown he didn't even try to hide from Daniel anymore. "Ready to step inside?"

Daniel decided staring at his shoes was a better plan. Not because he was afraid. He wasn't afraid of anything in this nowhere town. Adults found unresponsive kids annoying, Dr. Steve had told him, and being annoying suited Daniel just fine today. He reached a finger down to tug at the hole in the trashed sneakers his uncle had forbidden him to wear to school.

"Daniel? In my office. Now."

Principal Joshua White shut the office door as ten-year-old Daniel threw himself into the guest chair that was practically his second home.

Shrugging off a wave of discouragement he couldn't afford, Josh rounded his desk, giving the scared, defiant kid dressed in jeans and a dirt-smudged T-shirt his space. Josh remained standing as he reread his notes from the phone call he'd just concluded with Becky Reese's grandmother, Gwen Loar.

Becky and Daniel had mixed it up in class again today, and according to their fourth grade teacher, Mrs. Cole, Becky had instigated their latest tussle. Then Daniel had taken things way too far, as usual. Before Mrs. Cole could intervene, the confrontation had escalated into classroom warfare, complete with the kids throwing anything they could lay their hands on at each other.

Josh and the girl's grandmother had

discussed Becky's role in the altercation, trying to formulate a plan for better settling her into her new school. For compensating for the fact that a month ago Amy Loar had shipped the little girl off to live with Grandma, so Mom could dedicate 24/7 to her career in Atlanta.

Amy Loar.

Josh's memory produced an image of his childhood friend. Dazzling in white, her auburn hair a soft cloud of tousled curls, she was smiling at him from across the dance floor at their senior prom. Somehow she'd blossomed from his pal since kindergarten into the most beautiful girl in the room. A girl he'd suddenly wished he hadn't wasted so many years being *just friends* with.

After graduation, they'd left for their separate colleges, and their friendship should have slowly faded away.

If only it had been so simple.

Amy had always been ambitious. Growing up poor in the South had left its mark on her, and she'd been determined to do better. To be better. To ensure that she and her mother never again went without anything they needed. He'd always admired her beauty, brains and ambition. Right up until the moment she'd produced a big city fiancé who Josh had known instinctively was all wrong for her.

And how had he handled the situation? He'd done the unforgivable, made a jerk out of himself, and they hadn't spoken since.

She'd achieved her success, he'd heard. She'd carved out the dream life she'd wanted. Except her wealthy husband was out of the picture now. And as far as Josh could remember, being divorced and a single parent to boot hadn't been part of Amy's plans.

He refocused on his young visitor, shoving aside the unwanted trip down memory lane. It was April in South Carolina, and the kids in school were beside themselves with spring fever. All of them but this child. A study in shaggy blond hair and intelligent green eyes, Daniel sat sprawled in his chair, digging at the monstrous hole in the toe of his right sneaker. No doubt waiting for Josh to make the first move, so the kid could ignore him some more.

Well, let him wait a little longer. Nothing else had worked. Not exactly what they taught you at principal school, but it was worth a shot. Josh continued to flip through his notes, still standing.

"So?" Daniel finally sputtered, making eye contact for the first time.

Josh sat as if he was in no particular hurry to get to the point. He exchanged Becky Reese's file for Daniel's even weightier one. He didn't have to read through his notes. He knew Daniel's issues by heart: the struggles to conform and get along in the classroom; the confusion; the emotional explosions that so quickly built from simple disappointments. And the kid internalized each failure, each bit of negative feedback, making it that much more difficult for him to try the next time.

"So." Josh braced his elbows on the desk. "You and Becky got together this morning and decided to toss your classroom?"

Daniel shrugged and picked some more at shoes that looked like last year's Salvation Army rejects. "She started it," he mumbled.

"Someone else always does."

Josh shifted his shoulders, shrugging off the lingering weight of his own personal failures. The guilt still remained from the mistakes he'd made the last few years. The relationships he hadn't been able to save. But he was learning to let the past go and focus on making the best of now.

At least that was the plan.

But helping a child as angry as Daniel understand that loss and crushing defeat were just part of the game was a different story. What could he say that wouldn't sound like a bunch of psychological hooey?

Welcome to the club, kid. Life bites. Get used to it.

He gave his head a mental thunk.

"We've talked about throwing things in the classroom," he said. "We can't keep you with the other kids if we have to worry about one of them getting brained with a book —" he flipped through Daniel's file "— or your backpack. Or your shoe —"

"I didn't hurt anyone."

"You're down here almost every day, and you don't get along with any of your classmates — especially Becky Reese."

"She's a pain in the —"

"She's not your problem."

"She said —"

"She said that your mom was as big a loser as hers." Josh sighed. "Mrs. Cole told me, and I just got off the phone with Becky's grandmother. The girl owes you an apology, but you can't completely lose it every time someone mentions your mother. You and your therapist have talked about that."

"Good old *Dr. Steve.*"

Cynicism sounded awful coming out of the mouth of a ten-year-old.

"If you can't keep it together with the

14

other kids in class —"

"No one talks bad about my mom."

"Having temper tantrums isn't the answer." Josh was as disturbed as Daniel by what the little girl had said. It made him want to throw things himself, when up until a few months ago he'd been a pro at keeping his emotions and his job separate.

Everyone at school, including the kids, knew what Daniel had been through — at least part of it. A year ago, he'd come to them an unhappy child, after his mother moved them to Sweetbrook, a place Daniel had never seen before. Then she'd died in a single-vehicle car accident on New Year's Eve while driving under the influence. Rumors had spread in the four months since that perhaps she'd aimed for that telephone pole, after all, leaving folks in the community to pity even more the lost little boy left behind.

Sweetbrook might be small and antiquated by most standards, but tiny South Carolina communities took care of their own. People wanted to give Daniel the break he deserved. Everyone except Becky. From her first day in school, the child had seemed determined to bait Daniel with the one thing she knew would hurt him the most — trash-talking the boy's mother right along with her own.

Josh resented Amy Loar for dumping her problems in Sweetbrook, while she kicked back and did whatever she was doing in Atlanta.

"I know Sweetbrook has been a bum deal for you," Josh said with care. Sounding soothing and understanding was tough, when he understood next to nothing these days. "Moving here to be near family you don't know. Starting over. Then losing your mom the way you did."

Daniel's scowl rearranged itself into something fiercer. Something near tears.

Josh's chest burned. "But you have to keep your hands and things to yourself if you want to stay in school."

"When did this become about what I want? I don't *want* to be in trouble all the time, but that's what keeps happening." The kid looked up then, his green eyes glistening. "Maybe everyone would be better off if I wasn't here."

"That's not an option, Daniel."

Josh refused to let it be. He watched resignation crowd out the grief on Daniel's face, and he knew exactly how the boy felt. The situation everyone in Sweetbrook expected Josh to handle like a pro was speeding from bad to worse with each passing day.

He'd grilled the Family Services caseworker assigned to Daniel after his mother's death. He'd read every book available on dealing with kids with Daniel's issues. Josh was using all the tools at his disposal to help the little boy believe he was wanted. That he belonged here. That he could succeed. But the demons that drove Daniel to strike out every time someone got too close, every time the vulnerability he tried to hide swam to the surface, were unfortunately about so much more than losing his mother.

Josh's well-thought-out plans to help Daniel weren't making a dent. The boy's behavior was defying every logical step Josh took, just as his ex-wife's had, when she'd left to build the life she'd wanted away from him and Sweetbrook.

"It's going to get better, you know," he finally said, following Dr. Steve Rhodes's lead, even though the words sounded ridiculously shallow. Maybe if Josh kept saying them, he could will the platitude into reality.

Daniel's total lack of reaction announced that the kid wasn't born yesterday.

Josh checked his copy of Mrs. Cole's schedule. "Your class is at recess. You think

17

you and Becky can retire to neutral corners until the end of the day?"

A mumble and a shrug were all he got in response.

"Give it your best shot." Josh stood and walked around the desk, his stomach tightening at the realization of just how close he was to losing Daniel to whatever dark place he'd gone to after his mother's death. "We'll deal with the rest later."

He reached to smooth Daniel's bangs out of his eyes. The boy flinched, and Josh dropped his hand, fresh out of next steps.

Daniel inched to his feet, putting more space between them.

Josh let him go, like a principal should. He stared at his dress shoes, forcing his hands to stay in his pockets, when everything in him wanted to pull the lonely child close and hug it all better.

As if that had worked every other time he'd tried.

It was some kind of sick cosmic joke that he was Daniel's best shot at a normal life now. The kid needed love so badly, and neither one of them knew how to make sure he got it.

"Hey, buddy," he rushed to say as the ten-year-old reached the door. He hated the strained silence between them, almost as much as he hated the thought of Daniel leaving his office in worse emotional shape than when he'd come in. "Hot dogs for dinner again tonight?"

He held his breath, hoping Dr. Rhodes hadn't been placating him when he'd said to play the intense times loose and easy.

Daniel looked back, his eyes too old, too lost, and so much like his mother's the last time Josh had seen her.

The last time he'd seen his baby sister.

"Sure." The ten-year-old yanked open the door, his bored expression an improvement over the wariness that had been there just a moment ago. "Why not?"

Josh watched his nephew amble through the outer office and disappear down the hall.

What do I do now?

He'd asked himself the same question once before, when his wife had filed for divorce two years ago.

A decade into marriage, Josh had blissfully assumed he had the world under control. Granted, they'd had trouble getting pregnant. But with his family's money, they could have hired the best specialists in the world. They could have kept trying. But one day out of the blue, Lisa's bags were packed and she announced she'd been accepted to law school in New York. That she wanted

19

more than what they had together. Namely, a life of her own that didn't include him, his agenda for having a baby and his dream of raising a family in the small town he'd grown up in.

One minute he was standing in their living room listening to Lisa recite everything he'd never understood she needed, the next she was gone. And for the first time in his life, he'd had no idea what to do next.

Just like now.

Ruthlessly philanthropic, Josh gave away by the handful the White family fortune that had never bought him an ounce of peace, supporting organizations in the area that needed the money far more than he did. He was organized, compassionate and hardworking, even progressive by Sweetbrook standards. He could educate the one-hundred-and-fifty kids in his school like nobody's business. But none of that had won him points as a husband. His wife's unhappiness and longing for a different life had gone unnoticed and unchecked until it was too late. He'd made a mess out of loving her.

And now he was making a mess out of caring for his sister's troubled child.

"I know Becky's not happy there, Mama."

Amy Loar rested her head in her hands, her elbows atop the Kramer Industries files that would take her the rest of the night to organize for tomorrow's meeting. It was only Wednesday, but she'd already billed forty hours to her client's account that week. She had at least another forty to go. "I'd give anything to have her here with me."

She fingered the heart-shaped pendant dangling from the chain around her neck. Last year's Christmas present from Becky, back before things with Richard had exploded one time too many. Amy never took the necklace off now. It reminded her why she was doing all this.

"I hate to say it, because I know it's impossible for you to get away," her mother replied pensively. Amy could almost picture Gwen. Her close-cropped graying hair, originally the same dark red as Amy's, was always finger-combed into an unruly mess by this time of night. "But Becky needs you, honey."

Gwen Loar never meddled. She never passed judgment nor laid blame. So the touch of disapproval in her voice told Amy how dicey things were getting in Sweetbrook. Becky was staying with her grandmother temporarily, while Amy moved them from their pricey Buckhead condo into a two-bedroom apartment closer to her job in midtown. While she fought to get their lives back on track.

Gwen's tiny house, her life in Sweetbrook, had once been a slice of heaven for Amy. But growing up poor in the rural South had left a lot to be desired. For as long as she could remember, she'd longed to get out, to do better, to snatch for herself a speck of the security everyone around her took for granted.

So she'd earned her scholarships and attended college in Atlanta, only to meet wealthy, sophisticated, ten-years-her-senior Richard Reese during her junior year. At the time, he'd seemed the answer to all her dreams — a charming, successful man offering her marriage into a world she'd never dreamed of. But all dreams come with a price.

Now she was hoping the small-town life she'd turned her back on would work its magic on her daughter. If only Becky would give it a chance.

Just hold on for a little while longer, honey. I'll make everything up to you.

Amy checked the clock at the corner of her computer monitor and winced. It was almost nine. She'd meant to call home hours ago.

She forced herself to stop wilting into her desk chair, and smoothed a manicured hand across her expensive silk blouse. Her career uniform. One more tool she needed to get her where she wanted to be.

"Put Becky on the phone," she said to her mother. "Let her vent about what happened at school today. Blaming me for everything for a while will do her some good."

"I've tried to get her to talk." Gwen's sigh sounded like it came from her toes. "I tried all afternoon. But she headed straight to her bedroom after school and locked her door until dinner. She's finally asleep. I don't think it's a good idea to wake her and start things all over again. Maybe you could be here when she gets up in the morning? You could talk with her before the bus comes —"

"I can't come home right now, Mama."

"It's only a four-hour drive."

"I have the Kramer Industries sign-off meeting at three tomorrow afternoon. We're finalizing the proposal with the senior management."

She was a project leader for Atlanta's high-profile Enterprise Consulting Group, a position she'd had to fight for after her divorce. The partners had finally agreed to

23

give her this shot, and the Kramer account was going to land her the manager slot she'd declined three years running at Richard's urging. The promotion came with an immediate bonus and a hefty increase in her annual salary. And tomorrow's meeting was the last step before they presented the contract to the CEO in a few weeks.

"I can't pull out now for personal reasons," she said, trying to drown out the second thoughts that she never completely silenced. She was going to secure this promotion. She and her daughter were going to finally have some peace. "Phillip Hutchinson's watching me like a hawk. I have to stay on top of this project."

"Of course, you're right." Even though her mother sounded disappointed, her voice rang with the support and encouragement Amy had always depended on.

Simple, solid, no-nonsense living and unconditional love. Those were Gwen's gifts. The very gifts Amy hoped could break through her daughter's anger and confusion.

Gwen knew firsthand the sacrifices required of single mothers. Amy's father had died when she was just a baby, and Gwen had worked three part-time jobs some years to keep them off food stamps.

But she hadn't been able to soften the blow of having so little in a world where everyone else seemed to effortlessly have more. So Amy had worked nonstop making something of herself, vowing to build a better life for them both. And that's exactly what she'd done, even though Gwen had refused every offer Amy made to share her and Richard's financial success.

Her house was paid for, Gwen had argued. Her needs were simple. She had some savings, and she was still a part-time teller at Sweetbrook's one and only bank. Unlike Amy, she hadn't wanted more, as much as she'd wanted what she already had.

"I wish I had another solution, Mama. But I need this promotion. I don't mind giving up the condo, the car or that fancy private school Richard insisted Becky attend. But I can't afford to live in Atlanta on my current salary."

"Then move back home," her mother urged, as she had for months. "You two can stay with me until you find a job here."

"I can't ask you to do that. And I can't move Becky away from her friends for good and ask her to start over with nothing. Atlanta's the only home she's ever known. She wants to live here. I won't rip her world apart any more than I already have."

"There are worse things than having nothing, Amy."

"Yes. There's going back to Richard and asking him for money —"

"Of course you're not going back to him!" her mother interjected.

For years, Amy had kept the details about her marriage secret from Gwen. But her mother knew every ugly bit of it now.

"I have to prove to my daughter that a woman really can support her family on her own," Amy continued. "That Richard was dead wrong when he said we'd never make it without him."

She'd never seen her husband as angry as the morning she'd worked up the nerve to leave him. He'd controlled her every move for years. What she thought, and wore, and did, and with whom. Even how much she was allowed to focus on her career, insisting she curtail her responsibilities at work after Becky was born.

She'd tried to make the best of things when her marriage began crumbling less than a year after their wedding. She'd done everything she could to pacify Richard and save her dream of a perfect life with her perfect husband, downplaying the escalating verbal and emotional abuse. It took Richard striking her in front of their daughter before Amy had finally had enough.

Richard could have fought her for Becky. Considering his connections as a high-priced corporate attorney, he would have won. But his sights had been on a priority far more important to him than his daughter. If Amy would agree to his demands of no alimony and the minimum child support the law allowed, he'd let Becky go. The money would be paid lump-sum into a trust account for Becky's college tuition, not to be touched until she was eighteen. In return, he'd concede full custody, and Amy and Becky would be on their own — then maybe they'd wise up and understand just how much they needed him.

"You'll come back to me," he'd said in front of Becky the last time they'd seen him. "Once you're on your own and realize how tough the world is, maybe then you'll have some appreciation for all I've given you."

He'd set Amy up to fail, just for the satisfaction of watching her crawl back to him. And as usual, he hadn't concerned himself with their daughter, except for how he could use Becky to control Amy.

"I'm going to make things work for Becky here in Atlanta," Amy vowed to herself and her mother. "She needs to see me standing up to her father. She needs to understand that a woman doesn't have to put up with the way he treated me to be financially secure. She was there all those years, Mama, when her father belittled me, and I just took it. She watched me be a doormat for the sake of holding on to a man who didn't respect me. I can't even imagine what that did to her."

"But you're working around the clock now," Gwen reasoned. "What happens when the promotion comes through, and Becky moves back in with you? Will you have any more time to spend with her after you make manager?"

"I don't know. I'll figure it out." Whatever it took, Amy was going to be the strong woman her daughter needed her to be. Becky wasn't growing up afraid.

"But if you moved back here —"

"There's no work for me in Sweetbrook, Mama."

Amy's other phone line chirped at the same time that her computer dinged. She juggled the receiver between her shoulder and ear, checked the phone display and clicked the e-mail prompt with her mouse.

It was Phillip Hutchinson on both counts, Enterprise Consulting's senior partner, and her personal slave driver.

She didn't bother to read the body of the

e-mail or pick up the call. Not a man to worry about the constructive use of anyone else's time, Phillip Hutchinson didn't stoop to discussing details until those he'd summoned had quick-stepped their way to his corner office. His two-pronged bid for Amy's attention didn't bode well.

"I've got to go." She typed and sent a quick *I'll be right there* response to the e-mail. "I'll clear a few hours Saturday to come down for a day trip."

"Joshua White wants to set up a meeting with you and Becky's teacher on Friday —"

"Josh White no doubt thinks the entire world moves at the snail's pace he runs his elementary school." Amy winced at the anger in her voice, rubbing her temples, where a headache was building.

No one listening would have guessed she was talking about the best friend she'd ever had. The friend she'd told off when he'd dared to judge her decision to marry Richard and leave Sweetbrook behind for good. The friend whose angry kiss had almost tempted her to change her mind.

"Honey, I really think you should talk with the man. He's taken such a personal interest in Becky since she came here."

"I know he has."

Gwen had gone on and on about the time

Josh was spending trying to make sure Becky settled into his school. He sounded like a bang-up principal. And before their friendship had imploded, he'd always been there for Amy. But why did he have to pick tonight of all nights to work her mother into a tizzy about Becky's harmless antics at school? Wasn't there something more important for the wealthiest man in town to be doing besides shoving Amy over the edge of sanity?

"I'm sorry to saddle you with all this, Mama. If there was any other way . . ."

"I love having Becky," Gwen reassured her. "And she can stay as long as you need her to. But she thinks you've abandoned her. She needs to know that you want her with you, that you think this is the best place for her right now. That you care what's going on at school."

"I've told her how much I care. I tell her every time we talk." Another e-mail message from Hutchinson dinged for her attention. The subject line read simply, NOW.

Amy e-mailed back a polite *on my way.*

She was making compromises with her child she'd promised herself she'd never make. Her personal definition of hell. But sometimes a bad decision was the only alternative.

She hoped she wasn't wrong.

"I've got to go, Mama."

"You'll call Becky tomorrow?" In her mother's voice was that hint of the steel Amy had always admired.

Gwen was first and foremost a survivor.

Amy hoped she could be half as strong.

"I'll call tomorrow evening," she said as she stacked the Kramer Industries papers, shuffling the files into order. "Tell Becky I love her, and that I know she's going to do better with the other kids at school tomorrow. She'll be fine."

"I hope you're right."

"So do I." Amy closed her eyes against the doubt she couldn't keep out of her voice. "I love you both."

Her mother's "I love you, too," had barely sounded when her office door jerked open. Amy pushed to her feet and hung up the phone.

"Mrs. Ree— Ms. Loar." Phillip Hutchinson frowned in displeasure at his continued difficulty keeping her name straight. Even though she'd legally changed it back to Loar the same day she'd signed her divorce papers, he was still having trouble calling her anything but Reese. "I've got the Kramer IT director on the phone, and he wants to discuss the payout schedule."

"Those papers are right here." She shuffled through her folders, wincing as the one she needed slid from under the others. Papers fluttered to the floor between her and the desk. "Um, why don't you transfer the call down here?"

"Pick up what you need," he said with a shake of his head. "Leave the rest. I already have Jed conferenced in on the speakerphone in my office. If you're too overwhelmed to handle a client's unexpected requests, maybe we need to get you some backup on this project."

Amy returned the remaining folders to her desk with a slap and a cool stare.

She'd managed every detail of this project from day one. This was her baby, and no one was taking this opportunity away from her.

"I'll be right there," she said in as close to a civil tone as she could muster.

Mr. Hutchinson's eyebrow twitched upward, then he turned to leave. One final glance behind him at the disorganized mess covering Amy's normally immaculate desk told her he hadn't missed a single detail.

She dropped to her knees to re-sort the five-year pay-out schedule for the computer system and HR applications she was determined Kramer Industries would purchase.

Phillip Hutchinson. Richard. And Josh White. Why couldn't they just let her be? Why couldn't they let her win for a change?

With fear of failing yet again nagging at her, she marched through her doorway and down the wide hall that doubled as offices for the executive secretaries.

Everything around her looked expensive. Smelled expensive. Mahogany furniture glistened. She caught the subtle aroma of the polish the cleaning crew applied to keep everything sparkling. State-of-the-art computers and other office systems dominated each work space. Even the exquisitely maintained potted plants atop the desks had been arranged to present just the right image.

This was where the powerful worked. The world of success to which Amy had always dreamed of being a part. The Enterprise Consulting Group was where you wanted to entrust the future of your company's computer systems and human resource applications. Yet every square inch of the place was a prison Amy had never seen coming.

She mentally squashed her introspection and the melancholy that always followed close behind. So what if she wanted to be anyone but herself right now. So what if she wanted to be anywhere but where she was, doing what she was doing.

She was going to make this work, and she was bagging her promotion. She and Becky were coming out on top this time. They were going to be safe and out of Richard's control once and for all.

Unless you fail again, the little voice chimed in, right on cue.

No . . . not a chance. Not this time.

She was getting it right this time. Becky wasn't going to pay the price for her mother's mistakes. No matter what Amy had to sacrifice to get them through this.

CHAPTER TWO

"Yes, Mr. Westing." Amy nodded to herself, making adjustments to the project plan she was walking the Kramer Industries IT director through. "I'm confident your CEO will be more than pleased at the closing meeting on the thirtieth."

She withdrew a spreadsheet from her folder and slid it across the desk toward Phillip Hutchinson. The senior partner's slow nod as he reviewed the plans she'd sacrificed months of her life to produce, and his begrudging, "It all looks on target to me, Jed," were as good as a standing ovation.

"Good." Papers shuffled on Westing's end of the line. "Now, let's walk through the support contract again."

"Yes, sir." Amy dug out another set of papers. It felt incredible to be on top of her game. To be staring down the pressure and to have the right answer at every turn. To finally be in control of something, when the rest of her life was such a disaster.

"Let me fax you the schedule that details the two options." She handed Mr. Hutchinson the paperwork. "Take a look at —"

The cell phone at her hip started doing the cha-cha.

She grabbed it, grateful beyond words that she'd remembered to turn the thing to Vibrate. At the top of Phillip Hutchinson's list of meeting dos and don'ts was no, absolutely no, cell phone interruptions. But her cell was her connection with Becky and Gwen until she could bring her daughter back to Atlanta. Forget Hutchinson's rules.

The man's annoyed stare locked on to Amy. Her heart chose that moment to begin beating in her throat. She yanked the phone from her waistband, giving up any pretence of subtlety.

"Ms. Loar?" Mr. Hutchinson prodded.

The display revealed Sweetbrook's area code, but it wasn't her mother's number.

"Ms. Loar!" he demanded under his breath.

Oh, no. What was it she'd been saying to Westing?

The phone buzzed in her hand.

Becky! Something must have happened. Was that the number for the Sweetbrook hospital?

"I'm sorry." She passed her notes to Hutchinson. "I have to take this call."

"I'm faxing you those support schedules now, Jed." Hutchinson activated the fax machine at his elbow, his voice resonating professionalism. His eyes, however, raged with disapproval.

She forced herself to walk calmly from the room. She closed the door behind her and thumbed the Talk button on the still-shuddering phone, leaving her flawless spreadsheets, the countless hours she'd spent running and rerunning the Kramer numbers, to speak for themselves.

"Hello?" she said.

Please let Becky be okay.

"Hello?" an oddly familiar masculine voice echoed. "I was calling for Amy Loar . . . Reese. Amy Reese?"

"This is Amy Loar." She garbled her words as she sank into every mother's nightmare. Something might have happened to her child, and Amy was hundreds of miles away. "What's wrong?"

"What? Nothing's wrong, everything's fine," the man reassured her. "I mean, not exactly —"

"Who is this?" She finally took a full breath, as the initial edge of panic receded.

"Amy, it's Josh. . . . Joshua White."

She stared at the phone, a rush of childhood memories consuming her.

There was Josh, smiling and forever young, surely the handsomest senior class president ever elected, delivering his valedictorian speech at their high school graduation. Voted most likely to succeed. Brilliant. The only son of a wealthy Southern family whose forefathers had founded Sweetbrook over two hundred years ago. Josh had been so far removed from the reality of Amy's own childhood that the fact that they'd hooked up as kids and stayed friends through high school was still a mystery to more people than her.

And then she remembered the last time she'd seen him. His expression had darkened with disappointment, his voice angry and hurt as he passed his small-town judgment on her pending marriage to a man he didn't think was good enough for her.

"You're marrying him for all the wrong reasons," he'd said. "He won't make you happy."

"And you're an expert on me and what makes me happy," she'd retorted.

"I've gotten pretty good at watching you throw the important things in your life away in your pursuit of success, yes." His hands had

*shook as he cupped her cheek. "It makes me
sad to see you putting so much faith in this
guy and his money. His promises that this better life of his in Atlanta will make you happy. It
makes me . . . It makes me want to show you
what you could have if you came back to live
in Sweetbrook."*

*And before she'd known it, the anger in the
eyes of the man she'd secretly had a crush
on for years had heated into something new,
something that felt as forbidden and thrilling
as the kiss that had followed —*

"I'm the principal of the elementary
school in Sweetbrook," Josh said in the here
and now.

"I . . . I know who you are, Josh." She
checked her watch. "It's ten o'clock at
night. And I'm in an important meeting."

"I see." The friendly note drained from
his voice. "Your mother mentioned you kept
late hours at the office, but I thought by
now you might have time to talk."

"I'm trying to close a deal with an important client." Amy's cheeks singed at the
censure she couldn't believe she was hearing in his voice.

"What I've called to discuss about Becky
is equally important, I assure you," he
reasoned, "or I wouldn't have bothered
you."

As if taking time for her daughter was too much of a bother. Amy's spine stiffened.

Maybe he had seen Richard for the snake he turned out to be long before she'd wised up. Maybe Josh had been right all along, that her big plans for her life in Atlanta wouldn't make her happy. But he didn't know her anymore. He couldn't begin to comprehend the kind of trouble she was digging herself and Becky out of. Or how much she despised herself for each minute she couldn't be with her child.

"How did you get this number?" she asked, biting back her favorite childhood label for him when he was being a pain — *butthead.*

"Gwen gave it to the school when she registered Becky. I have it here in your daughter's file." He was full-on *Principal White* now, his voice as formal and as superficially polite as hers. "Just at a glance, I'd say the behavior problems and incidents Becky's racked up in just the month she's been with us constitute an emergency by anyone's standards. In case you weren't aware of what's been going on down here, I wanted to bring you up to speed."

"I'm aware of everything that's happening with my daughter. I talk with her every night," Amy snapped. "I'm very interested in her life, and I stay as involved as I can be."

"I wasn't judging you, Amy." He sounded genuinely hurt.

"Sure you were."

She'd been down this road before. For months now, as a matter of fact, ever since the mothers of Becky's friends first learned about Amy's increased hours at Enterprise after the divorce. The frenzy of unsolicited concern and advice that had ensued — after dance practice, at the car-pool stop to and from school, after birthday parties and sleepovers — had made Amy's decision to remove Becky from her exclusive private school even easier. They couldn't afford the tuition any longer, and Amy didn't need the daily reminder of how badly she was failing as a mother, no matter how hard she tried.

"I called to discuss Becky's issues at school," Josh offered, his tone edging toward reasonable. "Not to comment on your priorities as a mother, or your relationship with your daughter. I'd like to help."

"Look." Amy unclenched her jaw. Chided herself for overreacting. The man was just doing his job. She glanced at her watch again. "I've already spoken with my mother, and I'm just as concerned as you that Becky's having difficulty in school —"

"Then you're planning to be here Friday?"

"What?"

"For the SST meeting."

The door to Mr. Hutchinson's office opened. The senior partner stepped partially into the hall.

"Ms. Loar, I need you in here."

She raised a finger to signal for another minute. Turning her back as the door closed less than gently behind her, she gritted her teeth against the screaming tantrum that would be a really bad idea.

"Josh, I'd be happy to stop by the school as soon as I wrap up my project here. I don't know what this SST meeting is, but Friday's out of the question, I'm afraid."

"And I'm afraid we can't put this off." His statement resonated with the same determination she'd once admired. Only there was an unforgiving edge to Josh's controlled manner now. A harshness at complete odds with the easygoing charm that had tempered his personality when they were kids.

"We're just going to have to put it off." Amy took a calming breath. "I appreciate your call, and I'll make an appointment with the school admin for a few weeks from now —"

"You don't understand. We're having the

meeting Friday, with or without you. If you can't make the time to be here, we'll do what we think is best for Becky in your absence."

His disapproving tone snuffed out Amy's last attempt to keep the conversation polite, just as it had that night over ten years ago when he'd decided he knew what was best for her life.

Privilege and money had smoothed Josh's every step from childhood. After college, he'd returned to Sweetbrook to take his rightful place in his family's legacy of service and philanthropy to the community. He was principal of Dr. David C. White Elementary School. She'd heard his marriage had fallen apart a year or so ago, but beyond that it seemed his life had worked out exactly according to his master plan. How could he possibly understand what it was like to fight and struggle, and all the while know you're stuck in a no-win battle you might never escape from?

"I do appreciate your *courtesy.*" She nearly choked on the words. "But how exactly do you anticipate having a parent-teacher conference without the parent present?"

Butthead!

"The Student Support Team meeting is

43

for Becky's benefit, not yours," he explained. "It's a little more formal than you sitting down for a chat with her teacher. Your daughter's facing some tough challenges, and she's going to need all the help she can get. I'll be there Friday, along with her teacher, Mrs. Cole. So will our staff counselor. Together, we'll come up with a set of strategies that we hope will help school become a more successful experience for Becky."

"What challenges? What strategies? Becky's upset because of the hours I've had to keep the last few months. Because she blames me for how my marriage ended." Amy clasped the pendant dangling around her neck. "My daughter doesn't want to be in Sweetbrook, so she's acting out a little more than usual at school. I'll be there in a few weeks, then she'll settle back in here with me. Don't you think you're overreacting with this SST thing? Becky's going to be fine."

"She may not be, Amy. Not without some help." Josh's concern radiated across the crackling cell connection. Gone was the all-business principal who couldn't keep his intrusive opinions to himself. In his place was the friend whose shoulder Amy had cried on the summer her puppy had died in her arms after being struck by a car. Gwen had been at work, Amy hadn't had anyone else to turn to, and Josh had been there, as always. Steady, certain, unflappable. "Her teacher's concerned that part of Becky's acting out may stem from frustration over a learning disability —"

"What learning disability?"

"The purpose of the SST meeting is to discuss Mrs. Cole's suspicion that Attention Deficit Disorder may account for some of Amy's disruptive behavior in the classroom."

"Attention Deficit . . ." The muffled sound of the conference call going on behind her faded. Her surroundings shimmered to a hazy white. "I don't understand. . . ."

"We think Becky may be dealing with ADD, on top of the other issues you mentioned earlier."

On top of the other issues. . . . The words clamored through Amy's head. Issues that were *her* fault. On top of Becky losing her family and being separated from the life and home that were all she'd ever known. On top of her needing Amy the most, just when it was impossible for her to be there for her little girl. On top of all that, Becky might have —

"ADD?" she whispered. She didn't know

exactly what that meant, but she knew enough to be scared. She covered her mouth with a shaking hand. Tears threatened, blurring everything around her. "But I had no idea. . . . How . . . ?"

"It's going to be okay, Amy," Josh said. "We're going to figure this out."

His reassurance was like a lifeline, and she found his use of the word *we* wasn't as offensive as it should have been, given the way he'd been subtly pointing his finger at her moments before.

"Ms. Loar." Phillip Hutchinson was standing beside Amy. She had no idea how long he'd been there. "Mr. Westing has another question about the payout schedule. I need you to walk him through it."

The man was all but tapping his foot for her to hop-to.

"I . . ." Amy fought for words, fought against the sensation that her world was slipping out from under her.

"Amy, can you make the SST meeting?" Josh's voice sounded in her ear, cornering her, pressing for an answer with as much tenacity as her boss.

Her daughter or her career? Amy's plans to manage both had never seemed more unattainable.

"I'll be there on Friday," she croaked into

the phone, ending the call before Josh could say another word.

She turned to Mr. Hutchinson and squared her shoulders.

"I need to take a few days off."

"You can't be serious." He jerked a thumb over his shoulder. "I've got a nervous director in there, and you're meeting with their entire senior management at three tomorrow. You're not going anywhere."

"I have a family emergency. I'm leaving in the morning, as soon as I can wrap things up here. I'll be gone until Monday." She was already working out the details in her head. She'd spend tomorrow afternoon with Becky and Gwen, meet with Josh and his staff on Friday, get things back on an even keel over the weekend, then return to Atlanta by Sunday evening to catch up before the new week started. "I can video conference in on tomorrow's meeting. The rest I'll find a way to do from Sweetbrook on my laptop and smartphone."

"Sweetbrook? Where's Sweetbrook?"

"In South Carolina. It's where I grew up."

And it was the one place, despite all her plans to leave it behind, where she'd last felt safe.

She brushed past him and stepped into his office, pushing aside thoughts of every-

47

thing but the corporate director who needed to be placated before she could do anything else. Lucky for Amy, reassuring nervous clients was turning out to be one of her greatest talents.

If only her and her daughter's problems were as easy to resolve.

"Can I get you anything, Mr. White?" Mrs. Lyons asked Josh the next morning.

Josh lifted his head from his overflowing desk, trying not to be annoyed.

He and Daniel had to make it home on time this afternoon to whip the house into shape for their Family Services caseworker. This was their fourth home visit since Josh had been awarded temporary custody after his sister, Melanie's, death, and they needed to demonstrate they were making progress bonding as a family. Josh couldn't be running late because of paperwork, which meant he didn't have time to humor one overly attentive school secretary.

In the past, Edna Lyons had always been efficient. But she'd become downright doting since Melanie died and Josh had taken responsibility for Daniel. She'd progressed from straightening and organizing everything in sight to hovering, which she was doing right now.

She reached to restack the personnel folders he'd thumbed through earlier, as he considered applications for the vacant math-specialist position. He slid them out of her reach.

"Stop coddling me, Edna." He sat back and smiled as she huffed. "I'm fine."

"You're behind, is what you are. Have been for months. Both here and in that mansion your family calls a home." She scooped his wrinkled suit jacket off the chair he'd dropped it onto, smoothed the material and hung it on the coatrack. "You just don't know how to ask for help."

If only there was any real help for Josh's situation. He'd sold his own home after the divorce and moved back to the house he'd grown up in. His father, drifting through the final stages of Alzheimer's, hadn't even known his wife and son by that point. Josh's mother, frailer at sixty-five than most, thanks to the devastating toll Alzheimer's took on caregivers, had been at her emotional and physical wit's end. Josh had finally talked her into moving with his dad to an assisted living center about an hour away, in Demming, so the professionals there could help her handle the progression of his father's disease.

Melanie had come back to town with

Daniel somewhere in the midst of it all, the drama that always swirled around her adding to the strain of their mother's anxiety and Josh's messed up life after his divorce. And now they were all gone, all but Daniel. Josh visited his parents as often as he could, and he spoke with his mom each week. But all he'd tell her was that things were fine in Sweetbrook. He refused to burden her with either his or her grandson's problems. The woman had enough on her hands.

The lack of a family support system wouldn't have been a problem in the past. Growing up with emotionally absent parents had taught him independence from the cradle. After his divorce, he'd turned to his work and the kids at school to keep him busy. But now he also had Daniel to consider, and the boy's need for love and attention escalated more each day.

"Everything's going to be okay," he made himself say out loud as he got back to work. He hadn't asked for this kind of responsibility, but it was his nonetheless. Turning his back on his sister's child was out of the question.

"Oh, it'll be okay," Mrs. Lyons agreed in a not-so-agreeable voice. "Once you find a nice young lady to help you make a home for that nephew of yours."

"I don't need a nice young lady. What I need —" He initialed the page before him and flipped to the next, grunting at the memory of the string of *helpful* local women who'd tried to step in where his ex had left off "— is to get these pay sheets approved in time for you and everyone else to receive your checks on Friday."

"I heard Mary-Ellen Baxter's Tiffany —"

"Edna, have you by any chance started your own dating service?" He was only half teasing, and a bit too much of his irritation slipped into his voice.

"What?" She was a study in female indignation. At least she was no longer hovering. "I was only —"

"You were trying to fix me up with your best friend's single daughter." He dropped his pen, folded his hands and forced himself to smile at the good-intentioned woman who had caught him sneaking out of class in third grade without a hall pass — thus landing him his only stint in detention. "And while I appreciate you looking out for me —"

"I was looking out for the child." She pulled off dignified and embarrassed like a champ. "If you want to spend the rest of your life alone, that's your business. But that little boy needs some stability."

"You're a good woman, Edna Lyons." And she was. Gray haired for as long as he'd known her, always dressed in floral prints that did her Southern heritage proud. Tough on the outside, she possessed a marshmallow-cream center the kids in school rarely got a chance to see. "I appreciate you looking out for Daniel. But dating someone I don't have a hope of connecting with right now wouldn't end well for anyone."

The good-intentioned people of Sweetbrook had discreetly arranged for him to meet a parade of local beauties at various potluck dinners, or the Wednesday night trip he always took to the grocery to stock up for the week. Even at the school's Spring Fling a month ago. All of them were perfectly nice women, but none right for him. Because he wasn't interested. Not after losing Lisa and so much of what he'd thought the rest of his life would be built around. There wasn't a woman on earth who'd tempt him to go there again.

Suddenly, his last memories of Amy Loar muscled aside the images of the other women. Memories of Amy laughing with him, kidding him, making his day lighter just because she was in it. Then of her mouth, soft and giving, melting beneath his.

Melting away the anger and surprising hurt he'd felt at the thought of her marrying another man. He'd pulled her into his arms, wanting to hold on to something he hadn't realized he'd needed until that moment. And just for a second, it had seemed as if she was as lost in their kiss as he was. Then she'd shoved him away, almost crying, saying she would never forgive him for what he'd said. For what he'd done. . . .

With a shake of his head, he shifted to the edge of the chair and picked up the next time sheet.

You've got no time for daydreaming, man. No time for regrets about the past.

The mistakes he wracked up each time he tried to help Daniel and failed, filled more hours than he had in a day.

"I'll take care of these, at least," Edna said, a note of resignation lingering in her voice as she picked up the mail from his out-box and turned to go. "Do you want me to see that you're not distur—"

"Got a minute for me?" Doug Fletcher popped his head in, bringing Edna to a skidding stop.

She scowled up at the school counselor, clearly arming for battle. No one entered the principal's office unless she announced him first. But at Josh's approving nod, she turned away without a word.

"You have a curriculum meeting in ten minutes," she called over her shoulder. "You don't want to be late again."

Doug chuckled at her retreating back.

"You'd better watch your step for the next few days. She'll have her eye on you." Josh scanned and initialed the sheet before him. "What's up?"

"I just got a call from Barbara Thomas." Doug closed the door, then sat in one of the guest chairs. "She was asking for an update on Daniel."

Josh began stacking the unsigned reports it was clear he couldn't finish before his meeting. "We have a home visit scheduled this afternoon."

"Are things getting better outside of school?" his friend and colleague asked. Doug Fletcher was a top-notch counselor. The best. One of those people who could listen to you recite the alphabet and make it seem as if you were delving into inner truths he found fascinating.

"I'm starting to wonder if things ever will get better," Josh finally let himself admit. "Living with me, adjusting to this school —" he spread his hands "— none of it is getting any easier for Daniel. He still feels out of place. Like he doesn't belong here, no matter how much I try to convince him he does."

"He's hurting, Josh. The kid just lost his mother, and he was already having difficulty relating to people before that. I suspect it's an ongoing problem."

"Yeah. Dr. Rhodes thinks the same thing."

"Because of the father?"

"We're not sure. Melanie claimed the man was abusive, and the more I'm around Daniel, the more I'm convinced something happened." Josh's fists clenched at the thought of some jerk raising a hand to his sister and her son. "But Daniel won't talk about any of it, so we can't be certain."

"It would explain a lot of the acting out. The behavior that pushes people away before they get too close."

"Yeah, or maybe he just doesn't want to be here." Josh's fists clenched again. "I'm not exactly family man of the year right now."

"You're doing fine," his friend countered, repeating Josh's earlier assurance to Mrs. Lyons. Doug somehow managed to sound as if he meant it. "Just take it slow and give it some time."

"Yeah." Josh nodded.

His intercom buzzed long and loud, Edna's I-told-you-so signal that he was going to be late for the curriculum meeting, after all.

He threw his friend a long-suffering look as they stood to go. "Thankfully we have all kinds of free time around here."

Amy pulled up the driveway of her mother's place a little before three. Gwen Loar's tiny house looked more like home to Amy than her high-priced loft in the city ever had.

She dragged her garment bag from the 2002 Civic she'd purchased after trading in her Lexus, picked up her briefcase and nudged the trunk closed with her elbow. A wisp of a breeze lifted her bangs, a welcome relief from the early spring heat. Sweetbrook seemed overly warm after the milder temperatures in Atlanta. She closed her eyes and breathed in the scent of home.

There was a time, while she was in college, that she'd made it back to this place as often as possible. Then Richard had literally stumbled into her at the University of South Carolina, in the midst of a recruiting trip his legal firm was conducting on campus. She'd been a business major and not at all interested in a career in law. But Richard had been solid and steady, and magnetically handsome.

In his late twenties, he'd been on his way

to becoming his firm's youngest partner. Determined to win Amy's affection from the moment she'd sloshed her Coke all over his expensive suit in the student union café, he'd pursued her relentlessly, insisting they'd make a good fit. Flattered and awed by the success he wore so comfortably, she hadn't stood a chance once he turned on the formidable charm that had weakened the resolve of some of the most cynical juries in the South. Her mother had tried to warn her she was rushing into marriage. Even Josh had tried. But she'd been so sure Richard was her future.

After her graduation, they'd married in Atlanta, and she'd gone on to become the most promising of the young up-and-comers at Enterprise Consulting. Then Richard's arguments that they should have a baby sooner rather than later had begun. And with the arrival of Becky, Richard's passion for controlling Amy's life had shifted gears.

He didn't like the way it looked, having a nanny raising *his* daughter. Amy was too wrapped up in her career. Her place was at home, taking care of him and their child. It wasn't as if they needed the money she made. She'd clearly had her priorities out of place, he'd told her.

And so, by the time Becky was in preschool, Amy's *career* had morphed into little more than something to occupy herself while Becky was gone during the school day. Amy had passed up one career opportunity after another, even though she'd been more than qualified. She'd watched her peers' careers eclipse her own, while she was relegated to doing busy work on projects she'd rather have been leading.

She'd consoled herself with her family. With her husband's money and the financial security that had exceeded her dreams. Richard had assured her she had every reason to be happy. She was privileged. They were the envy of everyone they knew in Atlanta's supersuccessful business community. No matter that she became more and more terrified of her husband with each passing day.

When she'd finally woken from the haze of her abusive marriage, she found she'd been living a thinly veiled nightmare that was going to get worse before it got better. Not only did she have to find the strength to stand up to a man she'd let trample her dignity and self-esteem for years, but her best shot at financial independence was finding a way to be taken seriously in the world of corporate business, where she hadn't competed in years. And Amy hadn't just done this to herself. She'd dragged her daughter through hell right along with her.

How could she have been so wrong about what life had in store for her? Every mistake she'd made had been entirely her fault, because she hadn't wanted to see the truth in the people and things she'd built her happiness around.

Becky was right to blame her for being too much of a coward to leave Richard sooner. Amy had stayed too long. Her daughter had seen and heard too much.

"Amy!" The front door flew open. Her mom rushed out, arms wide. "You came. Why didn't you let us know?"

Amy dropped everything a split second before she was engulfed in her mother's sweet-scented hug. She couldn't hold Gwen close enough.

"I wasn't sure when I'd be able to get away," she explained. "I had a lot to take care of this morning. As it is, I'm waiting on a conference call my assistant's patching through to my cell."

She straightened the collar of Gwen's faded oxford shirt.

"This was Grandpa's, wasn't it?" She smiled at her mother's shrug. "That's one of the things I love about you, Mama. You never stop wearing hand-me-downs, no matter how many new outfits I buy you."

"I adore my old things. They're like memories I get to carry around with me all day." Gwen lifted Amy's garment bag and headed toward the house. "It might do you some good to look through your old closet. I bet there're lots of treasures hiding in there."

"Yeah. Everything will be just swell, as soon as I throw on a pair of my jeans from high school." Her briefcase in hand, Amy followed in her mother's wake. "Is Becky home?"

"Got off the bus about ten minutes ago." Gwen held the door for Amy to enter in front of her.

"Did things go better today?" Amy took the garment bag back and set it aside.

"She's in the kitchen having a snack. You should probably ask her yourself."

Amy turned from studying how much the walls of the tiny living room needed fresh paint. "That bad?"

"About the same." With another sigh, her mom led the way the few steps to the kitchen.

Becky was snacking on milk and a plate of Gwen's freshly baked cookies.

She looked so grown-up. So beautiful. So much like her father, with her dark hair and eyes, and her olive complexion. Had she gotten taller in the few weeks Amy had been away? Amy thought back to her last overnight visit, a hurried Saturday full of trying to help Becky understand why things had to be this way for now. Amy couldn't conjure up a clear picture of how her daughter had looked then. All she could remember was Becky's tears and shouts, and her own fear that her best was never going to be good enough.

"Hey, baby." She knelt beside Becky's chair.

Vacant eyes lifted, then shifted back to the plate. Becky dunked a cookie into her glass.

"I missed you." Amy ran her hand down her daughter's delicate arm.

"Whatever." Becky pulled away from her grasp.

Amy glanced over her shoulder. Gwen's slight smile encouraged her to continue.

"Grandma's been telling me a little about what's going on at school. I thought maybe we could talk about it this weekend. Maybe come up with a few ideas for making all this work better for you while you're here."

"You're staying the whole weekend?"

Their gazes connected again. But the doubt and hesitation filling Becky's brown eyes made Amy wish her daughter was still

61

pretending to ignore her.

"I'm sorry I haven't visited before now." She tried a tentative hug. The moment was so awkward, Amy wanted to cry. "I know this has been hard for you. I'd have come home sooner if I could."

"This isn't *home.*" Becky fought free of Amy's grasp, stumbling from the chair. She spun around, her arms crossed tightly across her neon-pink T-shirt. "Not that I have a home anymore, since you finally worked up the guts to throw Dad out. But I don't care about the condo or the apartment. I just want out of here."

"That's what your mom wants, too." Gwen stepped to her granddaughter's side and hugged her shoulders.

Becky melted against her and frowned at Amy. "Whatever. Just let me go back to Atlanta with you."

"I can't right now." Amy struggled to find a way to break through her daughter's unhappiness. To find different words than the ones she'd already said a hundred times. She was secure in her daughter's love. She and Becky would be okay once the dust settled. But that didn't erase the pain her child was enduring now — pain Amy never should have let touch her baby's life.

"We've talked about this," she said. "I've

barely moved everything into the new apartment. Our lives are still in boxes. And with this project at work taking up all my time, you're better off here for a little while longer."

"Work! That's all you care about. You don't want me around any more than Dad does."

"That's not true, honey." Amy longed to be holding her daughter herself. At least Becky was taking some comfort from Gwen. "I care about you very much. I'm doing all this to get us back on track. All I want is for you to be happy."

"Then get me out of this nowhere place." Anger laced every word the little girl hurled at Amy. "If you don't, I'll run away, I swear. I hate it here."

"You're not running away." Warning bells chimed in Amy's head. Like most kids, Becky could sense guilt a mile away. And she was a pro at using Amy's against her.

Time for tough-as-nails Mom to take the gloves off. She pushed herself out of her chair. "Your grandmother's taking good care of you, and you'll be back in Atlanta by next month. Back with your friends, and your stuff, and your new school. So please, why don't we skip the melodrama, make the best of the situation and talk about what's going on at school instead?"

Becky nibbled on her thumbnail, her outburst momentarily subdued. Amy didn't know which was worse, bearing the brunt of her daughter's threats and disrespect, or watching Becky slip into these scary patches of silence.

"Honey, I came down here so we'd have the chance to talk. So I could check on what's going on with you. Maybe I can help." She knelt again until she was looking up into her daughter's beautiful face. "I came because I'd do anything for you. You're the most important thing in my life, and I don't ever want you to think differently."

"Really?" Becky sniffed and wiped her nose with the back of her hand. "Are you really staying the weekend? Grandma said there was some kind of meeting at school tomorrow, but you couldn't come."

"Of course I'm staying. We're going to figure this out." The memory of Josh saying the exact same thing echoed in Amy's head. She took Becky's hand, tugging until the child's arm loosened and her hand dropped to her side. "I'll be at the meeting with your teacher tomorrow. But I wanted to talk with you first."

Her cell phone's high-pitched chirp made

them both jump. Becky jerked away, her expression fracturing into a mutinous scowl. Amy stifled a curse as she checked her watch. It was time for her conference call.

"I'm sorry, honey," she said as the dratted phone rang again. "I have to take this."

After gazing apologetically at Becky, she shifted her eyes to her mother, silently begging for some magical solution. But all she found in her mom's expression was a world of worry to match her own.

Amy stood and smoothed a hand through her daughter's chocolate-colored curls. "I promise. This evening, after dinner, I'm all yours. No cell phones, no interruptions, just you and —"

"Fine, whatever." The ten-year-old stomped away. "When you're ready to fit me into your schedule," she spat over her shoulder, "I'll be in my cell."

As Becky slammed her bedroom door, Amy slumped into a kitchen chair, then answered the still-ringing phone.

"I'm here, Jacquie," she snarled by way of a greeting, assuming her assistant was on the other end of the line. "Patch me into the conference room whenever you're ready."

"That won't be necessary, Ms. Loar."

Phillip Hutchinson's voice boomed over the line.

CHAPTER THREE

"The Kramer group has postponed the sign-off meeting until tomorrow afternoon," Phillip Hutchinson continued.

"Postponed!" Dread kicked Amy's pulse into a sprint. "What happened? Jacquie was supposed to call if there was a problem."

"I shared with the Kramer management that you had an unavoidable family emergency, and that you were out of the office today. I've bought you some time. Wrap up whatever you're doing, so you can be back for a five-o'clock conference tomorrow."

"But . . ." She closed her eyes and fought to manufacture order out of chaos. "Mr. Hutchinson, I appreciate your help, but I can handle this meeting long distance. Jacquie has my files. She'll be distributing the report and handling the audiovisual. And I'll be video conferenced. It will be fine."

"It will be fine unless something goes

wrong. This is the last meeting before we present the deal to their CEO on the thirtieth, and Alex Kramer is one of the toughest sells in the business. You can't afford to botch this. I know what's best in this situation."

Lord save her from men who knew what was best.

"Thank you, Mr. Hutchinson, but —"

"Then it's all settled." His tone announced just exactly what he thought of the word *but.* "I'll see you tomorrow by five."

Gwen smoothed a comforting hand down Amy's arm. Strength and support radiated from her touch.

"No, sir." Amy sat taller, fighting the impulse to back down. "I can't be there tomorrow."

"Ms. Loar —"

"Mr. Hutchinson." Her voice was boardroom direct, cutthroat calm. "I've given Enterprise Consulting my heart and soul for this pitch. The Kramer project is on time and under budget, and you have my personal assurance that tomorrow's meeting will proceed without incident."

It had likely been decades since anyone had dared to say no to Phillip Hutchinson. Deafening silence echoed the ringing in Amy's ears. She waited for a response that never came.

"My staff is more than capable of handling anything that arises in my absence," she assured him. "The project is in good hands."

"For your sake, Ms. Loar, I hope so. Your future in this firm depends on it. You're taking an enormous risk."

Amy blinked at the finality of his statement. At the thought of all she stood to lose, and how easily everything she was fighting for could vanish, all because of one mix-up.

"I have to be here in Sweetbrook. There's an important meeting at the school tomorrow afternoon I can't miss. I've promised my daughter," she added, another no-no in business — bringing her personal life into the workplace.

Which she'd never let happen. Until now.

"Do what you have to do," Mr. Hutchinson said. The uncomfortable rasp in his voice must have been his attempt at sounding supportive. "Take care of your daughter, take care of your family. Take care of the entire state of South Carolina. Whatever you need to do. Just get yourself back here by Monday."

"Yes, sir."

Amy ended the call and stared at her mother.

Her crazy little world had just taken an

even bigger twist into bedlam. One misstep at tomorrow's meeting, one crisis over the weekend that her staff couldn't cover, and her professional goose was cooked. Meanwhile, she had just over three days to find some common ground with her angry ten-year-old daughter and work things out at her school.

"I've got to talk with Josh now," Amy muttered, her next course of action clear.

"Why?" Gwen asked. "You have an appointment with him tomorrow."

"Yeah, him and Becky's teacher, and the staff counselor. I can't go in there cold. I need more facts, and I need them now." Her daughter's happiness and so much more was on the line. "Josh seemed so certain he understands Becky better than I do. Maybe he does. Where does he live?"

"Back at his family's house, ever since he divorced and his father became ill. His folks moved to Demming late last year." Gwen checked her watch. "He's probably home from school by now."

"Then that's where I'll be." Amy headed into the den for her purse, her mother following close behind. "Tell Becky I'll be back in a little bit. Maybe I can take her for ice cream after dinner and we can talk then."

"Honey," Gwen said as Amy opened the

70

door. "I don't think going to Josh White's house is such a good idea. He's been through a lot himself lately, what with —"

"This isn't a social call, Mama. I know I've been out of touch with things around here for the last few years, but I can't wait to catch up on all the gossip before I talk with him. Josh is the one who called me. I won't take up any more of his time than I absolutely have to."

Amy hugged Gwen's shoulders, then walked out to her car.

A twinge of sadness whispered through her at the thought of how little she knew about Josh's life now. He dominated the lightest, happiest parts of her Sweetbrook memories.

She'd never let him guess that her feelings of friendship had deepened into something more their last few years in school. She'd never let on how much that kiss they'd shared during their argument about Richard had affected her. After his harsh words that night, their friendship had fallen apart, and they hadn't spoken since. Not until yesterday, when she hadn't even recognized his voice.

She'd handled his phone call badly, partly because of her embarrassment that he was playing a starring role in her crisis with

Becky. But only partly. She'd distrusted him on the spot, and she'd said as much to his face. And no matter what had happened between them, Josh didn't deserve that. She owed him an apology. If it came down to it, she'd beg him to forget about everything but helping her the way he'd offered. She'd even weather more of his obvious disappointment over the mess she'd made of her life. Whatever it took.

Tomorrow's SST meeting had to be a success. That would leave her the rest of the weekend to work things out with Becky, as impossible as that seemed at the moment. But Amy had done the impossible before. She'd escaped from her marriage physically whole, albeit emotionally scarred. Surely she could make this work, too.

She had to.

"Give them back!" Daniel ripped the last of his clothes from the closet and flung them across his bedroom.

"They're gone." His uncle crossed his arms and leaned against the doorjamb.

True to his word, he hadn't come into the room. From day one, he'd said he wouldn't, not unless Daniel invited him in. He wanted Daniel to feel at home here. To know he had his privacy. To feel safe.

Whatever that meant.

Daniel crossed his arms, copying his uncle's stance. Anything not to let on how much a part of him wanted this guy to like him. But that wasn't going to happen. Things were too messed up. *He* was too messed up.

"So when you said my stuff was my stuff," he blurted, "that was just a bunch of lies!"

"Enough," his uncle barked. "Those shoes were falling apart. And I asked you to stop wearing them to school. You ignored me, as usual, so now they're gone. End of story. It's just a pair of shoes."

"*My* shoes." Daniel threw his arm wide. "*My* room."

"In *my* house."

He still hadn't stepped into the room.

"I'm sorry for raising my voice," he said. "And I don't like invading your privacy. But we have to come to some kind of compromise on stuff like this."

The man's patience had never angered Daniel more.

"Cut it out, okay?" He stormed toward the front of the huge house he still couldn't believe his mother had grown up in. "Knock off the *we're going to be a happy family or else* stuff. I don't belong here. You and my grandmother never wanted my mom here.

And you don't want me."

"That's not true." His uncle dogged him all the way to the front door. His hand flattened on the dark wood at the same time that Daniel turned the doorknob. "Where are you going?"

Where he always went when things got too real.

"Out."

Daniel yanked with all his might, pitting his strength against his uncle's. Closing his eyes, he shut out the man's concern. He didn't know why he'd lost it so completely about a stupid pair of shoes. Why he was always picking fights over nothing. Only it wasn't nothing.

He could handle his uncle angry. And when he finally pushed him too far, he'd be able to handle whatever the guy dished out. Daniel had taken worse.

But this wanting to let his uncle get closer, the sick feeling that rushed over him every time he tried . . . Surrounding him, suffocating him, just like the memories did. . . .

He couldn't take it.

His uncle stepped back, allowing the door to swing wide. Giving Daniel his freedom. The muscles that bunched beneath the rolled sleeves of his dress shirt made it clear just how easily he could have stopped Daniel if he'd chosen to.

"Okay. You're free to head out to wherever you go every afternoon. But your social worker's due here any minute for her home visit. I need you to stay until she's gone. She wants to talk with you about how things are going here."

"How things are going?" Daniel sputtered. "They're not!"

He shoved his uncle farther away and waited for him to finally snap. But instead of exploding, the man just stood there.

What a loser. Why wouldn't he do them both a favor and give up already?

"Whatever." Daniel snorted and sprinted away.

Let his uncle try to come after him. He could outrun anybody.

Daniel loped down the sloping front lawn, past the weathered brick pillars that flanked the driveway. The stone lions sitting atop the arched entrance growled silently, looking back at him with empty, lonely eyes.

His uncle was nuts if he thought family ties, and money and this moldy old estate would make Daniel feel like he belonged here. The man had been a creep to Daniel's mother, and now he wanted to play happy family?

Besides, hadn't he been paying attention?

Daniel didn't want to belong anywhere.

Josh was shoving the worst of the comics and discarded clothes back into his nephew's already bulging closet when the doorbell rang.

Barbara Thomas, Daniel's Family Services caseworker, was early. The doorbell rang again. Barbara didn't like being kept waiting.

Josh gave the fallout from Daniel's shoe meltdown a final glance and threw in the towel. He usually had the house straightened for one of these visits. But his nephew was getting more proficient by the day at trashing the place.

Josh pulled the bedroom door shut as he walked to greet the caseworker. Everywhere he looked, there were piles of books and toys, socks and shoes. Typical kid clutter that should have reassured him that things were getting back to normal, but he knew better. Daniel wasn't adjusting to either Melanie's death or living here with him.

He tugged at his rolled-up sleeves, reaching the front door as he shoved his dress shirt's wrinkled tail into his khaki pants. He kicked aside the backpack his nephew had dumped on the foyer floor. Pressing his palms to his eyes as the bell pealed again, he counted to five and opened the mahogany doors.

"Hello," Barbara said.

Her nod of greeting was as efficient as the rest of her. She wore a brown suit this afternoon. The black one must be at the cleaners. Same conservative white shirt as always, though. Narrow collar. Very no-nonsense. Not even a hint of jewelry.

Josh had worked closely with her for years, helping the kids in his school who'd needed more than a simple education. He and Barbara were colleagues, maybe even friends. But at this particular moment, she was the last person he wanted to see.

"Aren't you going to ask me in?" She peered around his shoulder. "I rang so many times, I thought perhaps you'd forgotten our meeting."

"No, of course not." He stepped to the side and gestured for her to enter. "I was just —" She tripped on the backpack that hadn't quite come to rest against the wall. He picked it up and out of her way. "I was just cleaning up a bit."

Her razorlike gaze touched on the furniture and piles of kid debris she'd already seen dozens of times.

"Have you given any more thought to my suggestion about a live-in housekeeper?"

she asked. "Finances can't be the reason you haven't."

"Yeah, I could afford a full-time maid." He dug his hands into his pockets, rocking back on his heels. "And I know things look a little crazy around here, but I'll get a handle on it. Theresa Cooper has been my parents' housekeeper for over thirty years. We're a little more than she can handle right now, and she only works a few hours a day, but she's family. I can't just replace her."

Barbara's expression revealed nothing as she digested his answer. She was good at that — keeping her opinions to herself until her input would do the most good.

"Is Daniel ready?" She pulled a folder from the briefcase that passed for her purse, and began leafing through it.

"Well, he was. But . . ."

"But?"

"He's not here. At least not now." Josh felt ridiculous. Inept and ridiculous.

"Didn't he know I was coming for a review?" She checked her watch.

"I think that played a big part in his decision to be somewhere else." Josh crossed arms. "That and the fact that he knew him staying here was important to me."

Her eyebrow jerked up. Her expression bordered on amusement.

"He didn't appreciate me telling him to get cleaned up and change into shoes that weren't falling apart," Josh explained. "He —"

"He resents you polishing him up so you can show him off to me?"

"Yeah. I guess that about covers it."

"So he told you what you could do with your meeting, and stormed off."

Josh shrugged. "He lights out of here almost every afternoon. Turns up again for dinner. I don't know where he goes, but it's somewhere he wants to be a lot more than he wants to be here."

"Good." Another one of her nods. She consulted her folder once more.

"Good?" He had just about had it. "You come here once a month and tell me to take things slow. That a boy abused the way my sister claims she and Daniel were needs time and space to settle in. But when I tell you that he can't bear to be in the same house as me, you're finally encouraged?"

"He stood up to you, Josh." She fingered through her notes. "And from the sketchy details we have of his past before his mother brought him to Sweetbrook, I can only imagine how much courage that took. You've remarked about how wary he is around you."

"He's downright terrified every time I touch him." Why had Josh let his mother's need to protect their family's reputation, her insistence that Melanie was exaggerating as always, shame his sister into silence about her relationship with Daniel's father? A man their mother had been mortified to learn Melanie had lived with for five years, but had never married. Josh would give anything not to be piecing together the disturbing details now. To have been there for Melanie when she'd needed him most. To understand what her son needed now.

"Daniel's nervous around all adults," he added, "but men especially. He watches every move I make, like he's expecting me to shout *boo* or something. Like he can't turn his back, or I might come after him."

"And when he first came here, he was nonresponsive and withdrawn if you confronted him directly." Barbara's gaze measured Josh's frustration.

"Yeah."

Just like Melanie had been.

"But this time, when you pressed him, he pushed back, at least for a moment."

Her words rattled around in Josh's head, then came together in a startling flash of clarity.

"Yeah," he repeated, amazed. "He actually

shoved me out of the way."

He and Daniel had taken a haphazard step in the right direction, and Josh hadn't even seen it.

"Good." She nodded and gave him a smile. She headed toward the back of the house. "Why don't we start with Daniel's room, then. I can usually tell from a child's personal space how he feels about his surroundings."

Josh's warm feeling of accomplishment fizzled, heartburn rushing to take its place.

Like a bloodhound, Barbara had sniffed trouble and was heading deeper into his nightmare. He shook his head and followed in her wake.

He was three steps from the bedroom when the doorbell chimed, then jingled again.

He bit back a curse as Barbara disappeared into Daniel's sty of a room. Relieved, actually, that he wouldn't have to witness her disappointment and shock, Josh turned and retraced his steps to the front of the house.

What now?

Amy pushed her rebellious curls behind her ear as she waited at the Whites' door. Sweat trickled between her shoulder blades.

She hadn't taken the time to change out of her sapphire-colored dress suit. That would have given her one chance too many to talk herself out of this.

She needed more information about Becky. End of story. And that made apologizing to Josh her first course of business. Asking for his help was the hard-to-swallow second step, but there was no avoiding that, either. She reached to press the bell a third time. Midring, the heavy door jerked open, revealing an all-grown-up Joshua White she should have been expecting but wasn't.

She'd been prepared for something along the lines of the boy she'd left behind. But the man before her was so much more than a replay of days gone by. Tall and classically handsome, broader at the shoulders, firmer at the jaw, Josh no longer sported the relaxed ease of the comfortably wealthy. The lines on his face spoke of responsibility and determination. Of a life not quite under his control, but he was determined not to give up.

Still blond and too good-looking by anyone's standards, dressed in rumpled but clearly expensive business attire, he stared at her for a moment before his pale-blue eyes widened with recognition.

"Amy?"

Just the sound of her name rolling off his lips with the same hint of Southern inflection as before made her incapable of saying anything in return. To her horror, her pulse gave a hiccuping flutter and her breath caught on some unexplainable obstruction in her throat.

What was wrong with her?

She realized a sappy grin was spreading across her face, and forced herself to stifle it.

"Amy?" he repeated. He checked over his shoulder, then turned back. "What can I do for you?"

"Oh, um . . ." She tucked back the hair that refused to stay where it belonged today. Straightened her purse strap on her shoulder. Fidgeted with the tail of her jacket like a schoolgirl. *Get a grip!* "I was wondering if I could have a few minutes of your time —"

"Not right now."

The coldness of his words washed over her. Where was the caring, it's-going-to-be-okay Josh from last night?

"I'm sorry." He winced and propped the hand not holding the doorknob on his hip. "I don't mean to be rude. But this isn't a good time —"

"Well, Daniel's room is certainly an odyssey into the mind," a feminine voice said from behind him. "And I was glancing through one of his homework notebooks. It looks like — Oh! I didn't mean to interrupt."

A middle-aged woman dressed in a nondescript brown suit stopped at Josh's side. Her gaze cataloged Amy's appearance, then she turned her attention to the man shifting his weight from one foot to the other between them.

"I'll leave you to your guest. But there's an important matter we need to discuss before I leave."

Amy watched the other woman walk into the sitting room off the hall. She and Josh had often done homework in that room, sprawling on the heirloom rug in front of an overstuffed couch and chairs, devouring snacks and trying to master the intellectual acrobatics required to complete assignments in geometry, history and American lit. Josh had tackled each assignment with ease, of course. He'd been brilliant, even in elementary school. A little bookish and preoccupied with making sure everything was perfect, but alarmingly smart. And he'd also been kind and genuinely interested in helping her do well. There'd been a lot of teacher in him even then.

She shook her head at the folly of looking

back, when she'd made such a disaster of everything since.

She squared her shoulders. Josh clearly had company to get back to. What had the woman said about his nephew? "I'm sorry to barge in like this, but I came to talk about Becky. I'd hoped you could tell me a little more about this SST meeting you've scheduled for tomorrow. Maybe give me some idea of what to expect. What to talk with Becky about tonight."

Josh chewed on the side of his mouth, glancing into the sitting room, then back at her. With a sigh, he dropped his head and opened the door wider for her to enter.

"Of course we can talk," he said. "I'm glad you've made it down for the meeting." The slight smile he gave her softened his features. His eyes, however, had her wishing she knew what was wrong, so maybe she could help. "I'm sorry I was so short on the phone last night. I had no cause to question your commitment to caring for Becky."

"Yes, you did." She tried to lighten the awkward moment with her own smile. His frown confirmed she hadn't quite pulled it off. "I don't blame you for jumping to conclusions, Josh. And I wasn't exactly on my best behavior. It's been a rough year."

He nodded his acceptance of her roundabout apology. A flick of his wrist allowed him to check his watch again. "Just give me a few minutes to finish up with my social worker."

"Your social worker?"

"No . . . I mean, yes." He tugged at his partially undone tie. "She's my nephew's caseworker from Family Services."

As if that explained everything.

He squinted when she didn't respond. Then his expression became guarded, as if he was bracing for an invisible blow. "You haven't heard, have you?"

"I didn't even know Melanie had a little boy." She measured each word carefully as she tried to keep pace with his shifting mood. "After the way we . . . the way you and I left things . . . Before my wedding, that is . . ."

She cleared her throat, remembering again exactly what they'd done the last time they'd seen each other, feeling saddened anew by the chasm that had stretched between them since.

"Well," she said, when Josh continued to stare. "After we fought, and I married Richard, I haven't really kept up with Mother's Sweetbrook gossip. Especially since my divorce. I've barely had time to think straight."

"Yes, well." The simple effort it took to breathe seemed to cost him dearly. "That woman in the other room is trying to help me find a way to give my nephew some chance at a normal childhood. If you'll just give me a few minutes, we can talk some more about Becky."

"Is Melanie okay?" Amy asked.

What on earth was he talking about? Why wasn't his sister meeting with her son's social worker?

"No." Josh turned toward the other room, leaving her by the front door. "My sister died in a car accident in January."

CHAPTER FOUR

Josh couldn't shake Amy's image from his mind as he tried to gather his thoughts enough to face Barbara Thomas.

It had been an unreal moment, opening his front door to a sophisticated redhead, who in a blink had transformed into a grown-up reflection of the girl he knew. Maybe if there'd been even a hint of the friendship they'd once shared, it wouldn't be so hard to accept this new, closed-off Amy. An Amy who had made every day of his childhood brighter. The Amy he'd driven out of his life with his own stupidity.

She hadn't even known that Melanie was dead. She'd had no idea that he was trying to be father and mother to a little boy who wanted nothing to do with him. The blue-eyed businesswoman cooling her heels in his foyer was like some kind of stranger that Josh didn't need to be dealing with today. Even if she still wore her auburn hair in waves that begged a man to bury his hands in them.

"I'm all yours, Barbara." He stepped into the sitting room, an agreeable smile plastered on his face. He came to a halt at the sight of his colleague flipping through one of the family photo albums his mother stored on a low shelf by the couch.

"I hope you don't mind." Her glance told him she knew otherwise. She closed the satin-covered book. "It was lying open on the table when I sat down."

Josh scanned the cluster of albums on the shelf. Several more were missing, in addition to the one in her lap.

"Daniel must have been looking at the pictures," he reasoned out loud.

It seemed a perfectly logical thing for the kid to be doing, trying to learn as much as he could about the people and places he'd come from. Except that Daniel flat-out refused to discuss anything about the family with Josh. He hadn't even wanted the picture of Melanie Josh had offered to let him keep in his bedroom. Yet he'd been secretly poring over photographs of holidays and vacations from aeons ago?

"Perhaps Daniel isn't as detached from you and this house as he'd like for us to believe," Barbara said, completing Josh's thoughts in that unnerving way of hers. She cocked her head to the side. "These pictures say a lot about how close you and your sister were growing up."

"That was a long time ago."

Before Melanie had run off and had a baby with someone he and his folks had never met. Before his mother had disowned her. When Melanie returned to Sweetbrook their mother had spent the last months of his sister's life reminding her of every mistake she'd made.

When Josh hadn't immediately stood up for his sister, she'd figured he'd sided with their disappointed mother. And that was the end of the special bond between big brother and little sister, which Josh hadn't appreciated until it was gone.

His stomach felt as if it was trying to digest broken glass.

He loved his family, but sometimes he wondered if the money they'd all been raised with had somehow damaged their ability to love the way the rest of the world did. It certainly hadn't guaranteed them happiness.

"Daniel never got to see his mom and me do anything but fight with one another," he finally said.

"Maybe looking at these pictures will help

him understand that it wasn't always that way between you two."

"Maybe," Josh agreed, though he couldn't get excited about the possibility.

He was more than a little amazed, actually, to be standing there having such a surreal heart-to-heart with someone he had to work with on a daily basis. Barbara's understanding expression held a glint of pity, and he could handle just about anything right now but being pitied.

"You said there was something important we needed to discuss." He crossed his arms and waited.

"Yes." She sat straighter on the couch and withdrew another folder from her cavernous briefcase. A blue one this time. "There's a snag in your petition to become Daniel's permanent guardian. His father is indicating an interest in custody, as well."

"Whose father?" Josh's confusion didn't last a full second. "You mean the jerk Melanie said knocked her and my nephew around? No way is that man ever coming near Daniel again."

"Your sister named him the boy's father on the birth certificate. That gives him solid legal grounds for custody. And there's no record of any of the abuse Melanie claimed happened."

"Melanie didn't file charges when they were together. For some reason, she was trying to make things work with the man. I think she hoped he would eventually marry her. Then the creep abandoned them, and it didn't matter anymore. That was five years ago. When she showed up here, my mother didn't want a scandal on her hands and forbade Melanie from even talking about the abuse she said she'd suffered. We . . . we were never sure how much of her story was true and how much was her attempt to explain away the mistakes she'd made. You know how many scrapes she used to get into. How she'd try to lie her way out of problems, until my parents came along to smooth things over."

He'd give anything for a second chance to earn Melanie's trust. To have believed her about Daniel's father from the start. Maybe he could have gotten her to open up about what had happened. But as usual, his mother's idea of dealing with the problem had been to protect the family reputation. Melanie had needed love and support. Their mother had instead doled out enough money for Melanie and Daniel to live in an apartment across town — under the condition that there'd be no more talk about Melanie's life before her return to town.

To their parents, wielding money and ignoring uncomfortable realities had been the solution to everything.

"But you believe her story now?" Barbara prompted.

"After the last few months with Daniel, yes." The guilt that he'd judged his sister so quickly never completely left him. That he'd taken her claims so lightly and spent so little time with her and his nephew before her death. He didn't deserve the faith she'd placed in him by leaving him custody of her son. "We may never know exactly what happened before Melanie brought him home to Sweetbrook, but I don't doubt for a second that my sister was telling the truth about the physical abuse."

"And Daniel refuses to talk with you about his father?"

"He barely talks to me at all." Josh dropped into an overstuffed chair.

"His counselor has relayed the same thing." Barbara shook her head, making notes in her file. "And I'm afraid that without Daniel's statement or concrete proof of your sister's allegations, Curtis Jenkins is well within his rights to visit his son, as well as petition to end your temporary guardianship."

"No way!" Josh was out of the chair and

pacing before he processed Barbara's stunned surprise. He was shouting at the person fighting in the trenches right alongside him. He cleared his throat. "How did the man even know about my sister's death? She hasn't spoken to him in years."

"I'm afraid that's my doing," Barbara replied in the civil servant deadpan that often masked more emotional involvement than she cared to let on. "I'm required by law to notify all immediate family in a custody matter like this. It took Mr. Jenkins this long to step forward, only because it's taken me months to locate the man. I finally found his parents in Shreveport and sent them a registered letter. Mr. Jenkins contacted me yesterday, and I was compelled to share with him the basics of Daniel's case, including the details of your sister's accident."

"And that's it?" Josh snapped his fingers in the air. "Just like that, the man can waltz in here and take Daniel away from me?"

"Of course not —"

"My sister wanted her son with me. Her will named me his guardian!"

"Of course, the judge will consider Melanie's wishes before a final decision is reached —"

"She was terrified of the man, Barbara.

Tell me that counts for something."

"Of course her claims of abuse will be weighed carefully." Barbara clasped her hands atop the folders in her lap. "But if you want your sister's allegations to carry much weight with the court, you're going to have to come up with something more than what you heard her say. Daniel will need to make a statement about the physical abuse. And you should start preparing him for the reality of seeing his father again."

Josh sat beside her on the couch, the total breakdown of communication between him and his nephew hitting home. "He won't talk to me. He won't talk to anyone. When he finds out Curtis Jenkins is coming here, there's no telling what he'll do."

"That's why I'm giving you a heads-up before his father arrives. So you'll have time to prepare your nephew. Maybe this will be the incentive Daniel needs to open up to you."

Josh could only stare.

Daniel needed someone he could connect with. Someone he could trust. And all he knew about Josh was that he was one more person who'd let his mother down.

"You know I'm on your side," Barbara continued. "I've sent the judge weekly briefs on how hard you're trying to make this work. There are positive signs that Daniel's bonding with you, even if the child's room looks like he trashes it on a daily basis just to irritate you."

"Thank you . . . I think," Josh replied, uneasy with her backhanded praise.

"And I assure you," she continued, "if there's any evidence whatsoever that Daniel's father is the kind of threat your sister claimed, it will be my personal mission to make sure Curtis Jenkins never gains custody of his son."

The fierceness of both Barbara's expression and her statement should have looked comical on such a tiny, unassuming person. But she was dead serious. She was the one ace up Josh's sleeve, but even she couldn't manufacture miracles. Daniel's cooperation was the wild card, and Josh had never had a stomach for gambling.

"When do you expect this Jenkins man to show up?" he asked.

"Within the week. That's the best I could tell from our conversation. You have the right to request a paternity test, and I strongly advise that you do. You'll also want to bring your lawyer up to speed, in case he has any other sugges—"

The peal of a cell phone interrupted her.

They glanced across the room to find an

otherwise silent Amy Loar standing in the doorway, a shocked, guilty expression on her face. It was clear as day why.

She'd been caught eavesdropping.

And who knew how much of his family's dirty laundry she'd managed to overhear.

Amy wanted to die. Drop to the floor, slither out of the house and back to her car, and die.

Mortified, at a total loss to explain why she'd been listening in on Josh's very private conversation about his sister, she turned around and made herself move into the hallway.

Melanie White had been abused. Her son, too, if Josh and the social worker's suspicions were correct. What Amy wouldn't give to forget every single word she'd just heard, for her sake as well as for Josh's. She hurried toward the front door and answered her phone, if for no other reason than to stop the infernal ringing.

"Hello?" she mumbled, her hand shaking as she lifted the phone to her ear.

"Hello . . . Amy?" her mother replied. "I can barely hear you, dear."

"What is it, Mama?" she whispered, hoping her voice wouldn't carry into the next room. "I can't talk right now —"

"Becky's gone, honey. Is she there with you by any chance?"

"What? No, of course she's not here." Amy checked her watch. "She was in her room when I left. Does she usually go outside to play this time of day?"

"She never plays outside. Hasn't made any friends to play with. She usually sits around the house all afternoon, reading."

"Then where could she have gone?" An avalanche of worst-case scenarios tortured Amy. "You don't think she'd really run away?"

"I don't know, honey. Is there any place she might have gone? Maybe somewhere you've told her about around here?"

"No, I don't think so. Have you —"

"I'll check my calendar at the office." The social worker stepped around Amy and opened the front door. Her cool glance conveyed her displeasure at Amy's earlier intrusion.

"I'll need to see Daniel within the next week," she said to Josh. "My report is due to Judge Hardy."

"I'll bring him by your office." Josh glowered at Amy, making her long to follow the other woman out the door.

The social worker left with a brief nod and another stern look in Amy's direction.

"Are you there, dear?" Gwen was asking. "Amy?"

"I'll call you right back." Amy ended the call and made herself face Josh.

"What do you think you were doing?" His complexion took on a reddish hue beneath the late-day stubble of his beard. "You had no business listening to anything that was going on in that room."

"I know." She clasped her hands and fought the emotion shredding her voice. "And I didn't mean to intrude, really. One minute I heard you yelling, and the next . . . there I was in the doorway."

Her feeble excuse sounded so lame.

Because it is!

"And then I heard what Melanie and her son went through, and I —"

"And you couldn't wait to hear more, is that it?" Josh dug his hands into his pockets, the motion so savage it was a wonder the seams didn't give way. Yet somehow his combative stance made him appear more sad than angry. "Just like everyone else in town, you had to know all the details about my sister's sordid mistakes, how it felt —"

"Trust me," Amy said over his tirade, shamed to the soles of her feet. "I didn't have to eavesdrop to know exactly how Melanie felt."

99

The silence resonating through the room screamed that she'd revealed way more than she'd ever intended. She smoothed the front of her silk suit jacket and swallowed what little air her throat would allow in. She fought to ignore the echoes of all she herself was still running from.

"You have to know, Josh . . ." She gazed up at his shocked expression. "I'd be the last person to judge Melanie for what happened to her and Daniel. For doing whatever she had to do to protect her son and raise him on her own."

Josh reached a hand toward her, his anger melting away. His brow furrowed when she edged out of his reach.

"Amy. I —"

Her phone jingled again.

"Becky!" She flipped open the phone. "Mama, is she back?"

"No, dear." Her mother sounded worried, but not yet panicking. "I'm going to walk through the neighborhood and ask if anyone's seen her. Is there anywhere you think she might have gone?"

"No. I can't think of a single place in Sweetbrook I've talked with her about. She's been so upset at the move, she didn't want to hear anything from me." Amy gave a start as Josh's hand settled on her arm.

Comfort radiated from his touch, from the concern warming his pale blue eyes. Just like when they were kids, and she'd instinctively known he was the one person in town she could trust more than all the others. She shied away, the voice inside her she never quite managed to silence warning that she couldn't trust anyone anymore.

"Wait, Mama. There is one place. I used to tell her about the tree house. The one by the Millers' pond. She knows that's where I went when I wanted to be alone."

Well, not quite alone. Recollection flickered across Josh's features. He remembered their secret hideout, too.

"When she was a baby, I'd tell her bedtime stories about daydreaming up there. You don't think . . ."

"It's possible. Her bus passes the Miller place on the way to and from school."

"I'm heading over there now." Amy ended the call and turned to leave.

"Becky's missing," she explained over her shoulder. "I've got to find her."

Josh stepped around her and opened the front door. With a raised eyebrow, he waited for her to move outside, then he followed, shutting the door behind them.

"You said you thought Becky might be at the Millers' pond." He checked his watch and waved for her to precede him down the winding walkway. "I've got at least an hour before Daniel turns up for dinner. Let's go find your daughter."

As Josh pulled his SUV away from the house and headed across town to the Miller farm, he glanced toward his passenger. The composed businesswoman who'd rung his doorbell was gone. In her place was a parent terrified for her child.

He'd offered to drive his car, not really expecting her to accept after their confrontation in the foyer. But Amy had acquiesced without a word. She'd even allowed him to help her step into the Range Rover, her focus clearly on Becky, her defenses momentarily down in a way that made it impossible for him not to do whatever he could to help, no matter how badly they'd gotten off on the wrong foot. She looked so small and miserable huddling beside him, the strength he'd always admired in her weakened by her fear for Becky. Maybe fear of even more.

She'd said she knew exactly how Melanie had felt. The empathy in Amy's eyes as she'd spoken . . . Something told Josh she wasn't just talking about her failed marriage or her own struggles as a single mom. His sister had survived an abusive relationship. Josh's fists clenched around the steering wheel at the thought of Amy living through the same kind of hell.

He hadn't liked Richard Reese and his slick, big-city indifference. But the man had seemed to care for Amy in his own way. He hadn't seemed like the type to —

"Becky was so angry at me before I left my mother's," Amy muttered more to herself than to him. Her fingers were fiddling nonstop with the heart-shaped pendant suspended from a chain around her neck. "Nothing I do, nothing I say, seems to make a dent anymore."

"We'll find her." He kept both hands on the wheel, remembering how Amy had skirted out of his reach when he'd tried to comfort her before. The lady wore her hands-off policy like a bulletproof vest.

"Sometimes kids need their space," he offered. "Daniel had just stormed away from me before you and Barbara arrived this afternoon."

"Daniel?" Amy's not-quite-focused gaze met his.

"My nephew." Josh took the left fork before Hudson's Bridge. "The last place he seems to want to be these days is in the house with me. Most afternoons, he takes off for parts unknown. Turns up for dinner every night, though. Becky will, too. Don't worry. Sweetbrook's still a fairly safe place."

"She said she'd run away if I didn't take her back to Atlanta with me."

"Kids say a lot of things."

"Yeah, but what if she meant it?" Amy gazed out the window at the passing farmland. "I haven't been home for more than a few hours, and my daughter can't wait to get away from me."

"She's an angry little girl," he agreed with a nod. He'd give anything to ease Amy's anxiety, but where would that get Becky? "How long has she been acting out like this?"

Amy stiffened beside him.

"You said you wanted to discuss her issues at school," he reminded her.

Her eyes narrowing, she sat straighter in the seat.

"It all started when she began to notice the . . . the problems between her father and me. I think she was seven or eight. By the time I divorced him, she'd graduated to hating him and blaming me for everything."

"Because you left her father?"

"Because I didn't leave him sooner." Amy stared at the dashboard, as if it was vital that she memorize every dial and display.

104

"It seems you were right about Richard, after all."

"Where's he now?" Josh asked, as if he understood. Meanwhile his list of questions was growing by the second.

"Out of the picture."

Her statement was determined. Almost menacing.

Josh recognized the tone. He'd heard it before, the few times Melanie had talked about Curtis Jenkins. As if the man was dead and buried. *Okay, no more questions about the ex.*

"Was Becky getting into fights at school before she moved in with Gwen?" he asked. "Was she picking on the other kids in her class?"

Blue eyes that had always been darker than his widened.

"No." Amy's lips trembled as she spoke. "Becky's always been so sweet, so open and friendly with everyone. That's part of what makes this so hard."

Amy's attention shifted back to the windshield, though he doubted she actually saw the pastureland rolling by as they left the town behind.

"Becky's changed over the last few years," she continued. "Since she realized things weren't right between her father and me.

Her behavior grew even worse after the divorce was finalized, and I had to start supporting us entirely on my own."

"Gwen said you work a lot of long hours." More disappointment than he'd intended made its way into his voice.

Amy's expression hardened. "Most single working mothers do, Josh."

She shook her head, as if he were about the stupidest man she'd ever stumbled across.

"To the point where their kids have to move to another state to live with relatives?" He sounded like a judgmental jerk. It wasn't his place to critique her life choices now, any more than it had been twelve years ago. But what else could he say in response to her circular logic? Amy was too smart to really believe that her success at work justified the damage she was doing to her relationship with her daughter.

"Don't you dare criticize me," she spat. "You don't have the first clue what you're talking about."

"Then explain it to me. 'Cause I can hear the guilt in your voice. You're blaming yourself for all of this, just as much as you say Becky is. But you talk like you don't have a choice. Like you really believe this job of yours is more important than keeping your daughter with you. You couldn't possibly need the money that badly."

"Spoken like someone who's been swimming in his inheritance his entire life. My *job* is the only thing standing between my family and our only other option. I either make this work on my own, or we go back to depending on Becky's father." She shivered at the thought, then pulled herself together right before Josh's eyes. "And if you were walking in my shoes, you and your moral certainty would compromise every last principle you had to make sure that didn't happen. Besides, if you're such an expert on raising kids, where's your family? Last I heard, you'd married your all-American girl straight out of college. Now you're living in your parents' house, raising your sister's child alone."

Josh took his turn staring out the windshield at nothing in particular. He deserved the question, after jumping down her throat. And if the fear in her voice was any indication, Richard Reese deserved to be beaten within an inch of his life for doing whatever he'd done to leave her literally shaking at the thought of going back to him.

"I never had kids," Josh said simply, hoping that would be enough. Which of course it wasn't.

"You and your wife . . . ?"

"Lisa and I couldn't conceive naturally." His jaw clenched as he spoke his ex's name. "Before we could try other methods, she . . . We divorced. Turns out we both wanted something else more than we wanted each other. She wanted a new life in a more exciting place, and I wanted a family here in Sweetbrook. It wasn't a recipe for a happy marriage."

"Ah. The career woman spurning the wealthy, small-town boy." Amy turned to look out her window. "That explains a lot."

Her sarcasm goaded him, as he was certain she'd intended. It was on the tip of his tongue to tell her that she was the one who didn't know what she was talking about. But then again, maybe she did.

The Miller farm came into view. The pond fronted the property, set back about a quarter of a mile from the road. The enormous oak that harbored the tree house held court at the water's edge. Josh swallowed the angry words he'd been about to sling at his passenger, and concentrated on leaving the asphalt behind and navigating the dirt path that would take them closer to the water.

"There it is." Amy pointed to the tree. "It looks exactly the same."

She shook her head in disbelief, reminding him that it had been ages since she'd
been back. Her attention zeroed in on the
tree fort.

"Do you see anyone in it? Please tell me
she's up there."

Anxiety and guilt turned her simple plea
into a prayer, reaffirming what Josh had
pretty much figured out already. Amy Loar
might be a woman sorely in need of a priority adjustment when it came to her child's
needs, but he'd been way off base thinking
she'd dumped Becky in Sweetbrook just to
get the kid out of her hair. Amy didn't need
him on her back about her decisions. She
was already raking herself over the coals.

And he'd pushed her too hard for the
details he needed to help Becky at school,
making Amy even more defensive. But he
took his responsibility to care for the children of Sweetbrook seriously. And that
included Becky, even if she was returning to
Atlanta soon. Especially now that he'd
learned more about the troubles hounding
both the girl and her mother. Something
about their situation added up to more than
just a bad divorce, poor parenting choices
and a rebellious ten-year-old.

He and Amy may have lost touch after the
fight he'd initiated about Richard. They

might be little more than passing acquaintances now, estranged friends that were getting on each other's nerves. And he had enough problems of his own. But he was sticking close to Amy until they found her daughter. And then he was going to do whatever he could to help.

CHAPTER FIVE

Amy was out of the Range Rover as soon as they'd rolled to a stop. She heard the emergency brake set, then Josh fell into step beside her as they made their way across the farmland they'd run through as kids.

"Someone's up there." Josh squinted up at the tree house, shielding his eyes from the setting sun.

Amy strained to see inside the fort. The structure sagged in places, warped with age. Its roof had been patched, and the chunks of wood nailed to the tree to serve as a ladder were a crooked mess.

"Becky!" Amy called as she sprinted to the base of the tree.

A rustling sound was the only response.

"Becky, honey. Your grandmother called. You've got her worried sick." Amy reached for the rickety step just above her head, prepared to scale the tree in her suit and stockings if her daughter refused to come down.

More shuffling sounds came, but nothing else.

Josh stepped behind her, giving the piece of wood she was clinging to a firm shove. It twisted in her grasp. "I don't know if these old steps are sturdy enough for an adult."

"Maybe not for you." She kicked off her heels and placed her foot on the wooden block closest to the ground. She pulled on the step above her and started to climb. "Becky, I'm coming up."

"Stay away from me," a child shouted down to them. It was a young boy's voice. "Leave me alone!"

"Daniel?" Josh called as she hopped back to the ground. "Daniel, is Becky Reese up there with you?"

"No!" An adorable little boy with sandy-blond hair and bright-green eyes poked his head out of the tree fort's door. The scowl on his face spoke to Amy of loss and loneliness. "Leave me alone."

"Daniel, come down here," Josh sputtered. "It's time to head home for dinner."

Amy's phone rang. She turned from the tree, leaving Josh to deal with his nephew.

"Mama? She's —"

"She just came home, honey." Gwen

112

sighed in relief. "She won't say where she's been, but she's back in her room. I'm going to try and get her to eat a little something."

"Oh, good." Amy covered her eyes with a hand that was shaking almost as much as her voice. "I'll be home as soon as I can."

". . . I'm not coming down," Daniel was shouting as Amy approached the tree once more. "And you can't make me."

"I'm coming up there," Josh replied.

"I said stay away from me," Daniel yelled back. "This is my tree, not yours. I hate you! And I'm not going back to that house again, ever!"

Josh scaled the first few steps, his motions effortlessly coordinated despite his size. Before Amy knew what she was doing, she'd grabbed his pant leg.

"Don't, Josh. You're scaring him."

She should stay out of this. She should ask for a ride back to her car, focus on her own problems and leave Josh to his. But the fear in Daniel's angry voice was turning her knees to jelly, and she couldn't walk away.

"I can't leave him up there." Josh jumped back to the ground, his face all rough edges and at-the-end-of-his-rope frustration. "I can't let him keep fighting me like this," he said, lowering his voice so his nephew couldn't hear. "Daniel has to start trusting me, before it's too late. Before his father gets here, and I have no way to keep the man out of our lives."

Amy motioned for Josh to follow her away from the tree and out of Daniel's earshot. "I heard your social worker say Daniel was warming up to you. What good's going to come out of you climbing up there and dragging him home kicking and screaming?"

"And you weren't going to force Becky to come home if you found her here?"

"We're not talking about me and Becky," Amy countered reasonably, even as her own demons swam closer to the surface, threatening with memories of feeling powerless and trapped the way Daniel felt right now. "We're talking about a scared, possibly abused kid who doesn't need one more person forcing him to do something, just because they're bigger and stronger . . . and they can hurt you in ways you never dreamed of . . . ways that no one else will know, because words don't leave marks. . . . And you'd never dare talk with anyone about it, because who'd believe you. . . ."

Breathlessness consumed her as it always did when she looked back. Fear she'd never completely outrun crept closer. She tried to clear her throat, to ease the lump of emotion.

The memory of Richard's belittling words, condescending verbal blows, still had the power to turn her into the kind of weak female she'd sworn she'd never be again. She'd promised herself she'd be brave from now on. Undaunted in the face of challenges, like her mother. Instead, here she had the chance to help a scared little boy, and she was turning into a hand-wringing coward.

Josh brushed at the bangs hanging in her eyes. Alarm bells sounded at the sensation of being touched, clamoring for her to run. To find a safe place where pain couldn't find her.

When she flinched, he dropped his hand to his side.

"Do you want to talk about it?" He glanced up at the tree, then back at her.

He knew.

He knew how much she had in common with his sister, and she had only herself to blame. She'd all but told him that Richard was no better than Melanie's ex. He'd no doubt filled in the rest of the story with his own imagination.

"Talk about what?" Resignation dripped from every one of her words. "How I let my husband convince me I was worthless without him? That I was lucky he'd married me, 'cause no one else would ever want me? That he was the only security I'd ever know, and if I didn't do what he wanted, he'd —"

Stop it right there, Amy.

She swallowed. The truth was too awful to say. Too awful to watch Josh hear.

"You don't have to tell me, if you don't want to." The compassion in his eyes held the hard edge of anger she'd seen only once before, when he'd tried to warn her she was making a mistake expecting Richard and his money to make her happy. "You can tell me whatever you want, but you don't have to."

"No, I . . . You . . ." Surprisingly, some of the panic eased at the thought of Josh being willing to listen. Not that she was so far gone that she'd consider rambling further. She'd already said too much. "Just believe me when I say I understand a little of what Daniel may be feeling. Please, let me try talking to him."

After the stunt she'd pulled back at Josh's house, she knew she didn't deserve his trust. But she couldn't bear the thought of what Daniel must be suffering. That the pain eating at her might be wreaking the same kind of havoc on a defenseless child. She was a grown-up, and she'd made her mistakes.

She would deal with the consequences. But Daniel didn't deserve any of this.

"Please," she begged. "If you're right about what happened to Melanie and your nephew, it may help him to talk with someone who understands what that can be like."

Josh's expression was unreadable as he absorbed all she'd said. And all she hadn't. He had a world of questions, she could tell. But instead of asking for the details she couldn't bring herself to give him, he offered a sad imitation of the smile that had once dazzled her.

"Okay." He shifted his gaze up to the tree house. "Give it a shot. You couldn't do any more damage than I already have."

"Daniel?" Amy asked, hanging on to the rickety steps that wound up the side of the tree. "I'm a friend of your uncle's. Is it okay if I come up?"

"Be careful," Josh cautioned from below.

She could hear him shuffling back and forth, waiting no doubt for her to plummet to the ground when the splintery wood she was clinging to gave out. He'd catch her if she fell. Amy was confident of it. The only thing that worried her was the damage she'd do when she landed on his head.

Holding on for dear life to the wooden

floor of the tree house a few inches above her head, she ignored the stinging in her fingers and made a pact with herself not to look down.

Don't be such a baby.

She pulled herself up and peeked through the surprisingly small door. "Can I come in before I make a pancake out of your uncle Josh? My arms are so tired I'm not sure I can climb back down right now."

The little boy scowled at her from where he sat huddled in the far corner of the wooden fort. His knees were pulled to his chin. His arms hugged his legs close. Golden light filtered through the patchy, hole-ridden roof. Comic books littered the floor around him.

"This is my tree house," he said, eyeing her precarious hold at the edge of the fort.

"Well, not technically." She gave up on waiting for an invitation, mostly because she could no longer feel her fingertips.

Squeezing through the square opening was an experience. Feeling the bark from the tree finish shredding what was left of her panty hose added to the moment. Yanking her non-regulation tree-climbing skirt back into place, she tried to wipe the worst of the grime from her hands.

She took in the sight of her four-foot-five

host, read the defensiveness he wore like armor, and knew in an instant the indirect approach was her only shot. She stood up, having to stoop to avoid hitting her head, and turned her back while she flexed her stinging hands. Silence filled the tree house as she searched the shadows, scanning the walls for something she hadn't thought about for years.

"Aha!" She gave Daniel her friendliest smile and waved for him to join her. "Have you seen this? The original owners left their names on the wall over here. So I guess you could say you're only borrowing the tree fort."

The little boy's squint suggested she'd lost her mind. But her smile continued to challenge him, and with a glare he joined her and read the words she pointed to.

The Sweetbrook Kids Club. Josh White and Amy Loar, Proprietors.

"I think your uncle and I were about your age when we built this place."

"But you could barely climb up here." The kid's total disbelief made her laugh.

"Yeah, when I hop in the shower later tonight, the scrapes up and down my shins will be all the reminder I need that I'm an old lady now." She shrugged. "But it's worth it if I can help your uncle get you to come down from this tree."

"Well, you can't. So why don't you leave?"

"Because if I do, your uncle is coming up here. And something tells me that's not exactly what you want."

She sat as gracefully as she could, given her attire, and began leafing through the X-Men comic book she found on the floor beside her. Actually, most of the superheroes gracing the covers scattered all over the place were of the mutant variety.

Daniel hesitated. The care with which he sat beside her, far enough away that she couldn't quite reach him, tore at her heart.

"The X-Men are cool," she said. She was still going for casual, but not so casual she sounded like a nutty adult trying to talk like a kid. "Are they your favorite?"

"They're okay." Daniel began gathering the rest of the comics into his lap. "Reading them's just something to do."

"Reading's good." She looked up. "Especially when you need to be alone. Is that why you come up here all the time?"

"What do you know about it?"

"Nothing." She handed over the copy she held, knowing more about it than she ever thought she'd be discussing with anyone, least of all a ten-year-old. "Except maybe I know a little about not wanting to be who

120

you have to be every day. It's hard to fit in when you don't feel like you belong. Kind of like the mutants who became X-Men, so they'd finally be able to help people instead of feeling like outcasts."

Daniel blinked at the stranger who'd invaded his tree house.

Correction, he told himself. This was his uncle's tree house. And from what the lady had said, she was the Amy who'd scribbled her name on the wall beside his uncle's — a million years ago. He glanced down at his comics, at the pictures of heroes who didn't belong anywhere.

"Who are you?" he asked.

"I'm Amy Loar." She stretched out her hand.

Like he was going to shake it or something.

When he just stared, she dropped it back into her lap. "I'm Becky Reese's mother."

He snorted and flipped open the comic on top of the pile. "Your daughter's a pain."

"Yeah, I've heard." The woman had a sad smile, like the smiles he'd seen on his mother's face after they'd run out of money and had to move to Sweetbrook. "But Becky's not like that. She's going through a rough time."

"She hates you, you know." Maybe that

would get her out of his tree.

"Becky hates the world right now." The lady sounded like she was trying not to cry. His own eyes started to sting. "Because she's been hurt. Not as bad as you, but she's hurting a lot just the same."

And there it was. That look, just like all the others who thought they knew him.

"Man! My uncle can't wait to tell the whole world how screwed up my life is."

And now, thanks to his uncle, Daniel had to put up with *the look* in his one safe place in this town.

"Your uncle didn't tell me anything," she explained. "I overheard something I shouldn't have, so don't blame him. He's very worried about you."

"So he sent you up here?" Daniel crumpled the comics between his fists, wishing he could squash the memories. "What, now I need a new shrink because I like to sit alone in a tree house and read comic books, instead of acting like I'm happy all the time?"

"I'm not a therapist."

"Then what are you doing here?"

"I asked your uncle if I could talk to you." She leaned forward and laid a hand on his arm. "I thought I might be able to help."

He jerked out of her reach. An ugly tear

slipped free, and he wiped it away with a shrug of his shoulder. "You can't even take care of your own kid."

"I'm trying." She brushed at the bits of bark on her skirt. "I'm trying as hard as I can."

Suddenly, it was Daniel who wanted to touch *her* and make it all better. Instead, he scooted farther away.

I'm trying as hard as I can.

"So what does any of that have to do with me?" he demanded, his voice as mean as he could make it.

She sighed and swallowed hard, as if she were eating some of the burned green beans his uncle had fixed as part of last week's healthy food kick.

"Daniel, I know . . ." her hand moved toward him again, but she pulled it back before she touched him ". . . I know what it's like to be hurt by someone who's supposed to love you. I know what it's like to feel like you can't trust anyone."

He was on his feet in an instant, dizzy with the need to run. The determination not to remember, not to feel the pain anymore.

The comics slammed against the wood beside her head before he realized he'd thrown them.

"Get out of my tree house!"

123

The tears were coming again. Tears always came with the memories. He couldn't let her see him cry. He never let anyone see him cry.

"Daniel . . ." She stood again, and he moved away so quickly he banged into the wall.

There were tears in her eyes, too. And there was something new in her expression.

Understanding.

"Leave me alone!" He didn't want to be understood.

She was too close. The memories were too close. . . .

He edged around her until he could crawl through the door, refusing to think of anything at all anymore. He'd never shimmied down the ladder faster. He'd never cared so little about the splinters the broken steps were leaving in his fingers. He hit the ground at a dead run and barreled into his uncle.

"Are you okay?" The man's hands caught him by the shoulders.

His uncle had really big, really strong hands.

Daniel should have been terrified. Instead . . . he almost wished those hands would pull him closer.

And that scared him most of all.

He squirmed free and sprinted toward the field beside the pond, his lunch a wad of fear in his throat. He was still close enough to hear the woman say, "Is he okay?" but he kept on running.

He was headed home, he realized, as he reached the main road and turned right. Back to his uncle's, the place in Sweetbrook he hated most.

But even going back there was better than staying here and remembering.

"What happened?" Josh asked as he helped Amy to the ground at the base of the tree.

She looked more worried than scared, which was a relief after the thundering crash and shouting he'd heard.

"I guess you were wrong." She headed for the SUV. "I'm clearly capable of doing plenty of damage on my own. Daniel couldn't get away from me fast enough."

Josh caught her elbow as she opened the passenger door. "Did he hurt you?"

"What? No." She disengaged herself from his grasp and settled onto the seat. "I tried to talk with him, hoping he'd calm down enough to go back home with you. But all I managed to do was make him angrier. He thinks you told me about what he and Melanie went through before they moved here."

"Well, at least you got him down from the tree. He was hightailing it home the last time I saw him." Josh braced a hand on the roof of the Range Rover and rubbed the other across his jaw. The need to reassure Amy felt right. Like old times, before he'd messed up their friendship so badly. "If I'd gone up there, we'd still be shouting at each other."

Her half smile almost looked like she meant it. "I was trying to help him, not drive him off."

"He was going to run anyway." Josh dug at a loose rock in the dirt with the toe of his shoe, remembering his earlier conversation with Barbara Thomas. "He gets that way when you push him to remember stuff he can't deal with. His therapist tells me it's a normal distancing reaction after a kid's lost a parent. Especially a child with Daniel's history. At least this time, he's angry at you and not me."

"Well, I'm glad I could help you out."

"Yeah." He snorted and fished his keys from his pocket. "Seriously, what did you two talk about?"

A crazy kind of jealousy struck Josh at the idea of Daniel connecting with a total stranger easier than he could talk with his own uncle.

Amy shrugged and stared at the wind-ripped surface of the pond. The late-afternoon twilight caressed her features, softening the texture of her skin until it resembled the fine porcelain filling his mother's curio cabinets. Amy's loneliness was a raw, tangible thing. "I told him I knew what it was like to feel totally out of place and not have anyone you can trust."

The honesty in her words grabbed at the soft inner part of Josh that she'd always been able to touch.

Years had passed since they'd been real friends, and he had no business prying where he didn't belong. But he found himself stepping closer, longing to have the right to hold her, so he could reassure them both that things were going to get better any minute now.

"Amy, look . . . I'm sorry about the crack I made back there about your job. I may not know what it's like to need to work to survive —"

Her laugh mocked him. "No, I don't suppose you do."

"But I do know that no amount of my family's money is going to fix my problems with Daniel. And I'm not as convinced as you are that this job that's taking up so much of your time is what you need for

Becky, either."

"What I need . . ." Emotion rippled her voice, even as she shrugged back into her business-as-usual persona. She turned in the seat until she was facing forward. "What I need is a ride back to my car, so I can go home."

He admired the composure Amy seemed to be able to call on at will. She must be really something in the boardroom.

"Home it is, then." With a nod, he shut her door and walked to his side of the SUV, letting the moment pass.

Focus on your job, man. You're supposed to be helping settle her child into school. Not trying to solve all her and Becky's problems.

Besides, waiting at home for him were hot dogs to boil and a decision to make about whether or not tonight was the right time to talk with Daniel about his father.

"Tomorrow's SST meeting is at one o'clock." He checked the digital clock on the dash as he fired the engine, and he got back to the issue that had driven Amy Loar to seek him out in the first place. "There's no way of knowing what's waiting for me at home with Daniel, and it's already getting late. It looks like you and Becky might be in for a rough night, too. Why don't you stop by early before the meeting, say around

128

noon? I'll bring you up to speed on every-thing then, before the others get there."

He felt rather than saw Amy droop into the seat.

"Thanks," she said simply.

A quick glance told him she'd closed her eyes.

"Becky's going to be fine. You're here for her now. That's what's important. We'll have things at school under control in no time."

"Yeah." Amy clenched the golden heart dangling around her neck. "That's you and me, Josh. We've got everything under control."

"You have a visitor," Mrs. Lyons said over the office intercom the next morning.

Josh swallowed a growl and looked up from the new mound of paperwork he'd been sifting through — plans for next year's third-grade-science curriculum. The com-mittee had made their recommendations last month, and his approval was required before new materials could be purchased. The committee chair had stopped by twice during the week, tactfully reminding Josh he was holding up progress. So after spend-ing an hour that morning talking with his lawyer about filing formal abuse charges against Daniel's father, in addition to requesting a paternity test, Josh had barred himself in his office to do the part of his job he liked the least.

Daniel's silent treatment last night, through dinner and beyond, had convinced Josh not to bring up the subject of the boy's father. Instead, he'd spent a sleepless night trying to find some right way, some right time, to break the news. And all he had to show for his troubles was a nagging headache that was threatening to blow wide open at any moment.

He checked his watch and did a double take. It couldn't be almost noon. The time fully registering, he remembered telling Amy to come an hour early for the SST meeting.

Setting his papers aside, he pressed the intercom button. "Tell her to come in, Mrs. Lyons."

He stood and straightened his tie, then his shirt. Then he decided to roll down his sleeves.

Get a grip, man! She's here for your help, not a date.

He was stepping toward the door when it swung open, and in walked a total stranger. The man gave Josh a shallow smile and held out his hand.

"Curtis Jenkins," he announced, his limp

handshake registering before his name.

Josh pulled back and wiped his palm on his slacks.

"I have a noon appointment, Mr. Jenkins." He turned his back, his anger from yesterday's conversation with Barbara Thomas roaring back. "You'll have to leave."

The other man's hand on Josh's arm stopped him. Josh jerked away, his skin crawling.

"Now there's no need to be unneighborly," Jenkins challenged, then he dropped uninvited into one of Josh's guest chairs. "I've stopped by as a friendly gesture, to let you know I'm in town, and that I'd like to see my son."

Jenkins's conservative suit should have given him a distinguished air. But to Josh, the man came off slimy. The urge to wrap his hands around Jenkins's neck made him collect himself. He leaned a hip against the desk and folded his arms.

He wasn't a violent person. He couldn't remember a time when he'd raised a hand to another human being. He was a rational, reasonable individual who preferred handling disagreements logically. But the man sitting before him had abused Josh's sister and her son. There was no logical solution to that.

"I wasn't expecting you for a few more days." He made a point of not sounding welcoming. "What do you want?"

The man's confident smile slipped, but only slightly. "I've come to see my son."

Josh's silence said volumes.

"You can't keep the boy from me."

"You abandoned him and his mother over five years ago, once you got bored using them as punching bags."

"I never laid a hand on either one of them." Jenkins brushed imaginary wrinkles from his jacket.

"That's not what my sister said."

"Melanie's not here to say much of anything anymore, now is she?"

Josh resisted the urge to take the man by the shoulders and shake him. "Daniel's living with me now. He's in my custody and —"

"*Temporary* custody, according to that Ms. Thomas I spoke with."

"It won't be temporary much longer. I've filed to adopt him. That's what Melanie stipulated she wanted in her will."

"Well now, there's your problem. The boy's mother should have consulted me before she went and did a thing like that."

Josh laughed. He felt like howling. "No judge is going to give an abusive, deadbeat dad like you custody of a child."

Jenkins schooled his features into a confident facade, sticking out his chest like a schoolyard bully whose bluff had been called. "I'm the biological father and that gives me rights, according to my lawyer. And I can provide that boy a good home. That's what the judge will see. I'm a respectable citizen, same as you. Even though I don't have your kind of money, I've got a job. I can give that kid a decent home. Plus, I'm his daddy."

"You're a violent, abusive jerk. And you'll never lay a finger on my sister's child —"

"I've got just as much claim on Daniel and Melanie's insurance settlement as you do."

"Insurance settlement?" Josh pushed away from the desk and straightened to his full height. It was a heady feeling when Jenkins shrank backward in his chair. "You heard about my sister's death, some crackpot lawyer dug up the information on the money she left behind for her son, and now you're here to latch on to a guaranteed meal ticket, is that it?"

Josh hadn't given Melanie's insurance policy a second thought since he'd deposited the settlement into a trust fund for Daniel.

"Let me make things perfectly clear," he said, mimicking one of Daniel's scowls. "If it's the last thing I do, you and your sleazy lawyer will never see a dime of Melanie's money."

"Don't get all high and mighty with me, Mr. White. Your bank account may be bulging, but that won't buy you custody. That boy and everything his mother left him belongs with me."

"How much?" Josh had never heard anything so depraved. "Name your price. How much will it take to get you out of our lives for good?"

"Nothing doing." Jenkins shook his head, his easygoing manner hinting at the hard-edged opportunist beneath. "I figure, given how much you seem to be taken with my son, he's worth a whole lot more to me than a one-time payoff. I'm just betting a concerned uncle like yourself will come through in a pinch, whenever I need a little help making ends meet."

Josh's fingers curled into fists. "If you think I'm going to bankroll you —"

"Oh, I think once I've got the kid, you'll do just about anything I ask, if you ever want to see him again."

Josh pulled the man up by his lapels, so hard that Jenkins's head snapped back.

"Don't mess with me. Don't mess with my nephew." A killer instinct he'd never known before raged higher. His vision narrowed to the flash of fear in the other man's eyes. "I'm about the last person you want to be threatening right now."

"Josh?" A soft voice penetrated the fury numbing his brain. A small hand pulled on his arm, yanking him back to the present.

Josh dropped Jenkins into the chair, his gaze locking on to Amy Loar's troubled features. Her hand still rested on his arm, her delicate strength the only reason he wasn't pummeling Daniel's father to bits. Josh closed his eyes and rubbed his hand across his face.

What was he doing? He'd been so out of control he hadn't heard her walk in.

"Is everything okay?" She glanced from one man to the other. A stylish jacket and chic black pants had taken the place of the suit she'd worn the night before. The gauzy designer jacket was the same reddish-gold as her hair.

Josh reined in the bewildering urge to touch her.

When Jenkins pushed himself out of the chair, Amy took a step back. Josh drew her to his side out of reflex. The arm he held trembled, and his anger flared to new life at her fear.

"And who is this beautiful young lady?" Jenkins's gaze slid over Amy's classic curves. His tone was Southern gentleman, with a slight leer lurking just below the surface. "She's not at all what I thought a country boy like you would be interested in."

"What?" Amy winced as she felt Josh's hand tighten on her arm. She eased out of his grasp, her cheeks burning at the stranger's last comment.

"Leave her alone, Jenkins." Josh's voice was so low that chills raced up her spine.

"From the stories Melanie told me," the other man continued, "I would have thought the wholesome, motherly type would be more your speed, White."

"Amy, this is Curtis Jenkins," Josh said, placing himself between her and the man he'd been about to beat to a pulp. "He's Daniel's father, and he's here to get his hands on as much of my family's money as he can."

"I thought he wanted Daniel back." Amy resisted the urge to turn and run for safety. Her head was spinning from the disjointed conversation.

"It's one and the same, isn't it, Jenkins?" Josh looked ready to explode again.

"Now, raising my son would mean the

136

world to me." Mr. Jenkins's smile was pure sincerity. "But I won't turn down the money that's my . . . his due. Caring for a child costs a fortune these days. It's only fair to expect adequate compensation for taking on the responsibility."

"Adequate compensation?" Amy's own outrage exploded at the calculation beneath that Southern-bred smile. "You make caring for your son sound like a business deal."

"And just what business is it of yours?" His steel-gray eyes hardened.

"I'm sorry, Mr. White." Mrs. Lyons, the school admin Amy remembered from years before, hurried into the office. She sent both Amy and Curtis Jenkins a look of quiet disdain. "I ran to the bathroom for just a minute or two."

"It's okay, Edna," Josh reassured her. "I was expecting Ms. Loar, and Mr. Jenkins was just leaving."

Daniel's father seemed to be deciding if staying and pushing Josh further would be of any use to him. Playing it safe must have won out, because he turned to go.

"Ma'am," he said to Mrs. Lyons on his way past her.

Josh sagged into his desk chair.

"Mr. White —" the older woman began.

"This is Becky Reese's mother, Mrs.

Lyons." Josh sat straighter and cleared his throat. "She's here for the SST meeting. Would you let us know when everyone else is ready? We'll be meeting in the conference room."

"Of course." Mrs. Lyons still looked like she wanted a little chat with Amy about barging into offices without permission, but she left in a swirl of quiet efficiency and closed the door behind her.

"So that was Daniel's father." Amy made a point of perching on the edge of the chair Curtis Jenkins had *not* been sitting in.

"That —" Josh slumped, the starch leaking out of his posture "— was the man who's going to take my sister's child away from me."

Chapter Six

"So my recommendation would be that you have Becky tested more thoroughly," Mrs. Cole said from where she sat beside Amy.

The SST meeting was finally drawing to a close.

The teacher's manner was calm and encouraging, her tone confident. The school counselor who sat to her right, Mr. Fletcher, possessed an equally effective knack for discussing disturbing information as if he were mulling over what was being served for lunch in the cafeteria that day. But regardless of everyone's efforts to keep things positive, Amy's anxiety for her daughter had only grown.

The facts she'd been presented during the hour-long meeting were clear. Her daughter was falling behind in courses she'd always excelled at. A once fun-loving, easygoing little girl was having difficulty making friends, and apparently spent most of her school day frustrated and in a bad mood that no one could penetrate.

If only Amy had had more of a chance to talk with Josh before the meeting. But by the time she'd arrived at his office and helped diffuse the confrontation with Curtis Jenkins, they'd been left with barely enough time to walk through his records of Becky's mishaps and misbehavior. Then the other staff had arrived, and they'd moved to the more formal conference room and the deluge of information about ADD had begun.

She'd always been able to finesse even the stickiest boardroom situations, but this was different. This was about her daughter, and everyone in the room clearly knew more about what was going on than Amy did.

"If indeed what we're dealing with is ADD," the fourth-grade teacher continued, "there are some wonderful treatment plans that can offer Becky relief from a great deal of the symptoms."

"You mean drugs?" The idea of doping her child into conforming in school made Amy's skin crawl.

She sought out Josh's reassuring presence across the table, as she had so many times during the meeting. When Mr. Fletcher had gone into detail about the most common symptoms of the disorder and how they affected a child's ability to focus and settle into the classroom, Josh had gifted her with the same half smile he did now.

"I'm not going to medicate my daughter so she's less of a problem for you in the classroom." Amy looked down at her clasped hands rather than at the teacher.

"That's not what Mrs. Cole was suggesting." Josh's tone was also full of understanding. But unlike the others, his reassurance didn't seem condescending. His support made her more relieved than she wanted to be that he was there. "Medication is one course to consider. But it, like the other treatment options, aren't implemented simply to control a child's behavior. They're meant to reduce her difficulty while she learns strategies to help her deal with her disorder. Becky's frustration and the effects her low performance and interpersonal issues are having on her self-esteem need to be addressed. Some children with milder forms of ADD can learn to tackle their obstacles without meds. And we don't even know for sure what we're dealing with yet. That's where the specialized testing comes in. Bottom line, we need to start helping Becky now, before school becomes even more of a negative experience for her."

Amy twisted her pen between her fingers as she reread the notes she'd taken throughout the meeting. She could handle this. She just needed to focus on the facts, not the panic and fear of failing her daughter. She could fall apart later, when she wasn't depending on a roomful of strangers for answers.

"And this testing. Would you do that here?" She fingered the stack of Becky's papers Mrs. Cole had brought from class. Papers that were half-finished and full of incorrect answers to problems her bright daughter was more than capable of handling.

"Yes, ma'am." Mr. Fletcher nodded. "We can do that here, or you might want to find a specialist in Atlanta."

"Well, I . . ." Not knowing what to say, not wanting to offend the good-intentioned man, she looked toward Josh. "I don't know. . . ."

"Doug's being modest, Amy," Josh interjected. "He's not only a nationally certified school psychologist, but his masters from Duke qualifies him to provide comprehensive evaluations in any number of areas. As well as personalized counseling when it's warranted. He can also advise you on modifying Becky's curriculum, if that becomes appropriate."

Amy looked to Doug Fletcher. "What kind of modifications?"

"The law provides kids like Becky with the opportunity to request greater curriculum flexibility in any public school in the country," the counselor explained. "For example, the Individuals With Disabilities Education Act mandates that special educational services and accommodations be provided in the classroom for anyone, when testing and performance show they are needed. Suffice it to say —"

"Hold on." She held up her left hand while her right scribbled away with wrist-numbing speed. She'd been up half the night surfing the Internet about all this, and the more information she recorded in her notebook, the more she realized she didn't know.

"Suffice it to say," Mr. Fletcher continued with an apologetic smile, "you have legal grounds to make sure Becky receives whatever accommodations she needs, whether in an Atlanta public school or here. And everyone in this room wants Becky to succeed, for as long as she's with us in Sweetbrook. Once we have a thorough understanding of the challenges your daughter's facing, we'll work together on an individual education plan she can follow here, and then take with her when she returns to Atlanta. It's clear from her standardized test scores that she's a gifted child." He ran a finger down a page of the report in front of him. "With the right kind of help, I see no reason why we can't reverse the decline we've seen in Becky's performance and her demeanor toward school."

Amy breathed through the rush of tears building behind her eyes. She wanted so much to cling to the man's assurance that they could make something better in her little girl's life.

"I don't want to talk to you. I hate you!" Becky had shouted when Amy returned to Gwen's last night. And the ten-year-old had refused to speak with either her mother or grandmother since.

"We can help her, Ms. Loar," Becky's teacher said. "More importantly, she can learn strategies that will enable her to help herself. School *will* become a successful place for her again."

Josh checked his watch. "Why don't I walk Ms. Loar through the rest, then she can speak with Becky and let us know their decision?"

"I really enjoy having your daughter in my class," Mrs. Cole said as she gathered her papers and rose. "I can tell she's frustrated, but I know she's a sweet little girl inside."

The other woman's smile seemed more genuine, as did Mr. Fletcher's as he shook Amy's hand and left. Or maybe their helpfulness had been sincere from the start.

Amy had come to the meeting prepared for battle, expecting the worst. Expecting to be judged, because she was sure that by now everyone in town knew of her divorce, her decision to remain in Atlanta while her daughter stayed here, and the toll the entire situation was taking on Becky. Instead, Amy had found herself in the presence of professionals as concerned about her daughter and as determined to help her as Amy was. Josh's staff was as amazing.

She couldn't remember why she'd imagined they would be anything less.

"You don't have to make these decisions on your own, Amy." Josh moved to the chair beside hers. "I'll help any way I can."

The tempting image of turning to him for support felt so familiar, just like when they were kids. And his clean, spicy scent teased her with the memory of the one time he'd pulled her close and kissed her as if he might never let her go. As if he'd wanted to keep her safe with him forever.

Panic raced through her on the heels of

the memory — a survivor's reflex to the temptation of accepting comfort and help that could so easily turn into more disappointment and pain.

Distance.

Distance was what she needed, not Josh's help. She couldn't afford to want anyone's help as badly as she wanted his.

She threw down her pen and shoved her chair away from the table so she could stand. Pacing, she chewed her thumbnail.

"Amy?" Josh prompted.

"What?" She turned back from the other side of the room.

"Have you thought about how you're going to discuss all this with Becky?"

Amy refused to let herself drop into one of the conference room chairs. "She's not talking to me at all right now."

"I know exactly what you mean." He settled deeper into his own chair and pinched the bridge of his nose. "I still haven't told Daniel about his father coming to Sweetbrook. It's kind of hard to do that, when the kid refuses to stay in the same room with me for more than five minutes."

In a rush, everything Josh was dealing with himself hit home. Amy felt about two inches tall.

"Josh, you shouldn't be spending so much

time on my problems. You've got Daniel's father to deal with. You need to be worrying about your own stuff."

"There's enough worry in me to go around," he assured her, but his smile lacked conviction. "Besides, we used to make a good team. Still do, it seems. I don't know what I would have done to Jenkins if you hadn't shown up and managed to get me away from him. He's a snake, and he deserves to be drop kicked back out of town."

The violence of Josh's words surprised her, though his outrage was perfectly understandable. Something in her expression must have relayed her shock. Hands that had been clenched on the table in front of him relaxed. The fury in his eyes cleared.

"Thank you for stopping me earlier," he said with a wince. "Given your . . . what you've been through, I'm sure it wasn't easy to step between Jenkins and me."

"No, it wasn't." She braced herself against the memory. "But I knew something must have been terribly wrong for you to be so upset, and I trusted you."

"So you'll trust me when I'm losing it with someone as dangerous as Daniel's father, but you've had enough of my help with

Becky's situation?" His expression darkened.

"I . . . It's not that I don't trust you, or that I'm not grateful for all you've already done."

"I don't want your gratitude, Amy. I want to help, like you helped me yesterday with Daniel. Your daughter's part of this school, a member of this community. That makes her partially my responsibility. Besides, do you really want to be sifting through all the testing and treatment options alone?"

"It's not that simple." He had to stop being so nice. "The idea of accepting help . . . especially from a man . . . I know it sounds shallow and mixed up, but that's not something I can do. Ever. Not again. I have to figure out what's best for Becky on my own."

Josh pinned her with a determined look.

The cell phone at her hip began buzzing. Amy grabbed at the excuse to stop rambling like a moron. She checked the monitor, made a mental note of the name of the junior assistant who was calling her from Enterprise, and turned the unit off. A look at her watch confirmed it was after two. She needed to contact the office before the rescheduled video conference call with Kramer Industries. She had to double-check the figures Jacquie had e-mailed over that morning.

"Why does it sound as if you'd rather have anyone's help but mine?" Hurt flashed across Josh's face. "If this is because I made an idiot of myself when you decided to marry, then please let me apologi—"

"No." She couldn't let him believe that. All he'd done was try to protect her from her own stupidity. "It's not about you, it's me. Don't you understand? I'm scared, Josh." Amy let her anger race at feeling so helpless. "It's this whole situation. It would be so easy to depend on you —"

"Then depend on me!" he sputtered. "We've known each other since we were kids. I'm your daughter's principal. Becky's in trouble, and you're out of your element here. You need help, whether you want to admit it or not. And I'm a friend. Lean on me as much as you need to."

"No!" The word came out too loud, too desperate. The thought of depending on anyone, for anything, even this kind man she'd secretly had a crush on since she was a teenager, made her want to run from the conference room. "You don't understand. I can't. I have to do this alone. If I let you help me, if — if I let you in . . ."

"Exactly how badly did Richard Reese

hurt you?" Josh's expression softened, even as his gaze heated with the same anger she'd seen when she'd interrupted his argument with his nephew's father. "Did your husband hit you? Did he hurt Becky?"

"No, he didn't beat me!" The words came rushing out, stumbling over themselves despite her resolve to never discuss her marriage with another living soul besides her mother. "Not with his fists, anyway. And the only person responsible for my daughter being hurt is me."

Amy was shaking, and she couldn't make it stop. The truth wanted out, and it refused to be silenced a moment longer.

"He didn't want much," she continued. "Just control. Control of me, our relationship, my career and every other part of my life. What I thought, what I wore, what I did and with whom. He was a pro at belittling and intimidating me until he got his way. And I let him. I stayed with him. Kept trying to please him, because by then I was too much of a coward to think I could make it on my own. And Becky saw the whole thing. Including the one night he finally did hit me, right in front of her, because he'd caught me talking alone with a man who lived nearby. Somehow, I found the strength to get out then. But it was too late. I should have left years ago, for my daughter's sake. But I was a coward, and Becky's still paying the price."

Her tirade over, she found Josh completely silent. Totally still. At least he finally knew it all. That the wreck her and Becky's lives had become was no one's fault but her own.

"I have a call to return." Amy moved to leave. She was about to fall apart.

Josh stepped behind her as she reached the door, but he didn't touch her.

"I'm so sorry for what you've been through." His concern washed over her. "I wish there was something more I could do."

Pressing her forehead against the cool surface of the door, she breathed in his compassion. He made her want to believe that there still were wonderful men in the world. Or at least one wonderful man.

"Good luck talking with Daniel tonight." She turned partially toward him, wanting him to know she was sincere. Finally, she reached out her hand to cup his cheek. "I know you'll find the right way to tell him about his father."

Josh stepped closer. "Amy —"

"I have to go."

Before I start bawling like a baby.

She made herself walk away.

Away from his kindness and concern.

Away from the temptation to let Joshua White into her world even further than she already had.

Josh watched Amy go, his pulse racing from the fear he felt for both her and her daughter.

Amy's ex might not have physically abused her, but the damage he had done to her spirit, and to the little girl who'd watched it all, had left deep scars just the same. Amy's hesitation to accept any kind of help, even from him, spoke volumes. Becky had been suffering in silence for years most likely, as she worried about a mother whose self-esteem had been battered by her father.

Josh could understand Amy's need for independence. He could even respect the courage it must have taken for her to pick up the pieces of her life after her divorce and move forward. But she and her daughter were paying an awfully high price for Amy's determination to do everything on her own.

He wanted to help this family, and it had little to do anymore with friendship, or his job as Becky's principal, or even a desire to make up for how he'd failed his sister. Things with Amy and Becky had become personal somehow, not that that came as a big surprise. The truth was his interest in

Amy had gone way beyond friendship a long time ago, when he'd faced the reality of her marrying another man, and realized just what he'd let slip through his fingers.

The tension sparking between them each time they were close enough to touch terrified Amy, and the last thing he wanted was for her to be afraid of him. He'd keep his distance, if that's what she needed, but he was still going to help her in every way he could.

Amy and Becky deserved hope and a better future, just as Daniel did. And Josh was tired of letting down the people who needed him the most.

Becky sat at the kitchen table and listened as her mom finished up whatever superimportant business call she'd been having for the last hour. Becky's stomach growled, demanding the dinner she knew she wouldn't be able to swallow.

Her mom had gone to that meeting at school today, the one with her teacher, Mr. Fletcher and Principal White. Becky had stepped off the bus this afternoon, ready for her mom's disappointed frown. After everything she'd pulled at school over the last month, plus her half-baked attempt to run away last night, she deserved it.

Only her mom hadn't looked disappointed, or even angry. She'd just hugged her and asked her about her day, then had disappeared into Grandma Gwen's room to prepare for some kind of video business meeting thing.

Her mom had seemed . . . worried, in a scary sort of way. Nervous. And her mom didn't get nervous. Not anymore. Not after she'd finally wised up and given Becky's dad the boot.

Her mom got sad sometimes, and she was tired a lot. But she'd been an it's-going-to-be-okay-no-matter-what-it-takes robot since the divorce. To the point that most days Becky just wanted to scream. But this afternoon, her mom had looked ready to cry.

They'd talk about the meeting at school later, she had said. After her work was finished.

What a surprise!

While Grandma Gwen hung laundry on the line out back, Becky was supposed to be doing her homework. Instead, she was about to break her neck, leaning back in her chair so she could listen to the conversation in the other room. The house was so small that working at the kitchen table, she could hear every word her mom uttered.

"Great job, Jacquie," she was saying. "E-mail me when you have the minutes of the meeting typed up. I want to review them before sending them on to Hutchinson."

There was a pause, then she added, "Yeah, I won't be able to get away until Sunday. But I'll be in the office first thing Monday morning."

Heat rushed through Becky. She'd known from the start her mom couldn't stay in Sweetbrook, that she had to get back to work so she could earn her promotion. That had to be their priority, now that they were on their own. But that didn't stop the sucky feelings that took over each time her mom's job yanked her away.

When were they going to have a normal family weekend, one without cell phones and laptops ruining everything?

There was nothing normal about Becky's family anymore. She didn't want her dad back, but she didn't want her mom working all the time, either. She stared down at the pages of her math book, at the homework problems she still hadn't finished. Long division problems. Endless columns of numbers and carrying and bringing things down.

Division was the worst. She knew how to do it the short way in her head. She could work out most of the problems without even using her pencil. But Mrs. Cole wanted to see her work, and by the time Becky got halfway through one of the problems that took half a piece of paper to finish, she was so confused she had to go back and start over.

With a growl, she crumpled her paper into a ball and threw it at the kitchen wall. The soft *whoof* it made on contact angered her even more. She gripped the edges of the math book, heard her mom still talking to her assistant in the bedroom, then sent the book hurtling across the room, too. It hit the wall with a satisfying crash.

The bedroom door swished open.

"Are you okay?" her mom asked, the stupid cell phone still growing out of her ear.

Becky rolled her eyes. She'd been trying to make it clear for months now that she wasn't okay. She didn't know how to be okay anymore. Everything was changing. Everything was out of control, and she felt more stupid and invisible by the day. Like maybe when she wasn't around, things were easier for everyone.

She shoved herself out of the chair and trudged over to her book. The spine, which had been hanging on by a thread, was completely messed up now, and there was a small tear in the wallpaper. Standing with her broken book in her hands, next to the damage she'd done to her grandmother's wall — damage she knew Grandma Gwen didn't have the money to have fixed — she stared at her mother and dared her to close herself back in the bedroom.

"We'll have to finish this up later, Jacquie." Her mom looked from Becky's latest screwup to the so-what frown she'd plastered on her face. "I have something important to take care of here."

CHAPTER SEVEN

"So you see, honey . . ." Amy smoothed open the homework her daughter had crumpled into a ball. They'd been sitting at the kitchen table, with her talking and Becky listening in obstinate silence, for over fifteen minutes. "A lot of the crummy feelings you've been dealing with at school may be because you're having trouble focusing on certain kinds of work."

Maybe it hadn't been such a good idea to start this conversation when Becky was so angry. But after the SST meeting, Amy thought she understood some of the frustration underlying her daughter's temper tantrums, and she had to show Becky that she was more important than work could ever be. So she'd changed out of her city clothes into one of the comfortable, outdated outfits hanging in her childhood closet, then she'd sat herself and her daughter down to talk.

"You mean I'm stupid, right? There's a news flash." Becky hugged her arms tighter around her middle, speaking for the first time since Amy began describing ADD.

Gwen looked up from pulling a meat loaf out of the oven.

"No, you're not stupid." Amy scooted her chair closer. Becky had a right to be angry. But Amy wouldn't allow her daughter the deception of downplaying her intelligence. She knew firsthand the damage that kind of nonsense could reap. "Both Mrs. Cole and Mr. Fletcher made a point of saying how bright you are, how high your standardized test scores are. It seems a lot of kids with ADD tend to be very intelligent. It's not about being smart. It's about the difficulties you're having in the classroom — why you have trouble following directions and keeping up with the other kids. It's about how confusing school seems to have gotten for you lately."

"So this lets you off the hook, is that it? I have ADD, I'm hopeless, so your job here is done? I'm surprised you're not heading back to Atlanta tonight. Why wait until Sunday?"

"Becky, whether you have ADD or not, it's not hopeless." Amy grabbed her daughter's hand and refused to let it go when

Becky tried to pull away. "Once we know a little more about what's causing you the most trouble, there are any number of ways we can get you the help you need. We can make things better."

She *had* to be able to make something better for her daughter.

"We can work through this," she insisted. "School doesn't have to keep being such a hard place for you."

"*We?*" Becky stopped trying to free her hand from Amy's grasp. Her entire body stilled. "How are *we* going to do anything? *You're* leaving on Sunday."

"We'll figure it out, honey." Amy watched Gwen walk over and pat her granddaughter's shoulder. "I wanted to talk with you about it tonight. Then I'll get back with Principal White before I leave and let him know where we want to go from here. Our first decision is whether you should stay in Sweetbrook for the testing you need, or if you should come back to Atlanta with me."

"You mean you want me back home?" The light flickering in Becky's eyes pierced Amy's heart.

"Honey, I've wanted you home from the moment I left you here with Grandma Gwen." She rubbed the smooth skin on the back of her daughter's fingers, remember-

160

ing the days when Becky had been a baby and Amy had had the luxury of holding her daughter in her arms morning, noon and night. Back when she could smooth away tears with a simple kiss. "I want you with me every day, all day long. But you have to work with me here. We need to figure out where you'll get the help you need the quickest."

"You mean I get to decide?"

"You get to be a big part of the decision," Amy corrected.

Her daughter needed to start believing she had some control over her life in school. Over her world in general. A need Amy understood far too well.

"Then I want to go home." Becky's expressive features prepared for battle.

"What about the support system you have here?" Amy used her business voice, counting on her daughter to engage the maturity that lurked just below the surface of her adolescent single-mindedness. "You have a principal, a teacher and a school counselor on your side, just waiting to help you. That's what the meeting was about today. All we have to do is give them the word, and they're ready to go. In Atlanta, we'll be starting over, enrolling you in a new school, finding a therapist to do the testing you need, then working with a new school administration on whatever strategies are recommended."

"You mean it'll be more work for you —"

"I mean, it will take more time before we can get you help, honey." Amy fought back her own frustration with the lousy choices facing them. "Here in Sweetbrook, you'll have people helping you left and right, starting now. You won't have to spend hours in after-school care because I'm working, or get used to a new teacher and new classmates. You tell me — which is going to be better for you?"

Gwen squeezed Amy's shoulder, then stepped back to the stove. "Why don't we have some dinner. It's after six, and I'm meeting some friends for a seven-o'clock movie. There's plenty of time for you two to work things out later, once everyone's calmed down and eaten a little something."

Becky pushed herself away from the table and headed for the bedroom she was sharing with her mom. "I'm not hungry."

The soft sound of her door closing was far worse on Amy's nerves than if her daughter had slammed it off its hinges again.

"Tell me what to do, Mama." Amy squeezed her eyes shut, pressing her fingers to the lids. She had notes to review from the Kramer call, which had gone extremely well. But work was the last thing she could face right now.

Josh was right. She was in way over her head.

"Becky's so angry," Amy murmured.

"She's so you." Gwen waited for her to make eye contact. "You're both scared, and neither one of you knows how to depend on the other anymore."

"Depend on her?" Amy did a double take. She picked at the ancient place mats Gwen always set out for dinner. "Becky's my daughter. She's supposed to be depending on *me.*"

"Maybe." Her mom stirred the canned corn she was heating on the stove. "But I think you're on the right track, letting her be in on the decision for handling her problems at school. It'll help her feel more a part of the process, once she gets over being angry about not going home with you on Sunday."

"I had no idea, Mama." The shaking started somewhere in the vicinity of Amy's shoulders, spreading down her arms to her hands as she covered her face. Tears had never been her thing, but it was getting harder to hold them back. "She's my child, and I had no idea she was struggling so much in school. It's no wonder she won't talk with me about it."

Gwen took the seat beside Amy, her quiet strength an anchor, as it had been so many times before.

The last year had been a marathon of survival. An all-out, gut-wrenching fight, first with Richard to achieve her divorce, then with the world in general as she found a way to succeed without his money. And even though she'd done it all for her daughter, where had that gotten them? Amy couldn't remember when she'd last checked Becky's homework or attended a parent-teacher conference. Where would she have found the time? This weekend was the longest stretch she'd had to focus on Becky in months.

"How could I not have seen this?" She wiped her eyes with the sleeve of what had been her favorite peasant blouse when she was in high school. "I knew Becky's grades were suffering a little, but I just assumed it was all the changes. The upheaval from me finally breaking off with Richard."

"Kids are good at hiding things." Her mother brushed at the small pile of cookie crumbs left over from Becky's after-school snack. "You did the best you could under the circumstances."

"I've ignored my own child." Amy shook her head. "And she hates me for it. She's been falling further and further behind in school, and I've been completely oblivious."

"She doesn't hate you, honey. She's desperate for your attention." Gwen folded her hands, facing the facts right along with her. "Two different things entirely. You both have plenty to work on, but —"

The phone rang, cutting Gwen off.

As her mother left to answer the call, Amy glanced at her daughter's bedroom door. She'd been so sure she was doing the right thing for Becky. That her job at Enterprise, her promotion, was what they needed to finally be free of Richard and the past. Starting over was hard work, but Amy was willing to do whatever it took.

But how much harder was it going to get?

"Honey," her mom said from the living room. "It's Josh White on the phone. It sounds urgent."

Josh hurried to answer his front door. It swung open to reveal Amy Loar.

"What happened?" she asked.

A day ago, she was the last person he'd expected to find on his doorstep. Tonight, she was the friend he'd called when he had nowhere else to turn.

He'd promised himself he'd help her family. Now he was hoping she could somehow manufacture a miracle for him.

"I'm sorry to pull you over here," he said. "I know you had a lot to deal with tonight —"

Amy silenced him with a small shake of her head. She reached an arm behind her and steered her daughter to her side.

"Gwen had movie plans," she explained. "So Becky came with me."

"You should have told me it wasn't a good time." He realized they were still standing on the stoop, and moved back so they could enter.

The beam of the porch light caught the fiery highlights in Amy's hair, adding an ethereal touch to her beauty and weakening his knees, which were already shaking from his disastrous talk with Daniel.

One look at Becky's closed expression halted Josh's wayward thoughts.

"Really, I've got no business dragging the two of you over here on a Friday night. It's just that —"

"You said it was an emergency." Amy blinked, her expression rearranging into the funny look she'd always gotten when they were kids, when he'd tried to explain some

166

bit of homework she hadn't understood. "Is it Daniel?"

Josh smiled down at Becky. "My house-keeper left some chocolate cake in the kitchen for tonight's dessert. Why don't you help yourself to a piece? The kitchen's down the hall." He pointed the way. "Once you pass the stairs, turn right. You can't miss it."

A nod from Amy sent the somber-faced little girl on her way. Becky dragged her feet, the slump in her shoulders telling Josh all he needed to know about how Amy's own evening had been going.

"Is it Daniel?" Amy repeated, her concern endearing her to him.

His blind panic for his nephew returned, and with it the urge to hunt down the boy's father and —

"Josh?" Her hand reached to smooth the rumpled sleeve of the oxford shirt he still wore from work, but she didn't quite complete the caress. Her soft, familiar scent reached out to him, though, offsetting the violent emotions he'd never had to fight so hard to control. "Did you tell Daniel that his father's in town? That he wants to take Daniel home with him?"

Josh nodded, stepping away so she wouldn't know how badly he needed her touch. Amy had made her boundaries clear, and he wouldn't push for more because of some selfish need for comfort.

"Is Daniel angry?" she asked, compassion filling those midnight-blue eyes.

"No. He's terrified. I've never seen him like this before."

"Where is he?" She glanced down the hall.

"In his room. Hiding in his closet, and I can't get him to come out. I called his therapist and his social worker, then I called you. You're the only one who was home."

Amy stepped back, startled. "Why me, if you've got professionals you can talk to?"

"Barbara's not answering her cell. I'm sure she'll call as soon as she gets my messages. And I left my number with the therapist's answering service. But I couldn't keep waiting and doing nothing. I mean . . ." He eased into the chair beside the hall table. "I'm trying, but I've totally messed everything up, Amy. From the beginning, I didn't listen to Melanie when I had the chance. And now that I have to get through to Daniel or lose him, nothing I say makes a dent. He's curled in a ball in his room, and I can't get him to come out. And I'm supposed to be convincing him to trust me, so he'll tell the judge what he remembers about his father. So I can keep Curtis Jenkins out of Daniel's life."

Josh started when he realized she was kneeling beside him. He searched her features, counting the minutes until she bailed and left him to finish screwing things up on his own.

"He ran from me yesterday, Josh," she said carefully, as if he were the wary child she'd come to soothe. At least she was still here. "He's going to panic when I show up in his bedroom."

"No, I don't think he will. Somehow, he knows you understand what he's going through. That's why he ran yesterday. He does that when people get too close. When the feelings build up. You weren't with him five minutes, and he hit the road. He knows . . ." Josh hated himself for what he was about to say, but he was a desperate man. "He knows you've been where he is now."

Amy stood and backed away.

He'd been too distracted when she arrived to notice the dark circles under her eyes, the fatigue her makeup had successfully hidden earlier in the day. Strain had etched the softness from her beautiful features, and fear was doing its own kind of restructuring. This wasn't fair to her. But he'd lost the luxury of being fair.

"You've been hurt, just like Daniel has,"

he made himself say. He swallowed as her eyes filled with tears. "And you're trying to piece your family back together, so the monster who did this to you can't ever hurt you again. Well, Daniel's monster is back, and my nephew's not going to talk with me about it. You may be the one person he'll listen to tonight."

He watched as she hesitated. As the strong professional woman he'd opened his door to yesterday warred with the frightened one who'd been damaged in ways he couldn't possibly imagine.

"Where's his room?" she asked, squaring her shoulders, her eyes still haunted, but her mind made up.

Josh had never seen anything so magnificent in his life.

"Thank you." He stood, reaching for her arm. She skittered away, smoothing wrinkles from the casual top she wore over a faded pair of jeans, both of which looked oddly familiar.

"This way," he said, grateful beyond words. Regretting everything this was costing her, he longed to draw her close until all the pain went away. Not that she'd be the least bit interested.

But somehow, he'd make this up to her. If she could find some way to help Daniel back from whatever awful place he'd slipped into, Josh would spend the rest of his life making it up to her.

Amy paused outside the scared ten-year-old's bedroom, terrified of what she was about to do. But from the first moment she'd heard about Daniel's tragic loss, she hadn't been able to walk away. She'd eavesdropped. She'd climbed into the kid's tree house. And now she was jumping into the middle of his troubles with both feet.

"Are you okay?" Josh asked at her elbow.

She nodded, his worry touching her with an eerie kind of understanding. He knew she wasn't okay, yet he trusted her with his nephew, anyway. Did he have any idea what that did to her? How just his presence tempted her to want even more? Another taste of his promise from so long ago to make her happy?

"Daniel?" She knocked on the partially open door. "Can I come in?"

When no sound came from inside, Josh nudged the door open.

It was a bit of a shock at first, seeing such a disorderly mess in the midst of the immaculate White mansion. Clothes and toys lay in jumbled heaps all over the room. It looked as if Daniel knew exactly how to get under his neat-freak uncle's skin.

"Stay here," she said to Josh as she stepped toward the walk-in closet, her heart already breaking for the defiant little boy hiding somewhere inside.

"Daniel?" She knocked on the closet's doorframe. "Anybody home?"

She zeroed in on a pair of filthy sneakers peeking from beneath the low row of pants hanging against the far wall. She settled on the floor a few inches away and drew her knees to her chest.

"You know, if I had a closet like this, I think I might hide out in it, too." The custom-shelved, recessed-lit cubby was half the size of her new bedroom in Atlanta.

The shoes slid farther behind the pants.

"Your uncle's pretty freaked, you know." Might as well give it her best shot, even if she was talking to herself. "About your father showing up in Sweetbrook, I mean. And he's worried about you sitting in here all alone."

The pants rustled, one of them falling to reveal half a tear-streaked face. Their eyes connected, then Daniel's ricocheted away. At least he hadn't run from her yet.

He wiped his face with the back of a hand.

"I know you're worried, too." She forged ahead. "I don't guess you're ready to talk about it or anything?"

His gaze collided with hers again, the silent fear there calling to every weak thing inside Amy that understood exactly what he was going through.

"You should have been there today when your dad showed up at the school," she offered, switching topics for both their sakes. "Your uncle Josh was so angry, I think he was about to knock the man senseless."

The gap in the row of pants widened. Green eyes glared in suspicion.

"No, really." She nodded her head, keeping the one-sided conversation upbeat, because she wasn't sure who would be the first to cry if things took another turn toward serious. "I've known your uncle for a long time, and I can't ever remember seeing him that angry. He got in your father's face, and he made sure the man understood that no one was taking you anywhere without going through your uncle first."

The way Josh had put himself on the line for his nephew had been amazing, no matter how much it had rattled Amy to witness the scene.

"You know what I think?" She paused, letting the seconds tick by, waiting for his reaction.

"What?" a gravelly voice finally asked.

173

"I think you're lucky to have someone like your uncle Josh looking out for you. So you don't have to hide in closets like this forever."

The thought of Daniel as a younger child hiding while his parents fought, maybe even to protect himself from his father, ended Amy's battle with her own emotions. Two tears escaped the corners of her eyes.

Daniel was picking at his left shoe now instead of looking at her, as if he was trying to pry through the canvas to get to his toes.

"So what about Becky?" he finally asked, the words coming out clearer this time.

The abrupt shift in topic caught Amy off guard.

"Is that what you're doing for Becky?" He looked up then. "You know, keeping her away from —" he shrugged "— you know."

"Yeah." Amy breathed through the lump clogging her throat. "I guess that's kinda what I'm doing. It's not exactly the same thing with Becky, but you guys are probably feeling a lot of the same stuff right now."

He snickered, the half smile on his face transforming him into one of the cutest kids she'd ever seen. He was going to be a heartbreaker when he grew up, just like his uncle.

"You know, Becky's pretty mad at you,"

he said, bestowing on her his ten-year-old wisdom.

"Yeah, kinda like you are at your uncle Josh."

"Yeah." Uncertainty flooded his expressive features. "I don't mean to be. But sometimes . . . I can't help it."

"That's okay." She stretched her legs out and leaned against the bureau drawers behind her, letting the conversation flow. Thankful that Daniel was no longer cowering in the darkness alone. "Sometimes losing your cool is all you can do. Especially when no one understands."

She felt him studying her, and hoped she hadn't gone too far. Where was the kid's social worker? His therapist?

"Yeah," he finally agreed, his voice stronger but still shaking. "It sucks not to fit in anywhere."

Amy glanced around at the piles of comics scattered about them. Cartoons full of misunderstood mutants and the superheroes many of them became. This brave kid had forever secured a spot in her superhero hall of fame.

She noticed photo albums scattered among the clutter around them, and opened one.

"These are of your mom and uncle," she

exclaimed. "Look! Here's one of me, one of the times I came over for dinner. I always had the best time here. It was so different from my house, so much nicer."

Daniel looked downright shocked at the idea of anyone finding the White mansion nice.

She kept flipping through the album, letting the silence between them stretch.

"So my uncle told off my dad, huh?" he finally asked, his little-boy voice almost back to normal. "I didn't think Uncle Josh knew how to get angry."

"I didn't, either," she agreed, turning to another page of pictures from a simpler time. "But I'm guessing he'd do just about anything for you."

The flash of envy she suddenly felt brought her head up, and she flipped the book closed. She had no business wishing she had someone looking out for her the way Josh did for Daniel. There was no place in her world for that kind of attention. Hadn't she told Josh as much at the school today?

"Whatever happens next," she said, leaning forward, "you have to know you can trust your uncle Josh. He'll be there for you."

"Yeah, maybe." Daniel gave a disinterested

shrug, but the fear in his features eased a bit.

Amy wanted to whoop in victory. She settled for sending the boy a conspiring wink. "You know what's better than losing your cool sometimes?" she asked, refocusing on her task of getting Daniel out of this closet.

"What?"

"Eating a huge piece of chocolate cake way past dinnertime." She gestured toward the closet door with her head. "Becky's out there downing a piece or two, if I don't miss my guess. Are you going to let her polish it off all by herself?"

She'd startled him again, she could tell. He eyed her warily, as if expecting her to turn into a normal adult at any minute, and not wanting to miss the transformation. Then he scrambled to his feet, and with that odd look kids saved for wacky grown-ups they didn't understand, he tore out of the closet, nearly barreling into his uncle for the second time in two days.

Josh stepped into the closet and grinned when he found Amy still stretched out on the floor.

Did he have to look more handsome every time she saw him?

"Comfy down there?" he asked.

"Seems I have a knack for sending children running." She struggled to her feet, struggled not to crave the reassurance just being close to him could mean to her again.

Facing the world alone was something she was getting good at. Something she'd told herself she wanted. But the world was becoming tougher to handle by the hour, and being around Josh so much was making *alone* feel a whole lot more lonely.

He offered her his hand, and nothing could have kept her from taking it.

"You're a miracle worker." The warmth radiating from him held her captive. His expression was a study in wonder. "I've been trying to get Daniel out of here for an hour."

Josh's clear blue eyes caressed her face. His thumb rubbed tingling circles on the palm of her hand.

The professional school administrator and the friend from her youth were nowhere to be found at the moment. All Amy could see was the ruggedly handsome man before her. A concerned, caring man who'd do anything to help his nephew. The man she'd forced herself to turn away from hours earlier.

What would it be like to feel those strong arms wrapped around her again?

It would feel like a really bad idea, she

warned herself.

He fingered the billowing sleeve of the raggedy peasant blouse she hadn't taken time to change out of before hurrying over.

"This looks familiar," he said.

"It should." She laughed, grabbing on to the distraction. "You got ink on it while we were studying for exams one year. Mother tried for days to get the spots out."

Josh's eyes crinkled with the memory, then dropped to the exact location of the still-lingering stain. With a chuckle, he pressed his fingers to the mark, caressing her rib cage beneath the cloth and causing her breath to catch. When his eyes tracked back to her face, his laughter had been replaced by a heat that rivaled the branding warmth of his touch.

"Why didn't I notice how good you looked in this shirt when we were kids?" he asked, appearing genuinely puzzled.

"I . . . I don't think I looked this good when —" she couldn't hold back a gasp as his fingers tangled in the hair falling across her shoulders "— when we were kids."

"Did you smell this good then?" He'd moved closer somehow, even though they were already standing too close because of the narrow confines of the closet. He hesitated, then the back of his hand smoothed across her cheek.

"Josh . . ."

She couldn't believe she was tilting her head upward. Craving the touch of his mouth against hers.

She should've felt crowded, trapped, as she stood there being held by such a large man in such a tiny space. But this was Josh. Her memories of the one other time he'd embraced her caused a flood of warmth mixed with confusion. Of needing more and never wanting to stop.

And in that moment, her longing for even a speck of something that was good took over. Just for a second, she wanted to step outside her world and grab hold of something that didn't hurt. And a part of her still believed, somewhere deep inside, that being with Joshua White could never, ever hurt.

"Josh?" she repeated as she felt his fingers tremble.

"Yeah?" He swallowed hard, holding back, though she could feel how much it was costing him.

He'd apologized for the kiss they'd shared when she was engaged to Richard. And he'd been nothing but a good friend since she'd returned home, no matter how the air sparked between them whenever they were together. He'd been careful to give her the space she'd insisted she needed.

But she didn't want space right now. She didn't want him to be careful.

"Aren't you going to kiss me?"

His eyes dilated, all that beautiful blue disappearing as his pupils expanded.

"But . . ." His hand clenched in her hair. He hissed as if he'd been burned.

"Please. Just one more time." She rose on her toes, her mouth coming level with his. She was out of her mind, but that was exactly where she wanted to be right now. "Please, don't say no, Josh. Please . . ."

She'd never be sure who erased the final distance between them. She'd only remember how his kiss had consumed her.

"Amy. You taste like heaven."

Her hands tangled in his hair. She wanted to anchor him to her so he'd never leave her.

Never leave her?

She tensed, the spell she'd fallen under fracturing as quickly as it had consumed her.

"Amy?" He inched away, as sensitive to her withdrawal as he'd always been to everything about her. He wiped at the tears she hadn't realized she'd shed. "Baby, please don't cry. Are you all right?"

"No!" she whispered, pressing her fingers to her trembling lips, because at any moment she was going to start screaming. "I'm not okay. I shouldn't be here . . . kissing you, breaking my heart over your nephew, letting any of this touch me. . . ."

"Because of your ex-husband?" Josh let her step back, then he shifted away from the open doorway. The still-logical part of her recognized that he was being careful that she didn't feel trapped. It wasn't the first time he'd done something like that in the last couple of days.

"You're afraid to let anyone close again, aren't you?" he continued when she didn't move. "Because of how Richard hurt you."

"No, because of me." She refused to sugarcoat the truth to save face. "I'm messed up, Josh. My entire life is a mess, because of choices made with my own free will. Because I was weak. And I won't let myself make those kinds of mistakes again."

"What are you talking about? You're one of the strongest people I know. None of what's happened is your fault, Amy."

"It is my fault," she retorted, knowing her anger was far safer than the softer feelings it replaced. "You think you know me, but you don't. I'm not strong. I'm a fraud. A weak, scared fraud who wants to run away from everything and start over. But I owe it to my daughter and myself to make our lives in Atlanta work. To do things right this time."

Finding that she could finally move, she stepped through the doorway. Joshua followed.

"And *right* means being alone?" He raked a hand through the golden hair she'd just feathered her fingers through. Frustration created a ridge of color across his cheekbones.

"Yes." The word lacked conviction, but she forced herself to say it anyway. "For me it does. I won't survive all this if I let myself be distracted from what's real. And as good as this feels —" she gestured between them "— it's not real."

When he took her hand, she realized just how much trouble she was in. All he had to do was pull, and she'd be right back in his arms. Right back where she longed to be.

And he thought she was strong.

"You deserve better than being alone, Amy. You deserve to let yourself be loved."

His sad, gentle smile tugged at her soul, even as he released her.

"Thank you," she said, grateful for the distance. Regretting more than he could ever know that this was how things had to be.

"No. Thank *you.*" The warmth in his voice caressed her. "For what you said to Daniel about me. If there's any chance he can learn to trust me —"

"He will." She would do everything she could to make sure of it. Josh and Daniel deserved the family they were just starting to make with one another. "He'll learn that you're the man he can come to for answers, regardless of what happened between you and Melanie. That you're the one who'll help this make sense for him. Just don't try to force him."

"And if I can't get through to him in time?" Josh's desperation to do right by his sister's child threatened to charm Amy right back into his arms. His fear that he might fail reminded her that no matter how hard you fought, some things would forever remain beyond your control.

"Maybe you can't make everything right for Daniel again," she said, smoothing her blouse and her pragmatism back into place. Life wasn't a fairy tale, and neither one of them could afford to forget it. "In that case, you'll have to do what I always do — bite the bullet, make your deal with the devil, then do the best you can. Sometimes surviving is the best you can hope for."

"Do you really believe that?" His concern for her, like his kisses, left her longing for more. "Is settling for mere survival really the way you want to live your life?"

"Life is what it is." She looked over his shoulder, toward where their kids were hanging out in the kitchen. Away from the temptation to want too much from a man who didn't need her problems heaped on top of the ones already burying him alive.

She'd help Josh with Daniel. But for both his sake and hers, what had passed between them in the closet could never happen again.

"If it helps," she said, remembering her earlier advice to Daniel, "get angry again, just like you did today with Jenkins. Let yourself get angry a little more often, and see where that gets you. Take it from me. Get angry enough, and you can do just about anything."

Josh watched Amy head for the kitchen, her shoulders back, her head held high. She was an amazing paradox — as brave as she was scared. And something told him she was worlds tougher than he was.

This latest flare-up with Daniel had knocked him for a loop, but Amy had come out swinging. And that made him like her even more.

The memory flashed of the taste of her lips. The strength of her spirit, which had been sucking him in for days. Her determination to make things work for her and Becky. Her protectiveness of Daniel.

A greedy part of Josh wanted a piece of all that fire for himself. His hands were still shaking from the need to kiss her again. He wanted her to stop denying how good they would be together. It was selfish, but he couldn't help wondering, as he followed her to the kitchen, what this family he was trying to make with Daniel would be like if Amy and Becky were a part of it, too.

He found the kids quietly gobbling over-size pieces of chocolate cake and watching cartoons on the tiny TV perched on the kitchen counter. They were sitting together while totally ignoring each other, but at least they weren't fighting. Amy was pouring herself a glass of water at the sink.

It was a taunting domestic scene straight out of his book of *not going to happen.*

The phone rang, and he turned to the built-in desk in the corner to pick up the cordless handset.

"Hello," he said, catching Amy's concerned glance.

"Josh, it's Barbara. I just got your message. What's happened?"

"We have things under control for now," he said as quietly as possible. Daniel tensed, regardless, even though the boy didn't look away from the TV. "Why don't we talk about it on Monday?"

"You told Daniel about his father being in Sweetbrook?"

"Yes," Josh replied, as Amy joined him. He braced his arm on the bookcase above the desk. "And as we expected, there were some . . . concerns."

"I'm glad Daniel knows, because I received a call earlier from his father." Worry leaked through the social worker's composure. "He says you threatened him in your office today. He's talking about filing an assault charge."

"He instigated the confrontation, Barbara." Josh ground his teeth as he resorted to his nephew's patented he-started-it argument. "Jenkins doesn't want his son. He's after my family's money. He came right out and said so."

Amy pulled at his sleeve. "Tell her I heard the whole thing," she whispered.

He covered her hand, which now clung to his arm, and to his relief she didn't pull away. At least she no longer shied away from his touch.

187

"I have a witness," he said into the phone. "She'll tell you Jenkins started the whole thing, and that he wasn't harmed."

"He says you threatened him."

"I made my intentions clear."

Which was totally not his style, but it had done the trick.

Get angry enough, and you can do just about anything.

"You have to keep it together around the man, Josh," Barbara warned.

"Then Curtis Jenkins needs to stay away from my nephew." He slapped his palm on the desktop, fighting the red haze misting before his eyes.

"This isn't like you." The caseworker's concern shifted to a full-fledged warning. "I think I can smooth this over, but you don't want a history of reacting irrationally on your record. Jenkins is coming off as the injured party here. Meanwhile, you've filed a formal statement claiming he's abusive. If you're not careful, the judge might see you both as a threat, and place Daniel in foster care until this whole mess is straightened out."

"That's ridiculous." No way was anyone placing Daniel in the child welfare system. "Jenkins threatened to blackmail me. He said that if I don't let Daniel go without a fight, and foot their bills to boot, I'll never see my nephew again."

"I understand, and I'll hold Jenkins off legally for as long as I can. But if the man wasn't motivated before, he is now. You should expect to be served papers challenging custody by early next week. Have you made any progress getting Daniel to talk about what he remembers?"

"No, Daniel isn't ready to talk about his father yet. And I'm not pushing him any more than I already have." Josh turned, to find both kids listening.

Daniel's loaded fork hung, forgotten, between the plate and his mouth. There was fear in the boy's eyes, but something else, as well. Something closer to trust than Josh had ever thought possible.

"But we're making progress," he said, biting the bullet and doing the best he could. Just like Amy, he wasn't giving up, no matter the odds. "And we're going to keep at it."

Daniel's tiny nod hit Josh like the highest high-five in NBA history.

From the start, Josh had been terrified of losing his nephew. First to the anger that had swamped Daniel after his mother's death, and now to Curtis Jenkins. And initially, Josh had hung in there more to make up for how he'd failed his sister than anything else. But not anymore.

This wasn't about guilt or responsibility. He wanted Daniel in his life. He wanted the boy to feel safe, to maybe even learn to want a family with Josh. And thanks to Amy's gentle words and the fighter's spirit, he and Daniel were finally moving in a positive direction.

He still might not be able to fix things for his nephew. There were no guarantees. But he wasn't letting Daniel go without one kicking, screaming, Amy Loar–size fight.

CHAPTER EIGHT

"Mom, did you ever have trouble . . ." Becky glared at her math problems the next morning. The series of words and numbers she'd scribbled on her latest homework paper had been torturing her since she'd first tried to solve them an hour ago.

"Did I ever have trouble with what, sweetie?" Her mom sat beside her at the kitchen table, tuned into the Internet on her laptop. Her head came up in response to Becky's question.

Another Kodak moment for the Loar family.

Becky tossed her pencil in the general direction of her math book. It bounced and tumbled to the floor. She slapped her hands on the table, flinching as her mother touched her shoulder.

"You mean did I ever have trouble finishing schoolwork?" Amy asked. "Even though I knew I was smart enough to do it?"

Becky blinked, then squinted in suspicion. She turned her mom's laptop so she could see the screen.

CHADD: Children and Adults with Attention Deficit/Hyperactivity Disorder, the Web page header read.

"Learn anything handy?" Becky asked, masking her surprise with the sarcasm she knew her mom hated.

They'd been sitting there all morning, working side by side in Grandma Gwen's ancient, spick-and-span kitchen, ever since her grandmother had left to work a half day Saturday at the bank. Her mom's nose had been buried in the laptop the whole time. Not doing her office work, it turned out.

"I've learned a lot that jives with what Mr. Fletcher and Mrs. Cole said yesterday." Her mom shifted her chair nearer and closed the laptop. "That a lot of ADD kids are incredibly bright, but they have difficulty handling certain kinds of schoolwork and classroom situations. What's sometimes thought to be lack of effort or interest is often due to frustration and withdrawal, because a child can't seem to get the information in her brain organized and down on paper."

Becky's eyes watered. Something tickled her nose. "You don't know that's me. You don't know anything about it."

"No, we don't know anything for sure. That's why the testing we talked about yesterday is so important."

Talk, talk, talk.

She and her mom had talked more in the past two days than they had in the entire last year. They'd talked before going over to Principal White's. They'd talked on the ride back. They'd talked until Becky had fallen asleep on the couch in the living room last night, and her mom had finally let her go to bed. They'd finally agreed over breakfast this morning to give it a rest, at least for a while.

Becky guessed their rest time was over.

"We can learn more about it once we get home," she declared. "I don't have to be in Sweetbrook to do that."

"You have teachers and school officials who know you here, Becky."

"You mean I have people like Grandma, who'll put up with me so you don't have to."

The pain that flashed across her mom's face made Becky feel like a brat. It had her blinking back more tears.

Who cared?

She straightened in her chair and shoved back the apology working itself free from

193

her anger.

As long as she got to go home, who cared?

Her mom suddenly got that look in her eye that meant Becky could knock off the guilt trip. "My only reason for sending you to Sweetbrook was because I thought this was better for you than shuffling back and forth between before- and after-school care in Atlanta. I can't help that I'm working twenty-four–seven right now. If we want to live in Atlanta, this is what it's going to take to get us started. Is that what you still want?"

Becky stared at the table and chewed at the ragged thumbnail that kept getting shorter and shorter. She really was a brat sometimes.

"Mom —"

"Do you still want to live in Atlanta or not?" her mom asked, in the voice Becky had heard her use over her cell phone when handling a problem at work.

"Yes," she mumbled, sneaking a peek at her mom's face.

"Honey, you know that when I left your father, I left with nothing. No credit, no savings, not even enough income to afford a decent mortgage."

Becky nodded, some of the anger returning. Her dad was a jerk.

"And you know that my job at Enterprise, this promotion I'm working so hard for, is the only thing giving us a chance to live someplace like Atlanta without me asking your dad for help."

"But you wouldn't do that!" Her mom couldn't be thinking about going to her dad for anything. "Not after . . ."

"I don't want to." She swallowed, her skin paler than before. "But I can't stand to see you this unhappy. And now, with the possibility that we're dealing with something like ADD on top of everything else, we've got to come to some kind of decision, honey. This weekend."

"That's not fair." Becky slammed the math book closed. "Why does everything have to be so final? I just want something to be the way it was before. I want to come home."

"And I want you home with me." Her mom's voice rose, too. "But I've been reading everything I can find on ADD since I got here. Your teacher's right. Your symptoms are almost a perfect match. The high intelligence that conflicts with low academic achievement in the classroom. The way you're having more difficulty with each passing school year, as the classroom structure becomes less and less flexible and you have to sit and concentrate for longer periods of time. The difficulties keeping your homework and your stuff here organized, like when you forget where you left your hairbrush four times in one morning —"

"So I'm stupid already! I get it!" Becky jumped to her feet, fighting the urge to hurl everything on the table across the room, including the dumb laptop.

"Sit down." Her mom grabbed her arm. "We're going to finish this conversation. I don't care how many temper fits you pitch."

Becky pulled against her mom's strength, fought not to hear the unhappiness in her voice. It was so much easier to be a pain than to listen, even when the last thing she wanted to do was hurt her mother.

Her mom had been hurt enough.

Becky dropped back into the chair.

"Honey," her mother said in a strained whisper. "You know you're not stupid. And I think, deep down, you know you need help."

Becky shrugged. No matter how hard she tried, she kept falling further behind at school. If that wasn't stupid, what was?

"And I *know*," her mother continued, "just how terrible it feels to need help, when it's been a long time since anyone's truly been there for you."

Becky bit her lip, trying to stop it from trembling at the thought of what her dad had done to her mom. What he'd done to them both. She dropped her head and wiped at her eyes, and her mom pulled her into a hug she seemed to need as much as Becky did.

"Do . . . do you hate him?" she finally asked, even though they never talked about her father. "I hate him so much."

Her mom hugged her closer. "I . . . I try really hard not to hate him. I don't like to think he has that kind of control over what I feel anymore. But I'll never forgive him or myself for what all this is doing to you. You deserve a happy childhood. You deserve a normal father —"

"I don't want him as my father!" Her mother's shoulder muffled Becky's sob. "I don't want anything from him, ever. Not even his name."

"I know, honey." Her mom smoothed a hand down Becky's back. "And I'd love for you to change your last name to match mine and Grandma Gwen's. But I want you to take your time deciding. I want you to be sure."

"I am sure." She sat back, mopping up the wet streaks on her face. "And I don't care what you say, I hate him!"

"You have every right to. Just like you have every right to be angry at me." Her mom ran a hand down her own cheek. She cleared her throat and gave Becky the look that always meant they were going to have one of *those* talks. "I should have left your father years ago. I never should have become so dependant on him. I let him convince me I couldn't make it on my own, and I kept you trapped right along with me. But I'm doing everything I can to fix things. You're right — it isn't fair. But this is the way things have to be. I'm stretched so thin in Atlanta, I don't have a second to myself. I'm lucky I didn't lose my job by coming here this weekend. And that's why I still think you're better off with Grandma for a while longer."

Becky made herself listen. Made the obnoxious girl inside her shut up for a minute. It *wasn't* fair, none of this was, but it wasn't her mom's fault, either.

"If we're going to make this work . . ." Her mom's words came out tired and tough at the same time. "If we're going to get our second chance in Atlanta, I need you to let the people here help you while I can't. I need you to grow up just a little bit more."

But an ugly thought wouldn't stop whispering in Becky's ear. What if she was so messed up no one could help her?

"Becky?" her mom prompted.

"What if I can't?" Becky asked. "What if I can't get smarter . . . ?" She made herself continue, because if she didn't say it now, she wasn't sure she ever would, and she had to know. "What if Daddy . . . What if it was me? I mean, I make everyone so angry here. I don't fit in. What if it was me he couldn't live with? Maybe it was me making Daddy so mad all the time."

"Oh, honey!"

She was back in her mother's arms in an instant, back where she wanted to stay, despite the mixed-up things she said when she was too mad to think straight.

"Don't ever think that." Her mom hugged her harder. "You're the best thing that ever happened to me and your father. It's not your fault he couldn't see that."

"I'm sorry." Becky clung to her mom's shoulders. "I'm so sorry. I want to help, Mom. . . . I really do."

"I know you do, honey." Her mom kissed her temple.

Becky had forgotten how good it felt to be rocked in her mother's arms. To feel safe, instead of scared and alone.

"Here." Her mom eased back and took off the necklace Becky had given her last

Christmas. "I want you to keep this until you move back to Atlanta with me. I've never taken it off, not once, since you gave it to me. Maybe it will help you remember I'm always thinking about you, even when we aren't together."

Becky fastened the gold chain around her neck with clumsy fingers. The cool feel of the dangling heart against her skin brought with it her last happy memories of what used to be her family.

An image of Daniel White's face flashed through her mind — the only person in Sweetbrook who was more in need of a hug and a special memory than she was. And the one person she owed a bigger apology to than her mother, if what she'd overheard last night was for real.

"Mom, is Daniel going to be okay?" she asked, wanting to think about anything but her own problems for just a minute.

Her mom hesitated before answering. "I don't know, honey."

"He's pretty mixed-up," Becky added. "About his mom dying and all. And now this thing with his dad. I haven't exactly been nice to him."

"Maybe you two have been at each other's throats for a reason."

Becky shrugged. "He didn't really fit in

with the other kids here, either. So we both were left out of groups a lot at school. And I guess it was easier to be mad at someone who felt worse than I did. . . ."

Becky felt sick.

When had she gotten so stuck on herself?

"You know," her mom said, "Daniel could really use a friend in Sweetbrook right now."

"Will he have to go live with his dad?" Becky's stomach rolled in the topsy-turvy way it always had when her dad started in on her mom. And Daniel's father sounded even worse than hers.

"I hope not. But it's going to be a tough time for him and his uncle for a while, regardless. That's why it means so much that Principal White's willing to go the extra mile to help you. You have to promise me to work with him and the other adults at the school."

Becky nodded, feeling both petty and somehow special at the same time. She'd made Daniel's life more miserable than it already was, but Principal White was still on her side.

"Then you'll stay here and do the best you can?" her mom asked.

"I'll try," Becky agreed, not sure how things could possibly get better at school. But she'd give it her best shot. It was time she started helping her mom, instead of making things harder. "So what was that website saying about ADD?"

It was only a little past eight the next morning when Amy settled her garment bag and laptop into the trunk of her car. Her heart bottomed out somewhere around her knees.

It got harder every time she left Becky behind, but Amy didn't want it to be any other way. She never wanted to get used to this.

She sighed and turned back to the house. Gwen held Becky close by her side. They were waiting on the porch to say goodbye.

"I'll be back as soon as I can," Amy said as she walked toward them. She didn't try to sound cheerful. She was done pretending this was a good solution. Becky was too smart to buy it, anyway. "It's only another week or so until I close the Kramer deal. And a few more after that to get the project off the ground."

She hugged her family close, soaking in the sound of the birds chirping in the nearby apple tree, the feeling of the Sunday morning sunshine warming Becky's hair. In her world of no-win solutions, walking away from the perfect feel of this moment was the hardest thing she'd had to do yet.

She stepped back and cleared her throat.

"Principal White said he'd set everything up with Mr. Fletcher at school. They can start the testing you need as early as tomorrow, and Mrs. Cole already has some ideas for modifying some of your class work, as long as you're willing to cooperate."

Amy had talked with Josh briefly on the phone yesterday afternoon to let him know that Becky was on board. He'd promised to oversee her progress personally and to keep both Amy and Gwen updated. He'd sounded as if he wanted to say much more, but he hadn't. They'd both said more than enough already.

"I'll try as hard as I can," Becky promised.

Amy hugged her again. "I knew I could count on you, honey. I'm so proud of you."

Her cell phone rang from where it was attached to the waist of her jeans. The jeans from high school Gwen had smiled to see Amy wearing for the second day in a row.

Her mom had been right. Amy loved wearing her old things. It was as if she was at home in her own skin again.

Becky stiffened as the phone rang once more, then she produced a stiff smile.

"Time to get back to work," she said, doing a lousy job of hiding how much she still hated Amy's cellular link to the office.

But Amy loved her for trying. She waved goodbye, then fished her phone from her waist as she walked to the car.

"Hello?" she said as she eased inside.

"Amy, I'm so glad you're there."

Jacquie sounded rattled. Not exactly Amy's favorite thing to hear at eight o'clock in the morning. She started the engine, the peaceful haze of her Sweetbrook Sunday fading.

"What's up?" She backed away from the house and waved to Gwen and Becky one last time.

"Are you sitting down?"

"I should hope so. I'm driving. I'll be back in Atlanta by noon."

"Better hurry. Thomas Fuller's in your office. He says he has Mr. Hutchinson's approval to review your files on the Kramer project."

"Why would Fuller care about Kramer Industries? He's buried under the HR redesign for Madison Toys."

"He finished that up on Friday," Jacquie whispered. "He's headed this way. I can't talk about it right now, but get yourself back here. I think Mr. Hutchinson's reassigned Fuller to your Kramer deal."

"What!"

The line went dead.

With a quick glance at the digital clock on the dash, Amy accelerated, racing away from her dreams of home and back to Atlanta — to the future and the security she was determined to provide for her daughter.

CHAPTER NINE

"And finally, let's hear about Kramer Industries," Mr. Hutchinson said at the conclusion of the Monday morning project managers' meeting. "You've gotten a fresh look at everything over the weekend, Thomas. Why don't we start with your take."

Amy seethed in her chair, isolated on the other side of the conference room table from both Thomas Fuller and Hutchinson. She'd driven straight to the office after Jacquie's call yesterday, to find Thomas instructing her staff on how to prepare for this morning's update. Thomas preferred a PowerPoint presentation, he'd been telling Jacquie, when Amy had stepped into *her* office. She'd assured him that a formal presentation wouldn't be necessary, that she'd kept Hutchinson in the loop from day one and a PowerPoint would be overkill for a two-minute staff meeting roundup.

Whatever she thought was best, Thomas

had said. He was just there to help. As if she needed a hungry, up-and-coming Enterprise star glued to her side. A walking reminder that Hutchinson was hedging his bets on the Kramer deal, in case she couldn't get it done.

"I think we're in pretty good shape," Thomas said. He nodded meaningfully toward her, then turned to address Hutchinson directly. "The video conference Friday was a bit of a concern, but it sounds like it went well."

"It couldn't have gone better," Amy interjected. "Jacquie did a great job here, and I was able to talk everyone through the meeting from Sweetbrook."

"Yes, you did a fine job under difficult personal circumstances," Mr. Hutchinson agreed in an overly understanding way. "I was pleased and a bit relieved at the outcome. It's unfortunate that you're having to juggle so many priorities. But now that we have Thomas providing backup, we can all rest a bit easier until Alex Kramer signs the contract."

"Yes, sir, I'm happy to have Thomas on board." Amy added the expected half smile of welcome. "He's an asset to my team."

And he's out for my job.

It would take Thomas maybe six months

to a year more of paying his dues, but he was on Phillip Hutchinson's fast track, looking project manager dead in the eye and powering forward, no matter what was in his path. And if Amy wasn't careful, he'd rip apart her bid for a manager's slot without even breathing hard. He was out to impress Hutchinson as much as she was, and the best way for him to do that was to *save* the Kramer project, once he'd pointed out any mistakes Amy happened to make.

"I'm heading over to Mr. Westing's office later this morning," she added, "to follow up in person and make sure he has everything he needs."

What she wanted to do was call Josh to get an update on Becky. Instead, she was going to put in the required face-time with the Kramer IT director, to make up for her professional lapse on Friday.

"Good." Hutchinson closed his portfolio and rose. "Take Thomas with you and introduce him to Jed. Why don't you both come by my office when you get back. I need to know where we are with systems development and legal."

"Yes, sir," Thomas said, closing his own notebook.

"Yes, sir." Amy left the conference room, her stride carefully nonchalant, while inside her stomach clenched at the thought of what her daughter was dealing with on her own that morning. But Becky was in good hands with Josh. Otherwise, there was no way Amy could have remained focused on what she had to do here.

"I want to help. You can lean on me as much as you need to. . . ."

And she felt as if she needed him more every day.

No, she corrected herself. *You don't.*

"Jacquie," she said as she swung into her office, memories of Josh's kiss still clamoring for her attention. "Let's get my files pulled together for the meeting with Jed Westing. And find me the PowerPoint from Friday. I want it on hand in case there are any remaining questions. The last thing I need is Thomas Fuller looking like he knows more about what's going on than I do."

This was her chance to get back on track, and she was going to make the most of it. No matter how much she wished she was in Sweetbrook.

"How did it go?" Josh asked Doug Fletcher as he stopped by the counselor's office after a morning meeting.

Doug and Becky should have just wrapped up their first stab at testing, so Becky could join her class for lunch. Josh was headed to his own office, where Daniel would be waiting to leave for a therapy appointment with Dr. Rhodes.

"Becky's a little skeptical how any of this is going to help," Doug replied. "Taking tests that she doesn't understand is only adding to her confusion. The good news is, she's cooperating, and she already knows something about Attention Deficit Disorder. Kept asking me questions. Sounds like her mother's doing a great job of making Becky feel part of the process."

"Amy's a fine parent," Josh agreed, proud in a way that left professional interest behind. "She's doing the best she can in the midst of a really bad situation."

"I can tell Becky worries about her mother. She seems to pick up on other people's emotions more easily than most ten-year-olds."

"Like mother, like daughter."

"What do you mean?" Doug asked.

"Becky's mom." Josh fought to keep his voice free of his attraction for Amy. "She's been a big help with Daniel. She seems to know exactly how to listen to him, like she can sense what he's feeling in a way that totally befuddles me."

"I heard about what happened with Daniel's father on Friday."

Josh grunted. He doubted there was a person in Sweetbrook who hadn't heard. "The man's bad news, and he wants custody," he said simply, not looking forward to talking with Dr. Rhodes later today, when they'd try to find some way to help Daniel talk about his memories of his dad.

"What are you going to do?" Doug asked.

"Keep my nephew safe."

Josh headed for his office, overwhelmed by the chaos of emotion building inside him. Watching his wife walk away had hurt so badly, his plan had been to feel as little as possible for a good long while. But then Melanie had left him Daniel, and Amy Loar had marched back into his life.

Amy . . . He needed her, no matter how much he tried not to. It was senseless and downright destructive to want another woman who in turn wanted a life elsewhere. But Amy had been gone for less than twenty-four hours, and he missed her so much he hurt.

He stepped into the school office, his gaze moving from the growing pile of phone messages on Mrs. Lyons's desk to where Daniel was huddled in the corner of the beige couch, closed off from him again. Obviously dreading the coming session with

Dr. Steve.

That's when Josh recognized the ugliest of the unwanted feelings pressing in on him — loneliness.

He'd never felt more alone in his life.

Amy trudged through the lobby of Atlanta's Georgia-Pacific Tower, heading for an elevator that would take her to the Kramer offices on the twenty-seventh floor. She knew Thomas Fuller was following close behind, mostly because the tiny hairs on the back of her neck remained on prickly alert every time the man was in the room.

She checked her watch, wondering if Becky's first meeting with the school counselor had ended by now. Amy had told both Gwen and Josh that she'd be in touch after work, but waiting to hear how things were going was killing her.

Jacquie, who was hustling beside her, had Amy's cell phone in her purse. A little added insurance. That way, there was no chance Amy would cave and try to cram in a personal call before her meeting.

She rounded one of the marble columns that flanked the elevators, Thomas Fuller's ambition driving her forward, and barreled straight into a three-piece, navy-blue pin-striped suit.

"Hey!" an annoyed voice said as the man it belonged to spilled his coffee down both their fronts. "Watch where you're going."

Hot liquid seared her skin through the flimsy barrier of her white silk blouse, but the pain barely registered over the assault of the man's familiar voice.

Backing away slowly, her survival instinct preparing her to run, Amy stared up into her ex-husband's angry eyes.

CHAPTER TEN

"Mr. . . . Mr. Reese," Jacquie squeaked over Amy's shoulder. The younger woman discreetly took her arm and prevented her from making a break for it through one of the revolving front doors.

Amy had filled her assistant in on the high points of her failed marriage. Once her divorce proceedings were in full swing, she'd needed Jacquie's help to cover things at the office while she was in divorce court. Jacquie had since then become one of the few female friends Amy had made in the workplace, and no one, with the exception of Amy's mother, was more protective of her where Richard was concerned.

"We're late for a meeting," Jacquie said as he stared disdainfully down at them both.

Amy searched her mind for something glib to say, some way to prove to herself and her ex that she wasn't about to vomit simply from being near the man. Instead she just stood there, shaking in her sensible, slightly feminine, just-expensive-enough-to-be-noticed executive heels.

"Our elevator's here," Thomas called from somewhere to her left.

One glance at his exasperated expression yanked Amy back to reality. She ignored the way Richard was studying the coffee seeping through her blouse, and walked calmly to where her colleague was holding an elevator. The scared victim within her begged her not to turn back. Her pride insisted she not take the easy way out.

"You'd better change that blouse before your meeting, baby," Richard practically shouted over the din of conversation surrounding them. Heads turned to look at him, then swiveled toward her just as she reached the elevator. Richard's leer shifted from her coffee-sodden breasts to her nylon-clad legs, then back to the hair she was now wearing loose and much longer, if for no other reason than because he'd liked it short and tidy. "You're a mess."

The doors swooshed shut, and the car rose toward the top of the classy, ultraconservative office building, where the city's top business people carried out their dance of confidence and power. A dance she excelled at, except her heart was racing and her palms were clammy, and she'd never felt more like she didn't belong.

She was free of Richard Reese, she reminded herself sternly. All she had to do was close this deal with Kramer Industries, and she was on her way. The future and the security she'd always wanted were finally within her grasp, waiting for her to reach out and take them like the confident woman she'd tried so hard to become.

But when the elevator finally dinged and the doors slid open, her breathing wasn't any less ragged. Her ears wouldn't stop ringing as she looked down the hallway toward the double glass doors that opened into the Kramer corporate offices.

One chance encounter with her ex-husband, one of his patented snide remarks, and all her insecurities were back as if they'd never left.

You're a mess, sweetheart. Go fix yourself up, so you won't embarrass me. . . .

I don't know why you insist on keeping that job at Enterprise. You don't have what it takes to succeed in business. They'll eat you alive if you try. . . .

You're lucky you've got me to take care of you. . . .

Why can't you do anything right? All I asked is that you have everything ready when my

*guests arrive, but you can't even do that. Just
look at you — you're hopeless. . . .*

"Amy?" Jacquie nudged her forward.
"We're here."

Thomas had exited before them and was
walking confidently toward the Kramer
suite, not bothering to wait for her.

"Amy?" Jacquie repeated.

"No," she said, shaking her head, which
only increased the noise inside. "I can't. Go
in without me. . . . Thomas is prepared.
Have him start the meeting."

"What?"

Amy looked to the left, then right, finally
zeroing in on the public restrooms that
flanked the central elevators. She shoved
her briefcase into Jacquie's arms and half
ran in the opposite direction from where
she should be going.

"Amy?" her assistant called after her.

"I can't," she mumbled, steadying herself
against the wall. "I just can't."

Amy pushed the bathroom door open and
stumbled inside, entering the first stall and
locking the door behind her. Sinking to the
floor, her back to the door, the skirt of her
suit twisted around her thighs, she covered
her mouth and fought the screams that

seemed to be building from the weakest part of her.

Why had she thought she could do this? What insane part of her had actually thought she could pull this off? One glance from her ex, one reminder of the pitiful person she'd been when they were together, and she'd turned into a trembling, hand-wringing weakling. What kind of corporate manager could she possibly make?

The memories grabbed at her. The anger, the arguments and the tears. The futile attempts to find the courage to fight back or leave. How many times had Richard convinced her she needed him? How many times had she gone crawling back, promising to try harder to make him happy?

She couldn't do this. She shouldn't be here. Closing her eyes, she focused on the one and only thing that could get her through the paralyzing fear.

Becky.

Her daughter smiled back from Amy's memories. Then came a flash of her little girl being held in Gwen's comforting embrace. Remembering that her family was happy and safe hundreds of miles away in Sweetbrook worked like a sedative on Amy's galloping heart rate. She reached for her necklace, then realized Becky was wearing it now, and the loss of her tangible link to her child nearly sent Amy into hysterics again.

Then from out of nowhere came the memory of Josh's hand touching her, his eyes full of concern, then filling with warmth as he bent to kiss her. As he showed her how it felt not to be alone.

The urge to feel his touch again was almost as intense as the need to hold her daughter.

Well, neither is going to happen right now, Amy, so get it together.

Don't you dare let Becky down!

Controlling her breathing, she pushed herself off the restroom floor, the panic attack receding enough for her to cringe as she brushed her hands down her skirt. Richard had been right; she was a mess. But she still had to make an appearance in the meeting with Jed Westing, so that's what she was going to do.

She stumbled out of the stall toward one of the tiny sinks, turning on the hot water. A glance in the mirror confirmed that the tears still streaming down her face had relieved her eyelashes of most of their mascara. The inky substance had melted into messy trails smudged on either side of her nose.

She scrubbed her hands beneath the

scalding water, longing to shower from head to toe from just brushing up against her ex. Then she grabbed a fistful of paper towels and went to work on her face.

"Amy?" The outside door creaked open and Jacquie poked her head in. "You okay?"

"I will be." She forced a smile as she turned, still rubbing at her ruined makeup. "I really blew it back there, didn't I?"

Jacquie shrugged as she stepped into the restroom. "I told Mr. Westing that you felt sick in the lobby and had to excuse yourself. He has no reason to doubt me."

"Yeah, but Thomas knows the truth."

"Thomas is a grunt. His job is to keep Westing happy."

Amy dabbed at the coffee stains on her blouse, then threw the wad of paper into the trash bin. How had she ended up here, hiding out in a corporate restroom instead of taking care of business? Counting on Thomas Fuller, of all people, to cover for her?

"What was Richard doing here?" Jacquie asked.

"The same thing he always does wherever he is, dominating everything in sight." Amy swallowed the panic bubbling up again. "Who knows how many clients he has in this building? I was bound to run into him eventually, even if he spends most of his time these days commuting back and forth to his New York offices."

"I couldn't believe it when I looked up and saw him towering over you."

"*You* couldn't believe it."

"I think you handled it well."

Amy gave her friend a disbelieving look.

"You held your ground," Jacquie countered. "The man's a jerk, Amy, and for years he enjoyed making you feel like you were worthless. The fact that you made it up the elevator before you fell apart is an achievement all by itself."

"Yeah, I'm a real all-star. Tell that to Mr. Hutchinson when he hears what happened."

"He'll understand." The sprinkling of doubt in Jacquie's tone matched the worry in her eyes. "So running into Richard threw you for a loop. It was just bad timing. Besides, this is only a follow-up meeting."

"A follow-up for a meeting I wasn't here for last week, Jacquie. Even though Mr. Hutchinson called me personally and asked me to come back for it."

"So? What does Hutchinson have to gripe about? You're in town now. You have things with Becky under control, and now you're focused on work. Richard's just a blip on the radar."

But was Amy really back to focusing exclusively on her job? Was Richard's power over her really a part of her past?

She studied her now makeup-free face in the mirror, trying to recapture a piece of the bravely independent woman she needed everyone around her to believe she'd become.

"Ready to get back to it?" Jacquie held the restroom door open.

Her forced smile of encouragement reminded Amy of how parents looked when they led children into the doctor's office and told them it wasn't going hurt.

Kids always knew better, and so did she.

"You feel like something to eat?" Josh asked as he braked the Range Rover in front of the house that afternoon and turned to Daniel.

Gone was the sullen, angry look the kid had worn for so long. In its place was the type of resignation that tempted Josh to hunt down Curtis Jenkins and exact retribution for every single thing the man had done to Daniel and Melanie.

"You know, I'm not going to let him take you away from me," Josh said when his nephew still didn't respond. "I don't care what I have to do, he'll never lay his hands on you again."

Dr. Rhodes had asked Josh to sit in on this afternoon's session. They'd talked over the phone ahead of time about Daniel's panicked reaction to the revelation that his father was back. Dr. Rhodes had suggested this meeting be with the two of them together, that it might help Josh find some way to bond with his nephew. If they were going to have any chance of getting Daniel to share his painful memories, Josh had to stop being the enemy.

But Daniel had spent the entire session slouched in the chair beside him, still as stone. Which left them no closer than before to having the information they needed.

"What makes you think you can stop my dad from taking me back?" the ten-year-old finally inquired.

It was a fair question, one Josh had been asking himself for days.

"Legally, I've done about all I can do for now," he admitted, clenching the steering wheel. "I've filed some legal papers and asked for a test to prove the man really is your father. And in her will, your mother chose me to be your guardian. That gives us some time. But my temporary guardianship isn't going to hold up for very long. Not unless the judge has a reason to think I'd be a better parent for you than your father."

Daniel was at least looking at him now.

"That's where you come in," Josh continued. "Mrs. Thomas says the only way we can stop your dad for sure is if you can tell a judge what you remember about living with your father. You've got to try to talk about what happened, Daniel."

The boy's reaction was immediate. His complexion completely drained of color. His eyes darted away, but not before Josh saw the fight-or-flight terror that filled them.

"You haven't known me for very long. And I know I hurt your mother, when she came back home and your grandma and I didn't listen to what she was saying about your dad." Josh shook his head in shame and regret. "I wasn't there for your mom when she needed me. But I'm here for you now. I . . . I'm here with you all the way. You're my family. Part of my sister, and that makes you part of me. You can trust me with your memories, Daniel. I'll do whatever it takes to keep you safe and living with me here in Sweetbrook."

The silence that followed seemed to last forever, but Josh was learning to let those kind of lapses work themselves out.

Finally, Daniel looked back at him.

"Are you and Becky's mom really

friends?" he asked.

"Yeah," Josh replied carefully, rather than redirecting the conversation back to Curtis Jenkins, where he wanted it. Lately, he'd started to wonder if a man could literally go out of his mind with frustration. "We've been friends for a long time."

"Just like you and my mom used to be friends?"

"Yeah," Josh hedged, remembering the missing photo albums from the sitting room he suspected Daniel had been looking through. "Something like that."

"And she and Becky . . . Her mom said Becky knew what it was like . . . you know. What it was like to feel the way I do."

Daniel's circular logic slapped Josh upside the head so hard his ears rang.

"Are you asking me if Becky's father was like your old man?" he asked.

Daniel shrugged.

"I don't know for sure," Josh said. "But I think she and her mom have had it pretty rough. Maybe that's why it's been a little easier to talk with Ms. Loar than it has been with me or Dr. Steve?"

"Yeah," Daniel said with another shrug. "I guess Becky's mom wasn't so bad. But she's gone now, right?"

"Yes, she's back in Atlanta."

They were talking, Josh realized. About what, he wasn't exactly sure. But he and his nephew were actually carrying on a seemingly normal conversation.

Daniel's words replayed in his mind as Josh drummed his fingers on the steering wheel.

I guess Becky's mom wasn't so bad.

Actually, Amy was the one person who'd been able to get through to Daniel. And she was the one person Josh had no right to ask for help again. But his other choices were quickly becoming nonexistent.

Which meant when Amy called for an update on Becky's progress, he was going to do the unthinkable.

At a quarter past eleven that night, Amy slid into the enormous upholstered chair that took up half her apartment's tiny living room. Unopened packing boxes that held the sum total of her and Becky's belongings sprawled around her. Her feet hurt, her back ached and her eyes were begging for one of the ice packs she kept handy in the freezer for late nights just like this.

She'd managed to finesse her way through the end of the meeting with Jed Westing, but she'd left with a new list of to-dos, many of which had to be addressed immediately.

Hence her extended night at the office, when she'd planned to head out on time for a change so she could call Josh for an update on Becky's day. But with Thomas Fuller at her side all evening, under the guise of learning as much as he could about the Kramer project and making himself useful, she hadn't had a private moment since returning to the office. And now it was entirely too late for her to be calling anyone.

The phone jingled on the table at her elbow, the sound deafeningly shrill in the late-night quiet. Amy reached for the receiver and froze, adrenaline pumping at the unwelcomed thought that it might be Richard calling to harass her some more about that morning. But Richard wouldn't do that. It wasn't his style. It would be so much more satisfying for him to sit back and wait for her to call instead. For her to beg him for another chance.

Almost hoping it was him, so she could rip into him as she should have at the Georgia-Pacific Tower, she jerked the unit off its receiver.

"Hello."

"Amy?" Josh White replied in that calm, soothing voice she'd longed to hear all day. "I hope it's not too late, but I've been trying to call for hours."

She checked her answering machine and slapped her forehead at the sight of the blinking message-waiting light.

"I'm so sorry. I didn't get a chance to call from work, and I just got home."

"It's okay, I know you're trying to catch up," he assured her. "I'd have called on your cell, but I didn't want to interrupt anything important."

"No, you should have. . . ." She sat back, mortified by how she'd behaved when he'd last reached her at work. "I mean, thank you for being so considerate, but I'd have paid money for the interruption tonight."

Just talking with him gave her a sense of peace she hadn't felt since . . . well, since they'd been together on the weekend.

How, in just a few short days, had he become her safe place again?

"Tough day?" he asked, his genuine concern wrapping around her heart.

"Nothing new," she hedged, banishing the memory of her run-in with Richard. "How about you? Any progress with Daniel?"

"No." Josh cleared his throat, paused, then cleared it again. "That's part of the reason I called. I mean . . ."

Something was wrong. She could hear it in the way he couldn't bring himself to talk about whatever was going on. Her heart sank.

"What is it, Josh? Tell me Daniel's father wasn't able to get custody already."

"No," he said. "It's just that — Amy, I'm supposed to be helping you here, not the other way around. Things went really well with Becky today."

"Good." She breathed a sigh of relief, almost feeling guilty because her problems seemed to be solving themselves, just as his were clearly getting worse. "You've made this so easy for us."

"Please don't thank me." He sounded annoyed for some reason. "You're just making this harder."

"Making what harder?" It was about half-past too late for her to be talking in circles. "What's going on, Josh?"

"I need your help," he blurted out. "You're the only one who's come close to getting through to Daniel so far, and it makes me sick to think about asking you for one more thing, with all the crap you're already dealing with. But I'm out of alternatives."

Instead of sympathizing, Amy's temper flared. "You mean to tell me, Joshua White, that after everything you've done for Becky, you don't want to ask me for help because *you feel sorry for me?*"

"Amy —"

"You always were a butthead, you know that? It may not seem like it right now, but I can be a pretty self-sufficient person."

Except of course when her ex glared in her direction, or for that matter when he was simply in the same building as her.

She shoved her internal editor aside.

"There may be nothing I can do to help you right now," she said, "because I'm stuck in Atlanta, and you're there. But you could at least ask me like you would any other friend. Stop handling me as if I'm going to break, Josh. I'm not a charity case."

No, but you're bordering on sounding like a shrieking maniac.

"Amy, I'm not trying to *handle* you. But we're not talking about a simple favor." He sighed, and in her mind she could see him raking his hand through all that gorgeous blond hair. "Daniel's still not opening up about his father. Not with me and not with his therapist. Things were a little better at his session today. I think he finally realizes how important remembering is, but . . . I'm not sure he can. No one's come close to getting him to talk . . . no one but you. He even asked about you today."

Amy shook her head, then realized Josh was waiting for a verbal response.

"Are you saying you want *me* to try and get him to talk about his dad? He doesn't even know me."

"He knows enough. You've opened your heart to him, Amy, both times the two of you were alone." There was awe in Josh's voice, along with something that sounded very much like envy.

"He knows you love him, Josh."

"Yeah, maybe, but he doesn't trust me. And I'm not sure I blame him."

Amy found herself at a complete loss over what to say next.

Petty as it sounded, she didn't want to be the one Daniel trusted. How could she help the little boy explore his own fears, when hers had all but eaten her alive just that morning?

"I want to help you and Daniel any way I can," she said, though misgivings were shredding her voice. "I really do, but —"

"You don't have to do this, Amy," Josh rushed to say. "Really, I can't even believe I'm asking. It's just that of all the people in the world for Daniel to bond with, it was such a relief he chose you. I can't think of anyone I'd trust more. . . ."

"Oh, Josh." She had to swallow before she could continue. "Thank you. . . ."

How long had it been since she'd been so

blindly trusted by anyone but her daughter? And even Becky had had reason to doubt Amy more often than not over the last few years.

"What do you need me to do?" she heard herself ask.

"Amy, you don't have to —"

"I know I don't have to, Josh. But I am. What do you need?"

"What about your work?"

"Well, it sucks right now, thanks for asking. But things are under control here. Or at least they will be, once I get a little sleep and come out swinging in the morning. I was already thinking about getting away early again Friday and coming back to Sweetbrook. Would next weekend be soon enough for me to talk with Daniel?"

She'd wanted to check in on Becky, anyway. It wouldn't be an imposition to see Daniel while she was there. Of course, that would mean seeing Josh again, too, and her pulse was already racing at the thought. But that wasn't the point.

Becky and Daniel, two kids who needed their worlds to stop spinning out of control — they were the point. Thoughts of being close to Joshua White again had no part whatsoever in her decision.

"Are you sure?" he asked. "This may be a

really bad idea."

"No, I'm not sure." She was scared to death of what facing Daniel's fears would do to the ones she was trying to bury within herself. "But Daniel can't go back to his father. I can't let that happen if there's any way I can help."

Another long pause made her wonder if Josh had wised up and changed his mind.

"I . . . I don't know what to say," he finally murmured.

"Say you'll keep doing a great job with Becky, which helps keep me sane while I can't be there. Then say you'll let me return the favor when I get home Friday."

"You're a strong woman, Amy Loar."

She laughed at the thought. "I'm a wuss."

"No." His voice hardened, even as it stroked the jagged edges of her tattered self-confidence. "You're a survivor, and I think I'm lucky I harassed you last week and dragged you back to Sweetbrook. I have no idea what I'd be doing right now without . . . without a friend like you to turn to."

Amy forced herself to focus on the word *friend*. Because that's all they could be to each other, and neither one of them was going to ruin things by wanting more.

His soft chuckle had her smiling. It sounded so good to hear him laugh.

233

"Butthead, huh?" he asked. "It's been a long time since someone called me that."

"Then it sounds to me like you're overdue," she retorted. "I'll see you on Friday. And I'll keep tabs on Becky through my mom. Just let Gwen know when Mr. Fletcher has the results he's looking for."

"You're my angel, Amy." Joshua's voice held a definite smile.

And you're mine.

"Good night," she whispered, alarmed by the unruly, romantic thought that had almost slipped out.

"Good night," he echoed, and the line went dead.

CHAPTER ELEVEN

Becky set her lunch tray beside Daniel's. He was sitting at the end of the table, as far away from the other kids as he could get, reading one of the comic books he always had with him. She scooted in beside him and opened her own book. Liking to read was one more thing she was learning they had in common.

It was Friday afternoon, and their class had just arrived for their twelve-thirty lunch period. She'd tried to stay out of Daniel's way all week. That hadn't been hard, since she spent hours each morning with Mr. Fletcher, then had to catch up with what she'd missed in class once she returned. A visit to the school counselor every day had sounded like a break — until the testing started. Mr. Fletcher was nice enough, but she couldn't do a lot of the things on his tests. She felt more stupid now than when they'd started.

She glanced at Daniel, who hadn't even said hi yet. She should apologize for everything she'd said about his mom.

"You wanna make a break for it?" she asked instead, opening her milk and stabbing her straw into the carton.

Out of the corner of her eye, she saw Daniel flinch, then turn to face her.

"What?" She poked at the watery mashed potatoes the lunch lady had plopped beside the block of meat loaf before Becky could say she didn't want any. "Don't tell me you haven't thought about it. Don't you want to just blow this place sometimes?"

Daniel was carving his meat loaf into chunks that looked like pet food.

"It doesn't do any good," he groused, drinking his milk straight from the carton. "Running away only makes it worse when you come back."

She gave up pretending to eat. "And just how many times have you run away?" she taunted.

"Every day for the last three months."

"Man," she said, actually impressed. She kept threatening her mom that she'd do it, but the one time she'd tried, she'd only had the guts to walk around the block and back. "If you want out of here so bad, why do you keep coming back?"

"Where else am I going to go?" He threw his fork down. "What is this? Get your kicks talking to the messed up kid day?"

"Who else am I going to talk to?" She swallowed a spoonful of applesauce, Daniel's screwed up life pointing a big fat finger at how hers wasn't as bad as she'd thought. "No one else in this place is going to understand what it's like."

"What what's like?"

"You know." She looked up. "Everyone telling you it's getting better . . . only it's worse than it ever was."

His eyes squinted at her.

"So you wanna make a break for it?" she asked again.

"You're nuts. We can't just walk out of here."

"Why not? You said you do it all the time."

"Not in the middle of school." He tapped his finger to his forehead. "You really are nuts. My uncle's the principal."

"So?"

"So! We're going to get caught!"

"So?"

Everyone was trying their best to help her. She understood that now. And she'd been trying as hard as she could this week, too. But she couldn't take this place anymore.

"Forget it!" She stomped to her feet.

Daniel's hand jerked her to a halt. The shocked understanding in his eyes had her sitting back down and pretending to play with her napkin so he wouldn't see how relieved she was.

"You're really up for cutting class the rest of the day?" he asked.

She nodded.

"We're going to get in trouble."

She shrugged. Her mom was supposed to be back in town by the time the school bus got home, and she'd be angry when she heard about this. But what was her mom going to do, ground her? It wasn't like Becky ever left the house, anyway.

"You know somewhere to go, don't you?" she asked. Someplace where she wouldn't feel like such an idiot.

"Yeah, I know a place."

"Good." She grabbed her lunch tray and walked away without checking to see if he was following.

And suddenly she didn't care. He could come with her or not. Either way, she was out of here.

She scanned the cafeteria for teachers, but they all seemed to be eating in the staff lounge. She located one of the monitors who kept the kids under control while the teachers took their break, and asked the elderly woman if she could go to the bathroom. The monitor nodded, only half listening because a group of second-grade boys a few tables over had launched into a food fight.

Over her left shoulder, Becky saw Daniel slip around the woman while Becky distracted her, then he headed for the side door that led to the hall. He jerked his head for her to join him, then he was gone.

Her heart beating so fast she felt it throbbing all over her body, Becky left the lunchroom behind. She'd pay for this later, but it was going to be worth it.

"Already?" Josh barked into the phone.

Edna Lyons popped her head through the open doorway. He held up a hand to stall her. He'd finally gotten Barbara Thomas on the phone, and the news wasn't good.

"Jenkins's lawyer filed the papers to gain custody. Be expecting a call from your lawyer about a hearing."

Josh sighed, motioning Edna into the office. "How long do you think before Daniel will have to talk to a judge?"

He initialed the expense forms in the folder Edna shoved under his nose, and handed them back to her. She made no move to leave.

"If you file for an extension, and you get lucky and catch Judge Hardy in a good mood, you can buy yourself a few more weeks," Barbara estimated.

"Are we going to get lucky?"

"I'll do everything I can." She sounded less than encouraging. "Any progress with Daniel?"

"He's sitting through the sessions with Dr. Rhodes now without acting out. Rhodes says it's a sign that he's finally beginning to trust me."

"That's great!"

"Yeah, except now Daniel doesn't say anything at all." In fact, they hadn't spoken since their cryptic conversation during the ride home Monday night.

"Mr. White?" Mrs. Lyons interrupted.

He'd forgotten she was still there. And the woman looked ready to rip the phone out of his hand.

"I've got to go, Barbara. Do the best you can with the judge."

"What is it, Mrs. Lyons?" he said, louder than he'd intended as he hung up the phone.

"Mrs. Cole stopped by a few minutes ago. She and her class were returning to their room after lunch and . . ." The normally direct woman hesitated. She was actually

240

wringing her hands.

Josh sat silently, waiting for the details of Daniel's latest scuffle. The kid had been lying low this week, his increasing withdrawal concerning Dr. Rhodes. It was almost a relief that there had been a new outburst.

"It's okay, Mrs. Lyons," he said. "Just tell me what Daniel's done, and I'll have a talk with him."

"Well, that's the problem." The woman worried her bottom lip between her teeth. "Mrs. Cole was wondering if Daniel might already be in here with you."

"What?" Josh pushed himself from his chair.

"He wasn't there when Mrs. Cole returned to take the kids back from lunch. She didn't think too much about it at first. She had one of the boys check the bathrooms, then thought maybe he'd headed back to class early. But . . ."

"But what?"

Curtis Jenkins wouldn't have the nerve to try and take Daniel from the school, would he?

"Becky Reese seems to be missing, too," Edna said. "Mrs. Cole's checking with the other teachers, but she was wondering if it's possible they might have run off somewhere together."

■ ■ ■ ■

Josh was waiting when Amy pulled to a stop outside the school at one-thirty. She'd just turned off the highway when he'd called her cell with the news about their kids. Instead of driving on to her mom's, Amy had given Gwen a quick call to let her know what was up, then she'd headed for the school.

She rolled down the window. Josh braced his forearms on the roof as he bent to talk with her.

"The last anyone saw of them was about an hour ago, so I'm pretty confident they're together." His expression was a mixture of apprehension and frustration. "One of the lunch monitors remembers Becky asking to use the restroom. No one saw Daniel leave."

"Why would they cut school?"

"Beats me, but it's the only thing that makes sense. Doug Fletcher said Becky was agitated this morning. The last of her testing took longer than usual. She was pretty frustrated by the time she left his office, and she was late meeting her class at lunch. My guess is she and Daniel got together and decided an afternoon off sounded like fun."

"Any ideas where they might be?" Amy

had taken a full day's work with her when she'd left the office that morning. Neither Hutchinson nor Thomas Fuller had been pleased that she was taking more personal time. She'd left them e-mail messages that she'd check in as soon as she arrived in Sweetbrook.

Guess that plan was moot.

"I have one idea," Josh responded, a half smile forming on his gorgeous face.

"Of course!" she exclaimed, reading his mind as easily as when they were kids. "The tree house."

"Give me five minutes, and we'll head over together." But he didn't immediately step away from the car. His smile grew softer as he studied her. "I'm really glad you're here."

Nerve endings sang to life at the memory of his kisses. Regardless of the circumstances, it felt good for her to be there, too.

Maybe too good.

CHAPTER TWELVE

"There it is," Daniel said as they stopped on the road next to the Millers' pond.

"You've got to be kidding." Becky gazed at the ancient fort perched in a tree down by the water. "I'm not climbing up there. I'll fall and break my neck."

"Don't be such a baby," Daniel sneered. She'd been so cool ever since they'd left the school. Now she was acting like a *girl.* "It's safe. Besides, if your mom could climb up there, you can."

"My mom?" Becky stared at him as if he had snot running out of his nose. Then she blinked in recognition. "So this is the tree house she told me about when I was little. Hey!" Becky's eyes narrowed. "How do you know she used to climb up there?"

"Never mind." He turned away, wanting to kick himself. Why, *why,* bring up her mother? Next, maybe they could have a nice long chat about his uncle. "I'm going up.

Stay here if you want to, I don't care."

"Now who's being a baby?" she grumbled. "Are you always —"

"Well, if it isn't a couple of the county's finest youngsters," a deep voice said from the road behind them.

The hair on Daniel's arms rose in recognition, even though it had been years since he'd heard that voice. He turned, pulling Becky a step or two away from the beat-up black truck they hadn't heard stop a few feet away. The man was smiling from behind the wheel, his arm propped on the open window. His grin showed off the gap between his two front teeth, and his nose was crooked.

Funny how the face looked like a stranger's, but the voice stunk of home.

"Aren't you kids supposed to be in school?" the man said, setting the hand brake. He slipped out of the truck, closing the rickety door and leaning back against the dusty metal.

"What do you care?" Daniel demanded.

Becky's arm trembled slightly, and he looked sideways long enough to catch the worry in her eyes.

"You know who I am, don't you, boy?" The man's smile looked even phonier when he winked.

Becky pulled against Daniel's grasp, as if she were planning to run. He held tight to her arm. Running wouldn't do any good with this guy. Daniel should know.

"If you think I care who you are," he said, "you're crazier than my mom said you were."

"Now is that any way to talk to your daddy?"

Becky flinched, then shrugged off Daniel's grip. She eyed his father up and down. "So you're the one Mr. White said would never lay a hand on Daniel again."

She turned up that snooty nose of hers. In the past, that same look had angered Daniel. At the moment, he wanted to applaud.

"Well, aren't you a little angel?" The way Daniel's father snarled the endearment had Daniel yanking Becky back another couple of steps, until she was slightly behind him.

The man's eyes honed in on him. "Your uncle tell you I'm here to take you home?" he asked.

"He told me he'd never let you take me anywhere." Daniel lifted his own chin, mimicking Becky's stubborn stare. Inside, he felt himself coming unglued. The storm was building, the anger and the hurt. The panic. The memories. "My uncle's got a lot of clout around here. He won't let you hurt me."

"Now, what makes you think I'd hurt you?" His dad stepped away from the truck.

Becky began inching back, pulling on Daniel's T-shirt for him to follow.

Daniel couldn't move, even though he felt like he was flying apart. The roaring in his ears drowned out every sound except the voice of the man walking toward him.

"Why don't you hop in my truck, and we can talk about it real civilized-like," the man said, easing closer.

"Don't touch me," Daniel whispered, while the words screamed in his mind.

The man's hand closed around his shoulder, and the dam broke.

"Don't touch me!"

Kicking, screaming, fighting, Daniel didn't care who he hit as long he got away. He had to get away. But his legs wouldn't run. So he kept on hitting.

Fight him off. Make him stop.

"Don't touch me!"

"Daniel!" another man's voice called from somewhere outside the panic. The unmovable mountain that was his father was yanked away.

"Keep your hands off him, Jenkins, or I'll —"

"Josh, don't," a woman's voice said as soft arms swept Daniel close.

The last of the fury cleared from his eyes, evaporating, until he was once again standing by the side of the road near the pond.

"Mom." Becky ran back to his side.

Mom?

The arms around him loosened and eased away, Becky's mom knelt beside him.

"Are you okay?" She brushed at the hair curling into his eyes. "Did he hurt you?"

Daniel leaned into her touch before he could stop himself. Her cool hand cupped his cheek.

"Sweetheart, it's okay," she said. "Your uncle's here. He's not going to let anything happen to you."

Still marveling at how unexpectedly good her touch felt, fighting to catch his breath, soaked with sweat, Daniel peered around her. A car had stopped just short of running his dad down. Both front doors hung open, and his uncle had his father pinned against the rusted hood of the black truck.

"You see?" Her own worried glance followed his. "Your uncle's got everything under control."

Daniel felt the shuddering start again from that awful place inside. The heat raging through him froze, settling in his stomach like a block of ice. Becky's mom tried to stop him, but he broke free.

He sprinted down the hill, falling when his foot sank into a hole, but he was up and moving again before he hit the ground. Someone yelled his name, but he didn't stop until he'd reached the base of the tree, just in time to puke up everything he'd eaten at lunch. Then he was scrambling up the splintery steps, desperate to disappear into the safety of the shadows inside.

"Stay away from Daniel," Josh growled in a voice that stopped Amy in her tracks.

Then she remembered that it *was* Josh, and she found the courage to keep walking toward the struggling men.

Josh had Curtis Jenkins pinned against the pickup truck. He seemed unable to let the other man go. Perfectly understandable, if he was feeling even an ounce of the anger that had consumed her when they'd driven up to find Daniel struggling in his father's grasp.

"Get your hands off me, White," Curtis Jenkins wheezed.

"Mom?" Becky tugged on her sleeve.

"It's okay, honey." Amy gave her a quick hug. "It's going to be okay."

"Should I go check on Daniel?"

"No. Just wait for me here, okay?"

Then she walked toward the angry men again, cringing inside while she kept her head high so Becky wouldn't see how terrified she was. Memories of Richard, of feeling helpless in the face of his anger, taunted her. But her memories were *her* problem. She wouldn't let them touch her daughter.

"Josh, Daniel's fine." She stopped a few feet away, her hand raised but not quite touching him. "Josh? Let the man go. Daniel's okay."

Josh took a deep breath and his grip loosened enough for Jenkins to edge away.

"You've made a big mistake, man," Daniel's father said. He looked around, presumably trying to find his son. "My lawyer's going to make sure the judge hears about this."

"Hears about what?" Amy grabbed Josh's arm as he stepped toward the man again. "That we drove up and found you trying to pull Mr. White's legal ward into your car, against the boy's will?"

"That's not what happened," the other man sputtered.

"Yes, it is!" Becky cuddled against Amy's side. Her tone dared Jenkins to keep lying. "Daniel told you to let him go, and you wouldn't."

"Why don't you have your lawyer relay

that to the judge?" Amy smiled down at her daughter's fierce expression.

"You've got yourself a spunky little lady there, White." Jenkins sized Amy up, then winked at Becky. "A right nice little family scene."

"Get in your car and go." Josh's voice was as dark as the dead calm that had finally reclaimed his eyes. He stepped sideways, effectively cutting off Jenkins's view of Amy and Becky. "Talk to whoever you like, but don't make the mistake of coming near anyone I care about again."

"Oh, I'll be nearby, all right," the other man replied. Amy felt his nasty smile, even though she couldn't see it. "Count on it," he called over his shoulder as he sauntered back to his truck.

Josh left Daniel's room later that night and closed the door behind him.

"Is he asleep?" Amy asked.

Josh nodded as he drank in the sight of her. He couldn't ever in his life remember being more relieved to see someone.

She should have gone home hours ago, as soon as they'd talked Daniel down from the tree house. But Becky had assured them she was okay. And she was safely at home with Gwen now, allowing Amy to drop Josh and

Daniel home. She'd stayed to help Josh make sandwiches that Daniel had barely touched. And she'd been waiting in the hallway ever since, while Josh settled Daniel into bed for the night.

Remarkably, the little boy seemed no worse off for the afternoon's drama. Once he'd calmed down enough to talk, he kept saying he was fine, the few times he'd spoken at all. Mostly, he'd lapsed back into the scary silence Josh had never been able to penetrate. There was no way to know what kind of damage seeing Jenkins again had done to the boy's progress in facing and talking about his past. They'd just have to wait and see.

"Josh? Is everything okay?" Amy asked.

He realized he'd been standing there like an idiot, staring at her. He inhaled to clear his head.

"I can't remember the last time everything was okay," he replied, wrestling away the fantasy of Amy Loar always being there, waiting for him. Stopping him from piling even more mistakes on top of the ones he'd already made. "I've never thought I was capable of physically hurting someone. But when I saw Daniel trying to fight that man off . . ." He clenched his fists, when what he really needed was to hold Amy against him

252

until he stopped shaking. "I could have killed Jenkins for daring to put his hands on my nephew."

"But you didn't." She stepped closer, and her strawberry scent soothed him as much as her voice. "You did what you had to do to keep him from hurting Daniel again."

"Just what the boy needs," Josh said with a harsh laugh. "Another man in his life who can't control his temper."

Her hand found his, uncurling his fist until their fingers linked together with excruciating perfection. "I know you're not used to having feelings this strong over-whelm you. You've always been so good at keeping your emotions under control. But you're not a threat to Daniel or anyone else, even when you're angry. Look how you've backed away from Jenkins, twice now. You're strong, but you use your strength to protect people, not hurt them. Daniel's a smart little boy. He'll understand the difference soon enough."

Josh opened his mouth to argue with her. But as the encouragement shining in her eyes worked its magic on him, he lifted her hand and placed it over his heart. Through his fingers, he could feel his pulse race. Or was it hers?

"Amy . . . Holding you . . . It's the only

thing that's come close to feeling good in my life in a long time. Maybe . . . maybe you'd better go."

There was no future in this for either of them, and he knew this wasn't what she wanted. But here she was, so close and so caring. How could he walk away?

Her deep blue eyes widened. She relaxed. Her breath hitched.

"Josh, I . . . This . . ." Her breath caught again.

"Don't," he begged. "Please, don't go."

"I feel like I'm drowning." She was so close. Her gaze, full of confusion and need, told him he wasn't the only one coming apart inside. He cupped her cheek, the feel of the delicate bones beneath his hand a reminder of how fragile his valiant little hero really was.

Curtis Jenkins's careless observation by the side of the road came back to him.

You've got yourself a spunky little lady there, White. A right nice little family. . . .

Josh shook his head, reminding himself that she wasn't his lady, and they weren't anything close to a family.

Miraculously, they'd found a way to help each other, and Amy had come back this weekend because he'd asked her to. But she'd come back for Daniel, not for him.

And her heart was set on a life somewhere else, just as his ex's had been. There was no logic in giving any part of himself to one more woman who couldn't make the kind of commitment he needed.

Which meant this had to stop. Now.

"I'm scared, Josh." Amy couldn't stop staring at his mouth. "This . . . whatever it is between us, it can't possibly go anywhere."

"I know. . . ." He shuddered, then began to inch away. He was doing the smart thing. He was being strong when she couldn't be.

They both had too much on their plates. Families depending on them, impossible situations to work through, and no time to find the answers they needed. Only it felt as if she'd die if she let him go.

"Don't." She clung to his arm to keep him close.

The fear and anxiety of the last few days were a lousy excuse for the enormity of the mistake she was making. But she didn't care. He'd been the best friend of her childhood. And in just a week's time, he'd somehow become an anchor in the swirling chaos of all the things going wrong in her world.

She needed him, no matter how much she didn't want to.

"Amy . . ." he whispered against her lips, and the broken way he said her name was the final straw for them both.

His mouth lowered and he kissed her, deeper than before. Longer. Sweeter. She clung to Josh, and sensed him shudder with the emotions swirling between them.

She felt her soul move.

Her heart shifted.

And in that moment, Amy realized just how much trouble she was in.

"I've got to get home to Becky."

"So that's it? You're not even going to try to give this a chance?"

Their hands brushed, and the tears that sprang to Amy's eyes nearly broke his heart for everything she was so determined not to let herself want. Well, he wanted more. This last week, she'd awakened a very big part of him that he'd thought would never love again.

"There is no chance. Not with me."

"Because you don't love me?"

Her head came up as if she'd been shot.

"I've already tried love," she said with a quivering sigh. "And you know everything you need to know about how badly that turned out."

"So try again." He took her hand, hoping

she'd calm down enough to talk. "I told myself I was done with relationships, too. And now I'm thinking maybe I was wrong."

"I owe my daughter better than to make another mistake like Richard."

Josh's hold on her arm tightened. "I'm not Richard. And you can't tell me that working yourself to death, alone, in Atlanta is giving Becky anything but more heartache. I see her at school every day, remember?"

"Are we back to that again? I'm giving my daughter the life she deserves." Amy yanked away from him. "The life and security she should have had all along."

"Whose security are we talking about, Amy? Becky's or yours?"

"Becky's." Her chin rose as she picked up her purse. "She's all I can let myself be concerned about now. My job and my promotion will give her what she needs. End of story. And that doesn't leave room for . . . for anything else."

"What if you didn't have to work so hard to give her what she needs?" he asked.

"What?" Suspicion shimmered across Amy's face.

"What if I can help you? Make it so you don't need that promotion? I have enough money —"

"Yes, you have money. And I suppose you could make Becky's and my problems go away, at least for a while." The sudden lack of emotion in her voice warned him he wasn't going to like what she said next. "But what happens one day soon when you stop wanting to help so badly, and I have to start all over again?"

"I'm not going to stop," he said incredulously, knowing it was the truth, even as he knew she wouldn't believe him. "I lo—"

"I'm sorry, Josh. I really am." She sounded both heartbroken and determined. "I know you mean well, but you and your money can't fix my life. I need to make a way for my daughter and me on my own. No short-cuts. No messing reality up with things that don't last, like love. No more mistakes."

She turned to leave, and all he could do was watch her go. He'd known from the start that he had no hold on her, and he should have known how much it would hurt when she walked away. Hadn't he been in this exact same place with Lisa?

"If you still want me to talk with Daniel," she said, her expressive features schooled in a businesslike calm, "I can stop by before I head back to Atlanta."

At his nod, she let herself out of the house and disappeared.

Sweet, beautiful, spunky Amy.

Her needs were leading her somewhere else. She couldn't have made that clearer from the start. She needed her career and her promotion, the success she'd wanted since they were kids. She was more determined than ever, after the hell Richard Reese had put her through. The last thing she wanted was a small-town relationship with Josh.

And yet he'd let himself fall headfirst in love with her, anyway.

CHAPTER THIRTEEN

Amy sat studying the spreadsheets she'd ripped from her briefcase after she'd returned to her mother's to find that Becky was already in bed. Dressed in a faded sweatsuit from her closet, one she was certain she'd last worn in gym class, she stared at the columns and rows of numbers, willing them to make sense. Willing her mind away from the perfection of kissing Josh.

Josh.

She'd needed him tonight in a way she'd never needed a man before. His gentleness had made her feel whole for the first time in ages.

She slid off her mother's faded couch, curled her body between it and the coffee table, and hugged her arms around her knees. What had she ever done to deserve finally having Joshua White become aware of her as a woman, just when neither one of them was in a position to play things out?

What had she been thinking? That kissing him again would somehow make everything better?

"Amy." Her mother stepped into the den and sat on the edge of the couch. "Honey, what's wrong? Becky was so upset when she got home. She said something about Daniel's father."

"She and Daniel ended up at the tree house after they left school." Amy raised her head. "We figured that's where they'd gone, but before Josh and I could get there, Daniel's dad had stumbled across them."

The memory of the scene she and Josh had driven up to made her shiver.

"Oh, no." Gwen stroked Amy's hair. They'd briefly discussed Josh's first run-in with Curtis Jenkins, and the knock-down-drag-out custody battle Josh was preparing to wage. "Didn't you say Daniel was afraid of his father?"

"Terrified." Amy shifted away from Gwen's touch. "And the man was trying to pull Daniel into his truck when we got to the Miller place. I thought Josh was going to kill him."

"It really must have been awful. I've never heard Joshua White so much as raise his voice, let alone physically threaten someone.

Is Daniel okay?"

"I don't know about okay, but Josh sent the man packing, and he has Daniel back home with him for now."

"Did you get a chance to talk with Daniel the way you wanted?"

"Not yet. Maybe in the morning, after I've finished grounding Becky for cutting class."

"She's worked really hard this week," Gwen reminded her.

"I know she has." Amy shoved herself off the floor to sit on the couch again. "And I want to read every encouraging thing in those notes Mrs. Cole and Mr. Fletcher sent home. But Becky can't think her unique situation means she no longer has boundaries."

"She understands that. I think she scared herself today."

"She was so brave, Mama." Amy had to smile. "The way she stood up to Daniel's father. She's a tough kid. She and Daniel both."

"How's Josh?"

Amy shook her head. "I don't want to think about what it would do to him to lose his nephew."

"It's a wonderful thing you're doing, helping that family."

"Yeah, I'm a big help." She puffed the hair

away from her face. "How can I help them when I can't even keep things in my own life together?"

"But Becky's doing better. And you said work is under control."

"Becky's a truant." Amy stood and walked across the tiny room. "And work's okay . . . I guess."

As much as working every waking hour could be okay. She had to be back in Atlanta by tomorrow night. All weekend, her staff would be hammering out the final details for next week's presentation. Her big shot. The pinnacle of all she'd been working toward for months.

What she'd just told Josh she wanted more than she wanted him.

"What am I doing?" She smoothed her hands down her age-worn sweatshirt. "I'm *this* close —" she pinched the air between her thumb and forefinger "— to having everything we need to be financially independent of Richard forever, but . . ."

"But?"

"But . . ." She fiddled with the handmade curtains she and her mother had sewn the summer before Amy had left for college. "Instead of focusing on what I have to do to finish this project, I'm sitting here wishing I didn't have to go back to the city at all. How mixed-up is that?"

"Maybe it's not so mixed-up." Her mother stayed on the other side of the room, while her words did their own crowding. "Not if the city and the job at Enterprise aren't what you want anymore."

"How can they not be what I want? How could I want anything else?"

How could another day shared with Josh bring on this kind of wishy-washy second-guessing?

"Maybe now that you've gotten some distance from your marriage —"

"Distance?" A harsh laugh forced its way out. "Yeah, I've moved on."

Her mother frowned.

"I ran into Richard the other day," she explained. "Literally."

"Oh, honey."

"He was condescending and superior, and it really messed me up. It left me more convinced than ever that I'm doing the right thing not letting him control our lives anymore."

"So what's the problem?"

"The problem is I keep coming back here." She couldn't even call up an image of her husband at the moment, to remind her of what was at stake. Instead, she was assaulted with memories of cool blue eyes deepening with emotion. A breathtakingly handsome male face, strong but gentle, determined but not domineering. "I keep letting myself want things that are no good for me."

"Like?"

Like depending on someone who makes me feel safe and needed and worthwhile. Like looking to anyone else for Becky's and my security.

"Like growing attached to things that can't be part of my life in Atlanta," she said out loud. "I'd be stupid to let my emotions take over again. Look at what that got me last time."

"Are you talking about Joshua White and his nephew?"

Amy nodded. "I can't turn my back on that little boy. If he doesn't talk about his memories of his father soon, he might have to go back to that awful man, and I can't let that happen. I have to help them. But this thing between Josh and me . . . I never expected it to be so confusing."

Understanding dawned in her mother's eyes, but Gwen kept her silence and waited for the rest.

"He's not for me, Mama." Amy looked around her mom's tiny house and felt anew the tug deep within for the simpler, uncomplicated life she'd known here. "None of this is for me. I may not like working in Atlanta and being so close to Richard, but that's where my job is. Where my daughter's life is. And I have a responsibility to her to make that work."

"I think what would do Becky more good than anything is seeing her mother happy for a change," Gwen countered. "If being in Sweetbrook does that for you, I'd say it's a step in the right direction. You could make a new life here."

"Not the life my daughter deserves."

Whose security are we talking about, Amy? Becky's or yours?

Josh's question haunted her, even though he couldn't be more wrong. Her daughter's happiness was her only concern. Her promotion and their life in Atlanta would provide that. Anything that distracted from that, no matter how much she might secretly want it, was out of the question.

"So I'll do what I can for Daniel," she reasoned out loud. "Then tomorrow afternoon, I'll head back to the real world in Atlanta."

The dash of skepticism in her mother's normally encouraging smile deflated Amy's floundering conviction even further.

"He's not for me, Mama," she repeated.

"Joshua White and his life here with Daniel can't be for me."

"Where are we going?" Daniel asked as Josh drove toward the Loar house the next morning.

"I told you," Josh said. "We're going for ice cream."

"With *them*?"

Josh chuckled, surprised by the sound almost as much as his nephew seemed to be.

Daniel shot him a give-it-a-rest glare that was light-years away from his fear after the run-in with his father. The kid was a fighter, and for a change he wasn't trying to inch as far away from Josh as he could get.

"Becky's mom's heading back out of town soon," Josh explained. "I thought ice cream would be a nice break for everyone."

Not to mention the fact that Josh couldn't wait any longer to see Amy again.

"I don't want to eat ice cream with Becky," Daniel grumped.

"You didn't seem to mind running off from school with her."

"That was different."

"Because you guys finally stopped taking potshots at each other long enough to be friendly?" Josh was still trying to understand

267

why the kids had done what they'd done.

"Maybe."

"Well, how has that changed since yester-day?" He watched as his nephew crossed his arms and stared at the homes rolling past the Range Rover's windows. "Are you worried about seeing her again after what happened with your dad?"

It was the first time Josh had brought up the subject of Curtis Jenkins since last night. He was risking upsetting the relative peace of the morning, but he was running out of both subtlety and time.

Daniel's gaze dropped to his lap. "I don't want anyone to know about him," the ten-year-old said in a little boy's voice Josh had never heard before.

"You have nothing to be ashamed of, Dan-iel." Not that Josh could even imagine what the kid was feeling. But he wouldn't let Daniel heap shame on top of everything else he'd endured. "And I don't think you have to worry about Becky using what happened to pick on you. The girl stood up for you after you headed to the tree house. So did her mother. I think you've made yourself some new friends."

A pause could last forever, Josh decided, as he waited for Daniel to either explode into his customary fit of anger or withdraw completely as he had after they'd left the Miller place last night.

"Just like you, right?" the boy asked instead.

"What?"

"They stood up to my dad for me," Daniel elaborated. "Just like you."

Josh was speechless for far too long, considering the simplicity of the statement. Or maybe it wasn't so simple, after all. Gratitude filled him for what Amy and Becky's presence in their lives had made possible. For the fragile bond growing between him and his nephew that he owed almost entirely to a spunky redhead who might not have come back to Sweetbrook if he hadn't badgered her into it.

"Yeah," he said. "They stood up for you, just like me."

He shook his head at the disturbing memory.

"Except they were able to stop your dad in his tracks without losing their tempers like I did. They just stared him down and told him where he could go jump."

"That's because they're girls," Daniel countered. "Girls are always confusing you with words. They talk so much, sometimes I forget what I'm thinking."

"Yeah." Josh's mouth tilted into a smile.

"Yeah, but girls like ice cream."

He pulled the SUV to a stop in front of Gwen Loar's house, relieved to see Amy's compact car sitting in the driveway.

He couldn't say who needed to talk with the woman more right now, him or his nephew.

"I don't know, Josh," Daniel heard Becky's mom say. He was standing behind his uncle, trying to look as if he didn't care. "You guys are welcome to come in for a little bit, but I'm not sure we have time for ice cream. Becky's grounded right now, anyway, for skipping class yesterday."

"But it's such a nice day outside," a lady with gray hair said as she stepped to the door. Daniel remembered seeing her at school once or twice. "How long could a trip to the Sugar Cone take?"

Becky's mom looked at the other woman without saying anything, then she glanced back at Daniel's uncle.

Daniel held his breath, actually wanting her to say yes — like he hadn't wanted anything in a long time. She'd been nice to him, and she somehow understood about his dad. And she'd stood up to the creep yesterday.

Could his uncle be right? Daniel wasn't

sure what a friend was anymore, but if that's what Becky and her mom were, maybe it wasn't so bad to have one.

She caught sight of him then, and her slow smile made him blink. His mom used to smile at him that way, as if just having him around was a good thing. The best thing in her day.

"I'm glad to see you're feeling better this morning, Daniel."

She looked back up at his uncle, then nodded her head.

"Becky . . ." she called over her shoulder. "How about some ice cream?"

CHAPTER FOURTEEN

"How's the chocolate with sprinkles?" Amy asked Daniel as they sat alone at the Sugar Cone.

She only had a few minutes — as long as it took Josh to walk Becky to the bathroom. She'd asked her daughter to excuse herself, had given her a look that begged her to cooperate, and Josh had been more than happy to make himself scarce right along with Becky. So Amy could have her moment of privacy with four cups of melting ice cream and a little boy she wanted to hug every time she looked at him.

"It's okay." Daniel shrugged as he inhaled another mouthful.

She licked her spoon with an extra-loud slurp. "Nothing beats butter pecan."

"Yuck." His nose crinkled.

"Well, I think it's decadent." She made a show of savoring the next bite. "It was nice of your uncle to treat us like this. I haven't found anything in Atlanta that comes close to the Sugar Cone's handmade ice cream."

A shadow of grown-up-size seriousness edged across Daniel's face. "I think Uncle Josh wanted to thank you for what you did yesterday," he said.

She'd never heard him say "Uncle Josh" before. The label sounded so perfect, she wished Josh had been here to hear it.

"You know." Daniel pushed the last half of his ice cream away. "For what you and Becky said to my dad."

Amy grappled for the right words, never in a million years expecting the little boy would bring up the subject of his father himself. She was thankful the outdoor eating area at the ice cream shop was empty because of the early hour.

"I'm sorry your dad scared you like that," she said.

Daniel shrugged as if to say the confrontation had meant nothing.

She'd never seen a tough guy look so lost.

"I guess it's not the first time he's acted that way, huh?"

"You get used to it." Fear haunted his eyes.

"You should never have to get used to something like that," she said.

Her own excuses had been just as feeble, the rationalizations she'd clung to as Richard's verbal abuse escalated over the years.

"We can tell ourselves it's not so bad," she continued. "If that's what it takes to get through the rough times. But you can't let yourself believe that things are always going to be that way."

Because that's when you start to give up.

Amy shook off her own warped memories and waited until she had Daniel's attention again.

"Promise me you'll never give up, Daniel. Promise me you won't let yourself believe you deserve to be treated the way you and your mother were."

"He . . ." Daniel looked around as if to make sure they were alone. He licked at the chocolate smudges at the corner of his mouth, then his shoulders slumped.

"My dad wants me back," he murmured so softly she had to lean closer to hear.

"He's not going to get you back, not if your uncle has anything to say about it."

"What if Uncle Josh can't stop him?" Daniel threw the question at her. "He may have tons of money, but that's not going to stop my dad. Nothing ever stops him. . . ."

The fatalism in that last statement propelled Amy to her feet. Good idea or not, she sat on the bench beside Daniel and rubbed his back, watching for any sign that her touch was spooking him. When he leaned into her, if only slightly, she felt as if she'd been given the most precious gift in the world.

"First of all," she said, determined to tell him what he needed to hear, and to make sure he actually heard it, "you belong wherever you're loved. And anyone with any sense can see that's here with your uncle in Sweetbrook. And don't underestimate your uncle Josh. There isn't much the man can't do when he sets his mind to it."

"But I've heard him on the phone with that social worker. Whatever he's doing, it's not working."

Daniel's tone begged Amy to tell him he was wrong.

"He hasn't tried everything, Daniel." She waited for the boy to look up. "There's one more thing he can do, but he's going to need your help."

Daniel inched away from her, shaking his head almost imperceptibly. She was close enough to see drops of perspiration break out on his forehead.

"Daniel." She took his hand and refused to let go. "It's okay. I'm not asking you to talk about the time you and your mom spent with your dad. You don't have to tell me anything at all. You have your doctor and your uncle for that, and it doesn't have to happen today."

His breathing slowed marginally. Birds chirped on some faraway branch. Otherwise, the world surrounded them with soothing silence.

"No one's trying to push you into anything you're not ready for. But you do have the power to stop your father. You and your uncle can make sure the man's out of your life for good. If you can find a way to let yourself talk about what happened, if you can trust the people who are trying to help you, there is a path through this."

"No." Daniel's eyes told tales he couldn't bring himself to face. "I can't. I've tried, and I . . . I just can't."

"You can't give up, Daniel." She squeezed his hand for emphasis. "You can't let yourself think you have no way out."

Daniel's glance over her shoulder warned of Josh and Becky's return. The little boy grabbed his ice cream and edged away from the table.

"Come on, Becky," he said over his shoulder. "Let's eat in the car."

Amy nodded for her daughter to follow. And bless Becky, she did, grabbing her ice cream on the way.

"Everything okay?" Josh asked as he

picked up his own cup. His frown told her he knew better.

Amy stood beside him, too aware of those rock-solid shoulders and how it had felt to cling to them. "I think I may have made things worse."

"I seriously doubt that." His gaze dropped from her eyes to her mouth, stalled there, then jerked back up.

"I wish I could do more," she said, meaning the cliché, even if it wasn't wise to grow more attached to this man and his heartbreaker of a nephew.

"You've made such a difference already, Amy. If Daniel manages to talk about his memories of his father, it will be because of you."

The intimacy of what Josh was suggesting — that she was somehow vital to him and Daniel — triggered the conflicting impulses to kiss him and run from him at the same time. The thought of being that integral to Josh achieving what was most important to him — his nephew's love and trust — sent tingles running through her.

But she had no business dreaming of having something that real, something as magical as owning a place in the life of a man who'd cherish her no matter what. She was done with looking to someone else to make her world okay.

"We should probably get back to the kids," she said, though she didn't have the willpower to move yet.

"When will you be back in Sweetbrook?" His gaze touched every curve of her face.

When I can look at you and not want to stay.

"After I close the deal I've been working on. The final presentation is Thursday, and if the CEO's decision is a yes, it'll take me another week or two to get everything in place for the implementation."

She'd thought Daniel's unhappy frown had been tough to swallow. Josh's brought tears to her eyes.

"Sounds like it's going to be a rough few weeks for everyone." He dug the toe of his sneaker into the dirt, then tossed his untouched ice cream into the trash. "You have your presentation. Becky's through with the formal testing, but Doug will still be evaluating her in daily meetings. And I'm about to go round one with Daniel's father and the judge."

"You can do it, Josh," she insisted. "You're going to beat that man."

"You don't know that." He sounded so much like his nephew.

"Yes, I do." She caught his hand with hers. "If anyone can do this, you can. You've always been the smartest person in the room, the most likely to bend the world to your will, and I've seen how much you care about Daniel. I have no doubt you'll send Curtis Jenkins packing."

Josh's thumb traced her palm, then he trapped the back of her hand against his chest.

"I'm afraid, Amy," he said. "At first, I took Daniel because I owed it to my sister to take care of her son. But now . . . I can't lose him. What if he's forced to go back to his father? If he doesn't learn to trust me, if I can't show him how much he means to me —"

"He knows." Amy smoothed her palm over Josh's amazing heart. "He's a smart kid, just like his uncle. The two of you will figure this out."

"I wish I had your confidence."

"Then I'll believe for you, how about that?" If she could leave Josh nothing else, she wanted to return a speck of the faith he'd always had in her. "Just like you always believed I'd make the grades I needed for those scholarships, all the while you were tutoring me until I got my SAT scores high enough. You knew I could make something of myself, and I'm just as sure that you've got what it takes to be a wonderful parent.

Just take it one day at a time. You'll see."

"We make a good team, don't we?" His smile was full of the past, when they were kids and she couldn't have conceived of not seeing Josh each and every day. . . . And of the present, when just last night he'd held her until she'd made him let her go.

She moved, but he held tight.

"Amy, I know you don't have time for a man in your life right now. . . . But if there's any chance . . . If a family's ever what you want again . . ." His widening eyes revealed he was as shocked as she by the loaded words that had just come out of his mouth.

Their kids were twenty feet away in his car. She was leaving for Atlanta in a couple of hours, where she planned to live and raise her daughter. He was happy with his small-town life, with no aspirations to ever move anywhere else.

"I . . ." He took a deep breath.

"Stop it, Josh." She yanked away, the cessation of contact causing her physical pain in the empty place that had once housed her heart. "You have your family, here in Sweetbrook with your nephew. And I'll be raising my daughter hundreds of miles away. You don't want a woman with my baggage in your life — someone who might never be able to love you back the way you want me to. So stop torturing both of us by thinking you do. There's never going to be another man for me. Period."

"Maybe there could be, if you'd give this a chance and let me in. You're as bad as Daniel." Disappointment filled his voice. "I don't mind the baggage. We can work through that. What we can't work through is you running away every time I get close."

"Then stop touching me! I'm not running away from you because I'm confused about what I want. I know what I want — for me and my daughter. And it's in Atlanta. The last man I let into my life nearly destroyed me. I'm not alone now because no one else has been interested since Richard. I'm alone because that's the way I like it."

"You know —" he picked up her ice cream and handed it to her with excruciating calm, as if they were casually discussing the weather "— after Lisa kicked my teeth in, that's what I thought, too. That being alone was the only way to be free of the pain."

It was a dead-on recitation of the mantra Amy had lived by since her divorce.

"But look at the second chance I've been given," he continued when she couldn't speak. "Maybe you're getting a second chance, too, if you could just see past this obsession you have for your job. What makes you so certain a promotion's going to make you happy?"

"I'm not looking for happy." She crammed her ice cream into the trash. "I'm looking to give my daughter a better life than I had. To make sure she grows up feeling secure and safe."

"And this career of yours is making the two of you feel secure?" He shook his head. "I don't think so."

"You don't know what you're talking about."

"Yes, I do. I was happily buried in my work when Daniel came along. I'd shut the whole world out. But he's the best thing that ever happened to me. Because of him, I can't imagine ever wanting to be alone again. And now that you've come back —"

"I'm not back, Josh." He flinched, but she forged on. Being kind wasn't what either of them needed. "I'll be gone for good before you know it."

"You can run away from Sweetbrook again, Amy." He stepped closer, every six-foot-three kissable inch of him. He brushed his lips to hers in a delicate caress that had her knees shivering. Then he leaned just a tad closer, until his lips hovered beside her ear. "You can tell yourself you can't trust me or my money any more than you could trust Richard Reese. But I don't think you'll ever be completely gone from Sweetbrook again. This place, and me, and everything you love here will be a part of you forever."

With the word *love* hovering in the air between them, he strode across the lawn, leaving her alone as she'd asked. It was like watching the promise of a new day being stripped away, just as she was facing the darkest hours of the morning.

Following him reluctantly to the Range Rover, watching him join the kids, who were enjoying their ice cream, Amy grappled for the determination she needed to keep her head about her and leave.

Josh painted a pretty picture. He was a strong man who loved kids, and he wanted to love her, too. And there he was, waiting to drive her and her daughter home. As if their families had already blended and were out for a morning of wholesome fun.

But this ideal snapshot of Sweetbrook serenity wasn't for her. Not anymore. Believing in a life like this had stopped being possible for her a long time ago. Maybe she *was* running away. Maybe she was deluding herself with the notion that she could be happy alone, building her life around her daughter and her work.

But as she'd said, happy wasn't really the

point anymore, was it?

And Josh deserved a woman who could return his feelings without the mistakes from her past ripping them both apart. A woman who still believed that love didn't have to hurt, and that romantic ever-afters really could be happy.

"Josh, did you hear me?" Barbara Thomas asked Monday morning. "The first session with Judge Hardy is set for two weeks from tomorrow."

"Yeah," Josh murmured into the phone as he doodled on the paper blotter that covered his desk.

Principal Joshua White, Mr. Let's Get Down to Business, was doodling while he toyed with the idea of asking Gwen Loar to watch his nephew after school, so Josh could drive up to Atlanta and confront the woman's daughter with the truth that he loved her.

"Joshua?" Barbara prompted again. "What's wrong with you? You have two weeks —"

"I know what I have to do in two weeks." He threw his pen onto the blotter, then sent the books stacked at his elbow sailing with a frustrated shove of his hand.

The ruckus they made as they hit the

linoleum floor and slid several feet wasn't nearly as satisfying as he'd have liked. He drummed his fingers on the desk, envying the people who managed to pitch temper tantrums and actually feel better as a result. He just felt childish.

"I'm taking Daniel over to Dr. Rhodes again tonight," he said, remembering the fear on his nephew's face as they'd discussed that very thing over breakfast.

Then Daniel had raised his chin and said, "Okay."

Okay.

The kid's simple, courageous acceptance had given Josh hope. A hope he owed in large part to Amy.

"We have several therapy sessions scheduled over the next few weeks," he explained to Barbara. "Outside of that, there's not much else I can do but wait for Daniel to come around."

"Oh, dear," the woman said. Never what you wanted to hear from your social worker. "I didn't realize you were seeing Daniel's therapist tonight."

"I called him at the end of last week, to set up some extra visits. Why?"

"Well, I was getting to that." She sounded as if she'd rather *get* to just about anything else. "I was hoping to schedule another home visit this afternoon."

"I know." Josh stood and turned his back on the temptation to find something else on the desk to throw. "I haven't brought Daniel to see you yet, but I figured therapy was more of a priority right now. I can bring him by toward the end of the week."

"Actually, I'm afraid I'll need to see him before then."

"Why?" The professional shift in her voice wasn't lost on Josh. "What's happened?"

"Jenkins's lawyer has requested a supervised visit between his client and Daniel," Barbara explained. "And the judge instructed me to make sure that happens within the next few days."

"What?" The terror of seeing Daniel fighting to get away from his father Friday afternoon returned in a searing rush. "Barbara —"

"Josh, I know this isn't what you wanted."

"What I wanted?" he bellowed. The constant stream of noise filtering in from the outer office screeched to a halt. Everyone within a hundred feet had probably heard him. Josh reined in his temper. "Jenkins tried to pull Daniel into his car Friday."

"I know." Her cool tone made it clear she was less than pleased. "Mr. Jenkins's attorney shared the father's side of the confrontation with me and the judge first thing this morning. Including how you physically threatened him — again."

"The child was screaming to be turned loose. What was I supposed to do?"

"You were supposed to keep your hands off the man, and then you were supposed to call me and let me handle it. We talked about this, Josh. Of all the times for you to lose touch with the reality of what you're dealing with. You don't have to convince me that Jenkins is a threat to his son, but it's what the judge thinks that's important. And right now, you're the one who appears unstable, not the boy's father. You can give me a statement with your side of the story, but that's not going to change Judge Hardy's decision to grant Mr. Jenkins supervised access to Daniel. I'll be present throughout the meeting, but the man is going to see his son."

"How much time do I have?"

"Today, maybe tomorrow. It will have to happen by Wednesday at the latest." She sounded as sickened by the idea as Josh felt. "I'm sorry. There's nothing I could do to stop it. I'd be happy to talk with Daniel ahead of time, if you think that would help."

"Nothing's going to help." Three days. He had three days. . . . To do what? "I'll find a way to tell him myself."

"What about Amy Loar?" Barbara asked.

Josh flinched. "What about her?"

"Jenkins mentioned there was a woman with you at the pond on Friday. And a little girl, too. I assumed that was Ms. Loar and her daughter."

"Our kids skipped school, Barbara. She came with me to try and find them."

"She's been around a lot in the last few weeks. And over the same time period, Daniel's become more cooperative, more open to talking about his father. Every time I turn around, she's there helping you."

"She has her own problems in Atlanta." Her own life. Without him. "And she's tied up with work all week. I can't drag her back down here to deal with this."

"She seemed very sensitive to the situation the one time I saw her at your house."

"I can't, Barbara. I'm not going to ask the impossible and have her feel guilty for saying no."

"Then you need to come up with some other way to break the news to your nephew. I'm putting Daniel on my schedule for Wednesday afternoon at five o'clock."

Josh didn't respond. What was there to say?

"I'm sorry, Josh. But maybe it's for the

best. This will give us a documented account of Daniel's reaction to his father, as well as the man's behavior toward the child."

"Great!" Josh felt the last shreds of his control slipping away. "Maybe you should bring a video recorder, so you can tape my nephew being forced to sit and chat with the monster that terrorized him and his mother!"

"Josh, don't —"

"Don't what, Barbara? Don't act like you're forcing Daniel to —"

"I don't have a choice, and you know it."

"Do I?"

"I'm not the enemy." She sounded hurt, and he almost cared. "I've done everything I can, but this can't be put off any longer. Whatever it takes, you have to get Daniel ready to see his father again."

Thankfully, she hung up before Josh could say anything else he'd regret.

Whatever it takes.

He laid both palms flat on the desktop, flashing back to the feel of Curtis Jenkins's shirt between his fingers as he'd pinned the man to his broken-down truck and told him he'd never be close enough to hurt Daniel again. Now, maybe partially because of that very lapse in control, Josh had been sentenced to personally delivering his nephew to the man.

With a roar, he swung his arms out, sending every last item on the desk flying.

CHAPTER FIFTEEN

Becky took a dripping plate from Grandma Gwen later that evening and dried it. Washing the dinner dishes was less of a pain than usual. Instead of grousing to herself about why her grandmother hadn't purchased a dishwasher like everyone else they knew, she decided it felt kind of good to be doing something so simple.

Every day, she found a new reason to like being at her grandmother's a whole lot more than she'd let anyone see.

School had dragged on forever that day, even though her testing was over. Now Mr. Fletcher wanted to talk about her schoolwork, and what she thought about things, and how she felt. It was exhausting, talking about herself so much.

By the time she'd gotten back to class, Daniel was gone. Mrs. Cole had said he and Principal White would be away the rest of the day. Which had left Becky sitting by herself at lunch. She'd kept busy the rest of the day, catching up on what she'd missed that morning. But waiting for bus call had been a nightmare without Daniel there to pester.

"Daniel and his uncle weren't at school much today." She twirled a raggedy, baby-soft towel inside one of the glasses her mother said she'd used when she was Becky's age. "You don't think there's some kind of problem with Daniel's father, do you?"

Her grandmother handed over another glass. "It sounds like you and Daniel aren't quite the enemies you used to be."

Becky shrugged. "I'm just saying it would be messed up if that guy actually did take Daniel away from Principal White."

"I'm not going to disagree with you there." Grandma Gwen pulled the stopper out of the sink, letting the soap bubbles gurgle away. "From what your mother's told me, Daniel should stay right where he is, with his uncle."

"He never talks about his own mom." Becky folded the towel and fingered the loose threads that had worked their way out of the frayed hem.

"Do you talk about your family and your dad with him?"

Becky slanted her a look that asked her to get real.

"I imagine it's the same for Daniel." Her grandmother took the dish towel and spread it over the edge of the counter to dry. "It's hard to talk about something that hurts that much. Maybe that's why you two are becoming friends. You can understand a little about how the other's feeling."

And that's exactly why Becky had missed Daniel today. It was like she could be herself around him, the same as she was with her mom and Grandma Gwen. He didn't think she was a dork for not being brainlessly happy all the time.

"Daniel and his uncle don't get along so good," she said.

Kind of like her and her mom sometimes.

"They've got a lot to work through." Her grandmother was watching her closely.

"How do you work through stuff, when nothing ever gets better, no matter how hard you try?" Becky took a chocolate chip cookie from the jar that had never once been empty since she'd moved in.

Grandma Gwen hugged her from behind. "You learn to lean on the people who love you, and you find a way to get through it together. You've got to learn to believe in your family, Becky. Nothing on this earth is more important."

"My family's gone," Becky said out loud for the first time, though she'd been thinking it for months. "It's all gone."

"No." Her grandmother's embrace grew fiercer, but she didn't try to make Becky turn around. "Your family's right here, with me. And back in Atlanta with your mom, where she's building that new life you both want. Family isn't about perfect marriages, or perfect parents, or perfect places. Family is about doing everything you can for the people you love. And your mom and me, there's nothing we wouldn't do for you, sweetie."

But her dad hadn't done everything he could for her or her mom. He hadn't even tried.

Becky had blamed her mom, because it had been easier that way. Because it hurt less when she was mad. But her mom wasn't the loser Becky had called her over and over after coming to stay in Sweetbrook. And being mad had stopped making her feel better weeks ago. She wasn't even sure she hated this tiny town so much anymore.

She'd never felt alone here, not really. No matter how hard she'd tried to make things miserable for everyone. Because, she realized, she'd had Grandma Gwen and her mom on her side.

Her family.

She turned in her grandmother's arms and hugged her back. For the first time, she felt lucky for the weeks she'd spent in Sweetbrook. Maybe she even wished she could stay longer than the short time she had left. That maybe she, her mom and her Grandma Gwen could be a real family, living together here and starting over.

Her thoughts returned to Daniel.

The kid's dad was a deadbeat, too. But unlike Becky, Daniel didn't have a mother anymore. Principal White was all Daniel had, and things weren't looking so good for them, either.

Where was Daniel going to find the family he needed?

"Excellent job, Ms. Loar," Mr. Hutchinson said at the end of what had turned into an all-afternoon planning meeting.

Amy discreetly checked her watch. Hutchinson had already caught her doing it once, and this wasn't the best time for her to appear as if her mind was anywhere but on his pet project. But six o'clock had come and gone a half hour ago, and she couldn't wait to talk with Becky, to hear how everything had gone at school that day. And she had to know how things were progressing with Josh and Daniel, too.

"Amy?" Thomas Fuller prompted.

She surveyed the boardroom. Hutchinson was waiting expectantly. Thomas's smile was growing more smug by the second, and the rest of her staff was trying not to look bored out of their minds. Obviously, someone had asked a question.

She cleared her throat. "Jacquie?" She turned to her assistant, trying not to look like a drowning woman grasping for a lifeline.

"Yes, Mr. Hutchinson." Jacquie nodded without missing a beat. She focused her attention on the man sitting at the head of the conference table. "The final draft of the project offering is ready to go. It includes documentation of the research and design we've done in conjunction with the Kramer staff, as well as the financials on the development, testing, support and equipment payout for the next five years. Plus the signatures we've obtained from each of the sign-off meetings."

"We're eighty-five thousand under the budget we projected up front." Amy took over, the bonus she'd been planning to secure for her friend and assistant increasing exponentially. "And we should have no problem completing the systems retooling two months before next year's deadline."

"So." The slight upward tilt of Hutchinson's mouth was a good sign. "You're confident we've secured their business."

"I don't see how they can say no." Amy turned her most professional stare on Thomas and dared the man to contradict her.

Everyone else at the table, having witnessed the growing tension as she and Thomas worked together over the last week, waited, as well. Her team had spent the last seventy-two hours finalizing the details for this presentation, going the extra mile for Amy without having to be asked. They understood her promotion was at stake, and had rallied behind her. All Thomas had to do to lose the respect of everyone in the room, including Hutchinson, was throw a wrench in the works now. Could the kid be a team player, or would his ego be his undoing?

He tipped Amy a begrudging nod, placed his pen on the table and folded his hands.

"I agree totally, sir," Thomas said from where he sat to Hutchinson's right. "Of course, Amy and the rest of her team will be working closely with the Kramer staff right up until the presentation Thursday.

But I don't foresee any stumbling blocks that would warrant your attention."

Amy hid her relief, content to watch the smiles spreading over the faces of the other ten people in the room.

"Excellent!" Mr. Hutchinson rose from his chair. The entire room stood to join him. "Then I'll expect daily updates, and I'll see the two of you at the closing meeting Thursday at three."

He nodded at Thomas, then stepped to Amy's end of the table and held out his hand.

"Fine job, Ms. Loar."

She shook it, feeling as if she'd just been told, *Welcome aboard.*

When he'd left and the conference room door had swung shut, she turned to the others and beamed.

"Great job, everyone." She began clapping, so proud of all they'd done.

The others clapped along with her. Jacquie, who knew better than any of them the sheer desperation that had kept Amy going for months, was close to tears. Even Thomas joined in the impromptu celebration, patting backs and shaking the hands of the associates closest to him.

It all seemed so right, so perfect. They couldn't take anything for granted until

Thursday's meeting, but it was actually going to happen, Amy realized. She and Becky were going to be okay. She was finally going to be free of the past.

But as wonderful as the moment was, she found herself checking her watch again. In the midst of the first taste of success she'd known in years, Amy's heart wasn't in it.

"Excuse me," she said to the group.

She couldn't wait any longer. She had to call home.

"Over easy or well done?" Josh asked, the same old joke sounding even more tired than he felt.

"Whatever," Daniel replied from the kitchen table, where he was finishing up his homework.

"Over easy it is." Josh turned off the gas burner and moved the bubbling pot of hot dogs to the side to cool.

Theresa had left a casserole in the oven that Josh would heat up later, but he knew good and well Daniel wasn't going to be tempted by whatever canned soup, chicken and broccoli concoction she'd magically morphed into a hearty meal. Good thing Family Services didn't much care what Daniel ate at this point, as long as the kid had three squares a day.

Josh caught himself staring at his nephew. Another session with Dr. Rhodes had come and gone with no real progress in getting Daniel to share his memories. Josh was closer every day to losing him, just as he and Daniel were finally beginning to settle in with each other. At this point, there was very little chance he could stop Wednesday's visitation with the boy's father.

He glanced to where the cordless phone sat on the tiled island, itching to make the call he'd promised himself he wouldn't make. Amy Loar had said her goodbyes. She was fighting for her survival in Atlanta. He had no business asking her to come back and hold his hand while he explained the inexplicable to Daniel.

It didn't matter that she was wrong when she'd said he didn't want a woman with her history in his life. He'd take Amy any way he could get her, baggage and all. But he wasn't going to pressure her any further. He'd made the mistake of not listening to his ex-wife's needs, and he owed Amy better than that.

The phone chose that moment to ring, its perky jingle mocking his dark mood. He grabbed it.

"Hello."

"Hey, Josh."

"Amy!"

Daniel's head lifted from his homework.

"Did I catch you at a bad time?" Her hesitant question had no business sounding so beautiful.

But heaven help him, it did.

"No. It's good to hear from you." And it was. He felt himself take his first full breath all day as he ripped open a fresh bag of hot dog buns and motioned for Daniel to come fix himself a plate.

"How was your day?" he asked, shaking off the tempting image of them as a couple, chatting like this every evening over a hastily prepared dinner.

"Great, actually. I think my promotion is a lock." Her voice was a little too bright. A little too forced.

"That's wonderful." He couldn't have been prouder, even though the promotion meant she was slipping even further beyond his grasp.

"How are things there?" she asked. "I just talked with Becky, and she said you and Daniel were out of school this afternoon. She thought there might be a problem."

"We're doing good," he replied for Daniel's sake.

Josh pulled the baking pan from the oven and scooped fries onto Daniel's plate, reassuring himself that potatoes were indeed vegetables. He tousled the boy's hair, the most affection he could give a kid who still refused to be hugged. At least Daniel no longer flinched every time Josh got within ten feet of him.

"Something's wrong," Amy stated. "I can hear it in your voice."

"Becky's still doing great at school, if that's what you mean," he said evasively.

"That's wonderful, but that's *not* what I meant. What's going on with Daniel and his father? I may be hundreds of miles away now, but I still care."

Her genuine concern made him want to crawl through the phone line and kiss her.

Josh checked that Daniel had returned to the table. The boy was engrossed in seeing how much ketchup he could consume with each fry, so Josh slipped into the hall with the phone.

"There's a meeting on Wednesday," he revealed in a half whisper. "A judge-mandated visitation with Daniel's father that Barbara Thomas can't make go away."

"Oh, no, Josh. Have you told Daniel?"

"No." Josh leaned back against the wall. "Not yet."

"Did things go better with the therapist today?"

"Not really." This afternoon's session had been especially disappointing, given how hard Daniel was trying to talk about his dad, but still couldn't. "The doctor says we're getting closer every day, but we're running out of time. I don't want to force Daniel to do anything, but —"

"Josh, you have to tell him he's about to see his father again."

"Now why didn't I think of that?" Josh snapped, blasting her with the irritation he'd been holding in since this morning's outburst.

He couldn't bring himself to tell Daniel. Not yet.

Maybe he was being a coward because he was afraid of losing the boy's trust once he admitted he couldn't keep Curtis Jenkins away. But Josh wanted to be the kid's hero, like the ones Daniel was always reading about in his comic books. Not another adult at the end of a long line of people forcing him to accept the worst and make the best of it.

"Josh, I didn't mean to upset you."

"No, I'm sorry." He sighed at the worry in her voice. "I've had a rotten day, but none of this is your fault."

"What are you going to do?"

"I'm taking Daniel back to his therapist

again in the morning," Josh said. "Dr. Rhodes is booked solid all day, but he managed to squeeze us in first thing, so we can give it one more try. Wednesday afternoon is soon enough to tell Daniel, if we still have no way to stop the visitation by then. There's no point in him worrying himself sick about it all week."

"I wish I could do something," Amy said in a low voice. "I wish..."

"Yeah. Me, too."

Man, did he wish.

He wished she was here with him and Daniel. That Amy could somehow let herself trust in the unknown she couldn't control long enough to see what she was leaving behind. He wished for a relationship with her that was a lifetime beyond the couple of kisses they'd shared.

He wanted it all. Amy and Becky and Daniel. He wanted them to be a family.

"I . . . I'd better get back to our hot dogs." He forced out the words, longing for the comfort of her touch.

"Oh! I should have realized I'd be interrupting dinner."

"Working late again?"

"Yeah." She gave a hollow laugh. "It's after six, and I'm just now taking my lunch break."

"It'll all get better after Thursday, right?"

"Yeah." The laugh was positively jaded this time. "Then Becky and I can start our new life."

"Doug Fletcher assures me we'll have Becky's evaluation by the end of the week. You'll be all set to start working with her new school when she returns to Atlanta."

"That sounds perfect," Amy replied without enthusiasm. She was doing what she did best, what he most admired her for — holding strong, even when it hurt.

"I'll talk with you soon, then," he offered, giving her the way out she needed. "Good luck on Thursday."

"You, too. With Daniel on Wednesday, I mean."

"Thanks."

"Goodbye, Josh," she said. Her words had an awful finality to them.

"Good night, Amy."

I love you.

The line clicked, and she was gone.

The hand holding the phone dropped to his side as he fought not to punch the buttons that would call her back.

He'd been married for ten years, but until he'd held Amy in his arms, he'd never truly understood the strength a man could find in a woman's softness. He knew he'd spend the rest of his life trying to forget that perfect feeling of wholeness he and Amy shared with each new touch.

He was in love with her. And Amy, her daughter and everything their families could have created together were slipping through his fingers just as surely as he was losing his fight to keep Daniel.

Chapter Sixteen

"Daniel? What are you thinking about?"

Daniel hated that question more than all the others.

They'd been there for almost an hour, he and his uncle and Dr. Steve. Talking a little, but mostly sitting and waiting. They'd come in first thing Tuesday morning, when they'd just been there last night, though his uncle wouldn't say why.

"Daniel?" the doctor asked again.

"My dad," Daniel blurted out. His stomach churned. "I'm thinking about my dad."

"Are you afraid it would make things worse if you talked about him?"

What was he supposed to say? Of course talking about it would make things worse.

Dr. Steve leaned forward. "You're trying so hard to talk about him now, even if we haven't quite gotten you there. Why the sudden change after the last few months?"

His uncle gave him a wink.

It was still a shock, how he seemed to really want Daniel around now.

"I guess maybe . . . talking about my dad might not be so bad anymore," Daniel said.

"Because it's better than the alternative?" Dr. Steve asked.

"The what?"

"Like talking about what scares you couldn't be worse than how it felt to actually see your dad last week?"

"Maybe." Daniel reached for the new hole he'd picked in his favorite black sneakers.

"Or maybe there's something you want now that you can't have until you deal with all the stuff you remember?"

"Yeah, maybe." Daniel glanced at his uncle again.

Uncle Josh didn't wink this time.

"And what is it that you want, Daniel?" the doctor asked.

Butterflies were beating away in his stomach. His eyes filled with tears.

"Daniel?" Dr. Steve asked. "This is a safe place. The things that are scaring you can't hurt you here."

Your uncle's not going to let anyone hurt you. . . .

Becky's mom seemed so sure each time she said that. And each time she'd said it,

Daniel had wanted to believe her a little bit more.

But he remembered his mom saying that they'd be safe, too, once they were in Sweetbrook. Daniel had believed her, but his grandmother hadn't wanted them here. And now his mom was gone, and his old man was back, and Daniel would never be safe again —

"I can't do it!" He exploded from the chair. Forget that he'd agreed to try. Forget all this stupid talking. Forget them all. "You can't make me!"

"Daniel —" his uncle began in a soothing voice.

Dr. Steve held up his hand, silencing them both.

"We can't make you do what, Daniel?" The therapist's eyes, when he got that look, made Daniel feel like the doctor could see every last one of his secrets. "Tell us what you're afraid of."

"Him, okay?"

The long glance exchanged between his uncle and therapist made Daniel groan.

"Not *him* —" He pointed to his uncle. "I'm not afraid of him. It's . . . it's my . . ."

"Your father," Uncle Josh finished for him. "Everything we've been trying to work through, the misbehavior and fighting at

309

school, the problems you've had settling in at the house, it all has something to do with what happened when you were younger and living with your mom and dad, right?"

"Yeah . . . No! Maybe. I can't . . . I can't talk about it."

"What don't you want to talk about it, Daniel?" the doctor pressed. "You know how important your memories are to your uncle keeping custody of you. And it's clear you don't want to go back with your father. What do you think has you scared so badly you can't do the very thing that will get you what you want?"

"Nothing." Daniel flopped back into his chair, suddenly too exhausted to do anything else.

"You're in control here, Daniel," Dr. Steve said for what seemed like the millionth time. "You don't have to let your father win this time, right?"

Daniel could only stare.

"That's right." Dr. Steve nodded. "You can stop him from hurting you this time."

Daniel laughed as he sneered at his uncle. "I thought you said that was your job."

His uncle frowned and shifted his shoulders. "I've tried, but there's nothing more I can do. Not without your help."

"Great. I'm supposed to help you."

"No, you're supposed to learn how to help yourself," Dr. Steve corrected. "That's what we've been doing for the last few months. Trying to get you to understand that you *can* be okay. That this isn't a hopeless situation. You're not as messed up as you think you are, Daniel. You've told me you think you're an outcast here in Sweetbrook. But you're not an outcast. You have a great home and all the support you need, and I think you know that now. You just need to make up your mind to do what you have to do to stay here."

Not an outcast.

Daniel thought of his stash of comics back at the tree house. Stories about misfits he'd thought were just like him. And for the first time, the idea of being out at the tree alone didn't sound so good. Instead, he wanted to be back at that stupid mansion of a house — with his uncle Josh.

You can *be okay.*

"Daniel?" Dr. Steve said from the chair next to him. When had he moved there? "What are you thinking about?"

Daniel could feel his uncle leaning forward, too. Could feel the memories creeping closer, and with them came the panic.

"I . . . I was thinking how much I wish . . ." he mumbled. "How much I wish I was ready to be okay. I . . . I want to be okay now."

The relieved smile on his uncle's face wrapped around Daniel. The man looked . . . Daniel didn't know, proud or something.

"Well, I'd call that a good start," the doctor said, checking his watch, a signal that their time was up.

"That's the best thing I've heard in a long time," Uncle Josh said. "Great job."

But Daniel could see the worry his uncle couldn't quite hide. Daniel's "great job" still hadn't been good enough.

Becky caught Daniel's eye as they waited for the lunch lady to fill their plastic trays with pizza and Tater Tots. Daniel jerked his head toward the back of the cafeteria, and Becky agreed with a short nod.

Together, their plates now full of one of the only meals that was actually edible in this place, they passed by all the other kids so they could sit alone. Daniel dropped his tray onto the table with a clatter and slumped on one of the benches that passed for chairs. Setting her food down more carefully, Becky sat beside him and waited. When minutes had gone by and he was still staring at the pizza like there were worms in it or something, she figured it was up to her.

"Maybe talking about your memories of your dad won't be as bad as you think." She did her best to sound as if she believed what she was saying.

He gave her his girls-are-stupid eye roll and tossed a handful of Tater Tots into his mouth. From the grimace that followed, Becky guessed that the cooks had skipped the suggested baking instructions again, figuring defrosting would be just as good as cooking them.

She leaned an elbow on the table and laid her head on her arm. Daniel had whispered to her during a morning break that his doctor thought they were close to a *breakthrough,* whatever that was. That Daniel was ready to talk about his memories of his dad. And he was scared of what would happen when he finally did. Like he'd go postal or something and finally scare his uncle off for good.

"I was pretty worried, too," she said, "when I first started the testing with Mr. Fletcher. My mom tried to tell me it would help, but all I heard was ADD, and I figured that meant I was stupid. So what was the point in testing? It would only prove what we already knew and make me feel worse.

It wouldn't change things."

Daniel's shoulders rose and fell with a heavy sigh.

"But talking about it is helping, I think. The tests, too. At least I'm starting to understand why I'm having so much trouble keeping up with you guys in class. The whole thing's kind of given me hope, I guess. Even if it does stink."

"It's not the same," Daniel said. "Talking about my dad's not going to make me feel better. Every time I try —" he shook his head and clenched his fists "— I always lose it."

"But the doctor said talking about it will help stop that, right? And you said yourself it would help keep your father out of your life so you can stay with Principal White."

"Will it?" Daniel pounded on the table. "What if it doesn't make any difference? What if talking about it and feeling like I'm going to puke from remembering doesn't do any good? Maybe after he hears everything, my uncle will be glad to let my dad take me."

"That's not going to happen. My mom said so." Becky bumped her shoulder into Daniel's. "Your uncle's not going to let your dad take you. You know that."

"Do I?" He snorted. "Maybe he'd be better off without me."

Becky understood Daniel's fear. She was afraid for him herself. But his doubt in Principal White made no sense. She'd seen how much Daniel's uncle cared about all the kids in school, Daniel most of all.

"That's the stupidest thing I've ever heard." She grabbed her tray and stood. "You're just scared, and blaming your uncle is easier than trying to fight back. I used to call your mom and mine losers. But at least they tried to fight. You keep giving up, Daniel White, and *you're* the one that's going to end up the loser."

She stomped toward the little window where the lady took their trays, and dumped hers off, her fingers worrying the golden heart her mom was letting her wear until she came back.

She worried she'd said too much to Daniel.

And a part of her was even more worried that she should have said more.

CHAPTER SEVENTEEN

"Barbara, I need a little more time. Just a day or two at the most."

Josh paced his office first thing Wednesday morning. He shouldn't be pushing his friend for special treatment this way, but what choice did he have? Daniel was one therapy session away from a breakthrough. Josh was sure of it.

But Dr. Rhodes was out of the office today and tomorrow, and he couldn't work them back in until Friday morning. Besides, he'd told Josh he'd done all he could do. That Daniel was ready. That what Josh should do was explain to his nephew about the visitation with Curtis Jenkins, then encourage Daniel to tell the judge what he needed to hear to call the whole thing off.

"Judge Hardy isn't budging," Barbara countered. "Jenkins's lawyer has lobbied the man every day for the last week. The visitation's happening tonight at five o'clock.

That's all the time I can give you."

Josh sat in one of his guest chairs. "What am I going to tell Daniel?"

"You mean you haven't told him he's meeting his father today?"

"No. I didn't want to scare the kid. He's so close to trusting me enough to talk about his memories. He just needs a little more time."

"There is no more time. Should I arrange for the meeting to be here at my office?"

Josh was up and pacing again. "Make it at the house. Maybe it will give us a home-court advantage."

What was he saying? Nothing was going to make this better for Daniel.

"You need to prepare the boy for this," Barbara said.

"I know."

"Josh?"

"I know, okay?" Where were his big plans now? His ability to handle things rationally and confidently? "I've got to go, Barbara. We'll see you this afternoon."

"Josh, I don't have to tell you how important it is that Daniel be there at five. I've been lenient up until now about him missing home visits. But meeting his father this afternoon is not optional. Daniel has to understand that."

317

"He'll be there."

Josh ended the call and faced the end of his road. No exits remaining. No more detours.

Between now and five o'clock, he either got his nephew to trust in him and the family they could make together, or he stood to lose one more person he'd tried to love but couldn't keep.

"Ms. Loar, I'd like you to join me for dinner tonight," Phillip Hutchinson said from Amy's doorway.

It was a little after nine in the morning, but she and Hutchinson had both been in the office since before six.

"I've arranged to meet Jed Westing at Remingtons," he added, referring to the midtown restaurant currently at the top of every upwardly mobile Atlantan's list of trendy places to be seen. "Sort of a precelebration celebration. Jed's given me his personal assurance that Alex Kramer's ready to sign off on our project tomorrow. Westing's very impressed with your performance these last few months. Told me himself he saw great things in your future."

It was as close to gushing as she'd ever seen Phillip Hutchinson. In his mind, she'd clearly graduated from her associate status

318

already. Add in the offer to accompany him to a business dinner that had less to do with the Kramer project than it did networking for future opportunities, it was as if he'd just announced with a megaphone that she'd arrived in the world of Atlanta corporate business.

She'd made it.

"You must be thrilled," Hutchinson said as he absorbed her shocked silence. "I know it's been a tough few years."

"Yes . . . yes it has." She stood and stepped around her desk. She took his offered hand and shook as expected. "I don't know quite what to say, now that this moment's here."

"We'll see you at the restaurant, then," he said. He paused. "Your daughter's still with your mother in South Carolina, isn't she? And things are settling down with her?"

"Yes." Amy blinked at his unprecedented foray into her personal life. "Becky's in Sweetbrook, and things are fine."

"Good." His smile was relieved. "Then there's no reason for you not to go out and celebrate tonight."

Only there was, she argued silently as he left and she returned to her desk. She didn't feel a bit like celebrating. She had everything she'd thought she and Becky needed, and she should be happy. But she wasn't.

Before, Sweetbrook had been just a place, a lovely place where her daughter would be cared for while Amy worked herself senseless. But Becky had found a home with Gwen. She was thriving, being doted on by a grandmother who loved her. She'd even told Amy when they'd talked last night that she wouldn't mind staying in South Carolina a little longer. For the first time, her daughter hadn't asked to come back to Atlanta. She'd sounded happy right where she was, almost as if she'd consider staying for good.

This pending promotion, Hutchinson's celebratory dinner, marked the beginning of the end of all that. Amy would have to settle Becky into a totally new school routine yet again. Not a helpful situation, according to her research into ADD kids. Becky needed consistency and stability while she came to grips with her disorder.

Instead, she'd be in after-school care every day, instead of taking the bus home to fresh baked cookies and some important downtime with Grandma Gwen. Amy would have to struggle to make sure she was there for regular meetings at school, and the equally important homework time that Gwen was currently covering. All part of Amy's plan from the beginning. All challenges she was sure she and her daughter would find a way to handle. All typical priority struggles for a single, working mom.

Only Amy didn't like the taste of typical anymore.

This brand-new life they were taking on, the life she'd thought they needed so much, came with an enormous price tag. One Amy was no longer certain she and her daughter could afford to pay.

And Becky's move back to Atlanta wasn't just going to be hard on the ten-year-old. Amy could almost feel again the perfection of Josh holding her, kissing her. He'd made her a part of something clean and wholesome again. And there was the unexpected friendship Daniel and Becky were forging, which, too, would fall by the wayside once Amy went home to Sweetbrook for the last time and took Becky away.

"You look a million miles away," Jacquie said from Amy's office door later that morning.

"Only a hundred or so." Amy massaged her temples as she stared at the picture hanging on the wall across from her desk. She should be in the midst of proofing the Kramer proposal — again. She knew Thomas Fuller was, just in case she'd overlooked something he could use to swoop in and save the day at the last minute.

But she couldn't do it. She couldn't play the game right now. Not when her heart was in Sweetbrook, with the people and the place she'd hours ago stopped trying to pretend she didn't crave in her life.

"It's home again, isn't it?" Jacquie sat across the desk. She looked uncomfortable, which wasn't her style. "It's tearing you up not to be back there with Becky."

If Amy massaged her head any harder, she was going to give herself a migraine.

"It's not just Becky, is it?" Jacquie guessed.

Amy's hands returned to the desk with a slap. Her assistant's intuition, until now a very valuable asset, really bit the big one at the moment.

"I'm just saying you've been like this ever since you talked to that Joshua White guy the other day," she explained. "And you're acting like Hutchinson's punishing you because he asked you to dinner with a client. You sold your soul for this promotion. You're allowed to let loose and celebrate for one night."

"I don't feel like celebrating," Amy snapped. "And there's no promotion, at least not yet."

Jacquie raised an eyebrow. "If you're still

not convinced you've got the Kramer CEO on the hook, why aren't you busting it getting ready to wow them at tomorrow's closing?"

The eyebrow remained raised as Jacquie's point sunk in.

"I . . ." Amy swallowed. "I'm not sure if I want to go to dinner tonight."

She wasn't sure if she wanted any of this anymore.

Jacquie carefully inspected her nails, looking for flaws that her once-a-week manicure guaranteed wouldn't be there. "Well." She stood with a careless ease that grated on Amy's frazzled nerves. "Since it's eleven o'clock, and Hutchinson's assistant just called to confirm you were to be added to tonight's reservations, I think now would be a perfect time for you to decide exactly what you *do* want."

Her meaningful stare made Amy squirm.

"Because if you take this mood with you to Remingtons," Jacquie continued, on her way out the door, "you might just blow the whole Kramer deal over cocktails. And then where will you be?"

Amy actually growled as she watched her friend leave, not annoyed so much at Jacquie's meddling as she was at herself. She couldn't really be considering giving up everything she'd worked so hard for here to start over again in Sweetbrook.

Could she?

Would Becky really be happier with the small-town life Amy hadn't thought was good enough until she'd gone back home? Was there really a family waiting for them in Sweetbrook, in the person of a man and a little boy who seemed to need Amy as much as she needed them?

Josh had made her no promises. And even if he had, people fell in and out of relationships all the time. Was she willing to take that kind of chance . . . again?

The thought of trusting in love again, trusting Josh and the feelings he claimed to have for her, stopped Amy cold. She'd be safer in Atlanta, where she had no ties but Becky, and no risk greater than keeping Thomas Fuller from setting his sights on her job. She'd be safe here, miles away from what loving and then losing Josh would do to her.

Which brought her back full circle to Josh's question. She'd explained that she couldn't commit to anything more, because the solitary life she'd planned for herself in Atlanta was more important — for her daughter's sake. He'd all but called her a

coward, and she'd told him he didn't understand.

*Whose security are we talking about . . .
Becky's or yours?*

CHAPTER EIGHTEEN

"I don't want to see him." Daniel said quietly as Josh sat with him in the kitchen after school.

"I've tried everything I can to postpone this," Josh explained. "But there's nothing more I can do, except help get you ready to see your dad this afternoon."

The boy shook his head in silence.

Josh would have preferred a good old-fashioned temper tantrum. He laid a hand on his nephew's knee, hoping the physical contact wasn't a mistake. He'd broken the news as soon as they'd gotten home from school, and in a way he was relieved that Dr. Rhodes hadn't been able to fit them in again today. The man was right. This was all up to Josh.

What he and his nephew had to do right now, no one could help them with. A memory of Amy's smiling face challenged the notion, but Amy couldn't be here for them this time.

"This is your home, Daniel," he said, grasping for the right words. "Ms. Thomas offered to have us meet your dad at her office in town, but I wanted you to feel as safe as possible. So he's coming here. We're going to show him that this is where you belong. We're going to get through this together, son."

Son.

Daniel's head snapped up, tears misting his eyes. Josh had no idea where the word had come from, and even less of an idea why it had taken him so long to say it.

"That's right," he said. "You're my son now. You don't belong to that man anymore. Your mother asked me to take care of you for the rest of your life, and that's what I'm going to do. You've got to find a way to believe that, Daniel, before your dad gets here. If you never trust anyone else in this world . . ." Josh's own eyes watered. His chest tightened. He longed for a real place in Daniel's life. A father's place. ". . . you've got to find a way to trust me."

Daniel slid his leg away from Josh's touch. "I don't want to see him," he said. "You can't make me see him."

"Unless we can give Ms. Thomas and the judge a reason for not letting your father near you, we don't have a choice." Josh curbed the urge to lean closer, wary of his nephew's unraveling nerves. "I don't want that man in our home, either."

"This isn't *our* home," Daniel retorted, the quivering of his bottom lip demanding that Josh tell him he was wrong. "It's not *my* home."

"But it could be," Josh pressed, desperate to make Daniel understand. "We can make this your home. And we can make sure your dad never has a place in your life again."

Daniel shot to his feet, his chair bumping into the wall.

"He . . . I . . ." Looking anywhere but at Josh, the boy grew silent, the building storm within evident in the way he squeezed his eyes shut and balled his fists. "When he got mad at me or my mom, he . . ."

Folding his hands together, Josh waited. The psychologist had said when this moment came, it would be an explosion.

The boy's sprint from the kitchen shouldn't have caught Josh by surprise, but it did.

"Daniel!" He bounded after his nephew, his pursuit no doubt terrifying the kid even more. "Daniel, don't —"

His nephew was already at the front of the house by the time Josh skidded into the hallway. The boy threw open the door, cast a defeated glance over his shoulder and stumbled outside.

Josh stopped short, his adrenaline-spiked heartbeat freezing at the sight of Daniel barreling straight into Amy Loar's outstretched arms.

Amy knelt and held the struggling little boy close, her eyes locked on Josh's shocked, hopeful expression as the man's long strides obliterated the distance between them.

"Shh . . ." she soothed, rubbing circles down Daniel's back while he kept up a halfhearted attempt to escape her grasp. "It's going to be okay."

Josh's hand came to rest on his nephew's shoulder, the touch instinctive and proprietary. A parent's touch. And at that moment she knew without a doubt that things were going to be okay for Josh and Daniel.

"You're here?" Josh said in a dazed voice. "But what about your work, your presentation?"

"I delegated the rest of the prep stuff to a colleague. I'll head back tomorrow for the presentation with Kramer Industries, but I couldn't just sit in Atlanta tonight. Not while you're dealing with all of this alone."

Not when her heart belonged here with

them, she stopped herself from staying.

She'd most likely ended her shot at a promotion by passing on Hutchinson's dinner with Westing and ditching the last of her Kramer work on Thomas, but she couldn't worry about that. Other things were far more important to her now, such as the child she held in her arms and the one waiting for her at Gwen's. And the man looking at her with so much love and adoration, she'd be content never to move from this spot.

If only she could be sure it could last. That she could find happiness here. Real happiness. The kind that didn't dissolve as soon as she started to trust it.

"What happened?" She placed her palms on Daniel's wet cheeks and raised his head until she could see his face. "Are you okay?"

"No." In a motion that shocked her and broke her heart at the same time, Daniel buried his head against her chest and held on for dear life.

"My dad —" he choked out over a sob "— My dad . . . hit my mom and made her . . . made her cry. Then he'd laugh. . . ." More sobs escaped. Daniel was shaking from head to toe. "And then I'd run and hide . . . but he'd come after me, anyway. And when he found me . . ."

Daniel's weight dropped fully onto Amy as she cradled him against her. All she herself had endured replayed in her mind as she held him. She'd barely survived her own taste of hell on earth, and it had messed her up to the point that she might never be able to trust in love again. How on earth did she help a child work through something so terrible?

Suddenly Josh was there beside her, holding her as she and his nephew clung to each other. And the healing warmth of his touch was exactly what both she and Daniel needed.

"It's okay," he murmured into her hair. Then he kissed her temple. Palming his nephew's head, he released a sigh.

"It's going to be okay now."

"May I speak with Ms. Thomas?" Amy asked the receptionist at Family Services, keeping her voice low as she used the Whites' kitchen phone.

Josh and Daniel were still in the little boy's room, curled around each other, Josh on the floor, Daniel huddled in his lap. Both were spent, both drained of the tears they hadn't been able to hold in. Now that they'd let themselves hold each other, both of them looked as if they might never let go.

Daniel's memories had trickled out slowly at first, each more horrifying than the last. Then the images of ugliness and darkness that had held him hostage for years began retching up in an escalating flood that had been as cathartic for him to admit as it was excruciating for her and Josh to hear.

"Call Barbara," was all Josh had managed to say, his eyes flashing rage at what his nephew had been through. "Try to get Jenkins's visitation postponed."

"This is Barbara Thomas," said a semifamiliar voice on the other end of the line. "May I help you?"

"Yes." Amy clung to her tattered wits. "Ms. Thomas, this is Amy Loar. I'm a friend of Josh and Daniel White."

"Yes, Ms. Loar," the other woman said with slow recognition. "We met at Mr. White's home, a few weeks ago, wasn't it?"

"Yes. Well . . ." Amy swallowed her mortification at the scene she'd caused that day. "I'm at the White home now, and Josh asked me to give you a call —"

"Is there a problem?" There was a brief pause. "I'm meeting the boy's father there for a visit in a little over an hour."

"That's why I'm calling. Daniel's had a breakthrough that Josh is hoping will change the judge's decision about visitation."

"What kind of breakthrough? Is Daniel finally talking about his father?"

"Yes, and it . . . it was terrible." The queasiness in Amy's stomach flared. "And I'm sure if you and the judge could hear just part of it —"

"You don't have to convince me, Ms. Loar. I've been on Daniel and Josh's side from the start. But Judge Hardy is going to need to see the boy himself."

"Please, can't we do that tomorrow? Daniel's so upset." Amy couldn't imagine making him go through everything a second time in front of a stranger. "I'm not sure how much more he can take today. Can't you speak to the judge for us?"

"I understand," Ms. Thomas assured her in a voice that didn't sound encouraging. "But there's no other way. Jenkins's lawyer has the judge convinced that Josh is coaching Daniel to say things that will interfere with his father's custody petition. The sooner we get Daniel in to see the judge, the better. How quickly can you have them here?"

"I . . . I don't know. I'll have to check with Josh."

"Tell him he's got an hour." Ms. Thomas forged onward. "I'm calling Mr. Jenkins's lawyer and asking for an emergency hearing in the judge's chambers. Whatever you have to do, get Josh and Daniel in a car and get them over here."

"I'll . . . I'll do the best I can." Amy had never felt more powerless.

"Do whatever you have to, Ms. Loar. You seem like a good friend, and I'm not sure the Whites will be able to do this on their own. That family needs you now."

Family. Josh's family. The family he'd said he might want to share with her. A family for her and Becky, as well as for Daniel. And they needed her.

A familiar urge tingled through her, the compulsion to run from the temptation to belong to something that real again. But equally as strong was the determination not to fail Daniel and Josh. Or her daughter. The determination to fight. Not because she was afraid of the past this time, but because maybe, just maybe, she was finally ready to fight for the future.

"We'll be there within the hour," she said, punching the phone's off button.

CHAPTER NINETEEN

"I have a right to be in there," Curtis Jenkins bellowed as he paced up and down the hall outside Judge Hardy's chambers.

"Keep it down." The man's lawyer looked as if he was trying not to do some yelling himself. His client was being an absolute jerk.

Amy was trying not to look at them. Her nerves couldn't take much more of being so close to the abusive man who'd done those horrible things to Daniel and Melanie.

By the time she had driven Josh and a disturbingly quiet Daniel to the courthouse, Jenkins and his lawyer were there waiting, ready to pounce. Jenkins's blustering, his demands to talk with his son, had started the moment they'd stepped off the second-floor elevator.

Josh had hustled Daniel toward the judge's door, too preoccupied with protecting his cowering nephew to respond. Jenkins had, of course, followed them into the office, making a scene out of defending himself against charges he was supposed to be innocent of.

Thankfully, Ms. Thomas had assessed the situation and immediately recommended that, for Daniel's sake, he be allowed to talk with the judge with only his uncle present. So there they were, Amy and Daniel's social worker sitting side by side on the straight-backed bench outside the judge's door, enduring Curtis Jenkins's antics as it became clearer by the minute he was about to lose any chance of permanent custody of his son.

And each minute that went by hammered away at Amy's resolve to stick this out and fight for the life she and Josh and their kids could have together. Every ugly word that Jenkins muttered, each a bit louder than the last, reminded her of why she'd been so determined to be alone. Of the excruciating pain she'd endured when she'd been naive enough to give Richard Reese her heart and her future, only to watch him rip them to shreds.

"If you don't keep it down, man," the lawyer warned again, "you're going to finish ruining what's left of your chance here."

"What chance?" Jenkins stomped over to

Amy, who shrank away, despite her best efforts not to show her fear.

Familiar territory. Too familiar.

Had she really thought the past was gone, just because Josh said he loved her? Just because she wanted the ridiculously happy life together he'd tempted her with?

"You've got your little finger in this, don't you, honey?" Jenkins asked, leaning closer. "You've found a man with money. Are you enjoying taking my boy away from me, you little —"

"Step away, Mr. Jenkins." Barbara stood, all five feet of her, and stared the man down. "If you don't, I'll have an officer physically remove you from the building."

The man sneered, looking more the bully than ever as he edged closer to the diminutive woman who'd dared to point a finger in his face.

"Nobody shows me the door, you hear me?" He moved to raise a hand in the air, but it was suddenly yanked behind his back by a guard, who'd appeared from nowhere.

"Get your hands off me!" Jenkins's struggles increased as the burly cop locked the man's wrists behind his back. "I haven't done anything. You've got no right."

"Take him downstairs, if he insists on staying until the judge makes a decision," Barbara instructed. "If he continues to be abusive and refuses to leave the building, find something to charge him with until I'm done here."

"Sure thing, ma'am." The officer turned the still-cursing man away and half dragged him down the hall.

"You're on your own, man," the lawyer said as Jenkins and the officer passed. "You're nuts."

"Are you okay?" Barbara sat beside Amy again and placed a hand on her shoulder.

Amy flinched, horrified by her rudeness and, worst of all, by her inability to pull herself together.

Curtis Jenkins hadn't hurt her. He hadn't even come close to hurting her, thanks to Barbara. But that didn't stop Amy from feeling attacked. Violated. Threatened. Lost to the memories of another angry man blaming her for things beyond her control, yelling at her and telling her she was worth nothing and never would be.

She pressed her hands to her ears, but the voices wouldn't stop. She should be over Richard. Over all she'd lost and how weak she'd been. But it wasn't over. It would never be. Jenkins's taunts, joined now by Richard's, grew louder in her head until they drowned out everything else, including

Josh's declaration of love and his dream of a new beginning for their families.

But it was her own little voice that chanted loudest, reminding her that she'd never have the courage to believe in that kind of life with him.

Struggling to her feet, she headed for the elevator. She couldn't be here anymore. Not in the courthouse with Curtis Jenkins. Not in Sweetbrook with Josh.

"Where are you going?" Barbara asked. "Josh and Daniel will be out any minute."

Amy forced herself to keep walking.

She had to try three times to press the elevator button before the light came on. She owed Ms. Thomas an explanation. Only there was none. All she could do was run.

"You're a very brave young man," Judge Hardy said. "Not many kids your age would be able to talk about these things with me."

Josh had watched the man's frown deepen throughout the interview. First as they'd listened to Curtis Jenkins's explosion in the hallway. Then even more as Daniel had hesitantly repeated everything he'd already shared with Josh. The judge's sympathetic anger would have relieved Josh, were it not for the toll the situation must be taking on his nephew. And Amy. He hated having to leave her in the hallway to deal with Jenkins. He hated having to leave her at all.

She had come back. For Daniel, and maybe for him. Josh wasn't certain, but once he and his nephew got out of here, he was going to find out. And if she still wasn't convinced they had a future together, he'd find some way to get through to her. This time, she wasn't going back to Atlanta thinking he and Daniel didn't really need her, or that she could live the rest of her life without letting herself need them.

He squeezed his nephew's knee. Daniel had talked himself into silence several minutes ago. Nothing else to say.

How could there be?

He'd been terrorized. Bullied and threatened, and punished for things that couldn't possibly have been his fault. Or Josh's sister's, for that matter. And he'd witnessed his mother being beaten by the man who was supposed to have loved them both.

"Tell me you've heard enough," Josh demanded of the judge.

If Judge Hardy minded the anger amplifying Josh's words, he didn't show it. Instead, he directed a smile of encouragement at Daniel.

"Well, Daniel. It's obvious how much your uncle wants you to stay with him. And if that hubbub in the hall was any indication, your dad seems to want you back, for what reason I'm not exactly sure."

"Money," Josh replied. "He wants Daniel, because he knows I'll make sure my nephew has everything he needs for the rest of his life, whether he stays with me or not. And to Curtis Jenkins, that means money."

"Well, that certainly adds a wrinkle to things." The judge nodded to Josh, then returned his attention to the ten-year-old. "But you see, Daniel, none of that really matters to me right now. Because with everything I've heard, you still haven't told me the most important thing I need to know."

The man's eyes twinkled at the child. He was the personification of acceptance and warmth.

"What?" Daniel finally asked.

"I understand what your uncle and your father want. Now I need to hear what *you* want."

"What?" Daniel repeated.

"What do you want, young man? Where do you want your family to be? Where do you feel like you belong?"

Josh watched his nephew swallow the word *family*, and braced himself for the fallout. The kid had been pushed too far today. Too much had been unearthed from his past. It wasn't a good time to ask for the impossible, like Daniel believing in the concept of family again after all he'd been through.

"I . . ." Daniel sat straighter in his chair and slid his knee away from Josh's touch. "I don't know."

"Are you sure?" The judge folded his hands together. "Because it's very important to me to understand what you think about all this."

Daniel blinked and glanced sideways toward Josh.

"I want . . ." he stuttered. "I want . . ."

Josh held his breath.

For Daniel, admitting he wanted anything must seem like an open invitation for more pain. Watching Amy's losing battle with her own insecurities had taught Josh that, if nothing else.

"It's okay," he said, knowing it would never be okay again if he lost this little boy. "You don't have to want anything right now."

"I want to belong . . ." Daniel crossed his arms and stared at his sneakers. "I don't know . . . I guess I want to belong in Sweetbrook."

Judge Hardy smiled. "Mr. White, how

does that sound to you?" he asked, keeping his focus on Daniel.

Josh couldn't speak. He was certain his jaw was hanging somewhere in the vicinity of his knees. He scooted to the edge of his chair, as close as he could get to his nephew.

"Are you sure, son?"

"I . . ." Daniel's chin wobbled. His mother's chin used to do that when she was upset. "I want to stay with you, Uncle Josh."

Uncle Josh.

Daniel had called him "Uncle Josh."

Instincts drove care and reason from Josh's mind as he scooped Daniel into his arms and held on as if he'd never let the kid go.

"I want you, too, son." He sobbed when two little arms wound themselves around his neck. "I want you, too."

Amy sat in the tree house, her business suit rumpled about her, trying to pull herself together before she ventured home to face her mother and Becky. Or was she saying goodbye to this peaceful place and the memories that filled it?

It was close to seven, and dusk was threatening, but the waning sunlight hit the openings in the wooden slats around her at just the right angle to keep the inside of the tree house illuminated. One particular beam of gold slanted across the tiny space, spotlighting the names she and Josh had carved in the wall as kids.

"Mom?" Becky's voice found its way into the tree house from somewhere below. "Mom, are you up there?"

"You guys wait here." Josh's voice reached her ears, then the sound of him climbing the tree.

She didn't want to see him, not now as she faced the reality of all she wanted but wasn't strong enough to reach for.

This morning, she'd let herself believe there was a chance she could make love and family work with him. That she could find comfort and a new beginning in coming home each night to a partner, someone she could trust with her whole heart. Yet here she was, still running. And she wasn't sure she'd ever be able to stop.

Josh might be kind and loyal, but he'd never be happy with half of her heart. And that's all she'd be able to give him. He'd already been burned by someone who couldn't trust and believe in the things he believed in, and she wasn't going to let herself hurt him that way, too. If she was too weak to believe in things like lasting love and commitment, then at least she could be strong enough to end this now, rather than causing him more pain down the road.

"Amy?" Josh squeezed through the kid-size door and then knelt beside her.

The lightness in his eyes, the tilt of his mouth gave her hope that things had gone well with the judge. Then his expression wrinkled into a frown.

"Barbara told me what happened with Curtis. I'm so sorry I left you to deal with him alone. I never meant for you to be frightened like that."

The perfect smell of him tempted her to lean closer until he had no choice but to hold her. Instead, she wiped at her smudged makeup and sat as tall as she could.

"No, I'm fine," she assured him. "Barbara took care of everything. I just couldn't . . . I needed to . . ."

"You needed to climb a tree?" he teased, but even he couldn't make her smile right now.

"The judge upheld my custody of Daniel." Josh took her hand and squeezed. "All that's left is the formality of a hearing. And Barbara's filing a restraining order against Jenkins, that he's not to come within a hundred feet of Daniel again. The last the court officer saw of him, he was peeling out of the parking lot, saying sticking around this hick town wasn't worth the money."

"I'm so glad, Josh." Amy squeezed back, then made herself let go. "You and Daniel deserve to be happy."

His smile slipped. "Just Daniel and me? What about you? Don't you deserve to be happy?"

"Josh . . ."

"What are you doing up here alone and crying? We won. Daniel's free, and I couldn't have done it without you. The kids are waiting down on the ground. I told Daniel we'd go out for pizza to celebrate, and he actually smiled. But when I got to your mom's to pick up you and Becky, you hadn't made it home yet. I drove over here on a hunch, but for the life of me I don't understand why you'd want to be up here alone at a time like this."

"Maybe I like being alone," she snapped.

"If you wanted to be alone so badly, why did you come back today?"

"Because . . ."

Because I couldn't stay away.

"Because there's something you need here, that's why," he finished for her. "Don't bother to deny it. I saw your face when you were holding Daniel at the house. You belong here, Amy. You belong with us."

She stood in a rush and bumped her head

on the roof. Stooped over, she faced off against Josh.

"Do you need a new project to work on now that Daniel's problems are solved? Is that it? I'm messed up, so you're going to fix me, too — just like you did your nephew? Well, news flash, Principal White — I'm not fixable."

"Amy, where is this coming from?" He tugged on her arm until she settled back onto the floor. "I don't think you're messed up. I'm not trying to fix anything. I —"

"Well, I am messed up. I'm broken, Josh. And I can't do this. You and me and Becky and Daniel, making a family together. It's a nice dream, but I can't do it. It would never work between us, so back off."

"Do you love me?"

"It doesn't matter."

"It matters a lot. What you think, what you want, that's all that matters to me. If you're saying that you don't love me —"

The fierceness in his words, the insecurity in his eyes, drew her in.

"Of course I love you, Josh." She folded her legs under her and fought for the right words. "And Daniel, too. I don't know how I'm going to leave and never see him again."

"Then don't leave. Stay and we'll work this out."

"Josh —"

"I know you've been hurt, Amy. And you're scared. You have every reason to be, but we can work through that. I'm not asking you to give up anything. Not even your career or your life in Atlanta."

"Oh, so now you're going to move to a city the size of Atlanta and be happy without all this?" She waved her arms to encompass the jewel-like textures the dusky sunset was painting on the walls around them.

"You did," he said. "You've been gone for years. When you came back, I thought maybe there was something in Sweetbrook good enough to keep you here. But if you have to live somewhere else to be happy, then Amy, I'm going with you. I'm done losing the people I love. I don't care what I have to give up."

"Josh, listen to me. I can't be part of the kind of relationship you're looking for. I thought I could finally be free of my mistakes with Richard, but it's not working. Everything still scares me. Becky's and my new life in Atlanta. The thought of all of us together and everything that could go wrong . . . It all terrifies me. And you deserve better than that. You deserve a woman whose past doesn't destroy everything she touches."

"What if what I deserve is you?"

She sighed, her heart breaking for him. "You need to find someone else, Josh."

"Not going to happen." He leaned in and feathered a kiss across her lips, his taste filling her senses even as he moved away.

"Josh." She had to stop him. "You make me want things I don't think I'll ever feel safe enough to believe in. Happy families. Sharing my dreams with someone and trusting him not to use them against me one day when things start not working."

"Then we'll figure out how to make you feel safe, Amy. Together. You can't keep pulling away from me forever, and I'm sure not going to let you off the hook this easily."

"Easy? You think this is easy?"

"No, I think it's harder than I could possibly imagine." His expression softened. "Today I watched a ten-year-old boy be more of a man than I've ever been. This kid, who hasn't let me near him since his mother died, found a way to open up and accept that he wanted to try again. He told the judge he wants to be with me. He called me *Uncle Josh.* He . . . he let me hold him today, Amy. Can you believe that?"

"Yes." Smiling at the new beginning he and Daniel had been given, she caressed his cheek. "You're going to make a wonderful father, Joshua White."

"And I'll make just as good a husband this time around, Ms. Loar." He trapped her hand against his face, then planted a kiss on her palm. "If Daniel's willing to give me a shot, how can you say no?"

She tried to pull away, but he held firm.

"Josh, you don't know what you're saying. You're just feeling grateful for my help with Daniel, or you're feeling sorry for me, or you're wrapped up in the moment. Either way, I don't want to be there one day a month from now, or a year from now, when you wake up and realize that marriage to someone as messed up as me isn't worth it. I can't go through that again. Not with you."

"Amy, because of you, because of what's inside that heart you think is so messed up, I have a chance with Daniel. For that alone, I'd follow you up a thousand trees, or to Atlanta, or across the earth, if that's what it takes to keep you. But that's not why I'm here."

"It — it's not?"

"No, it's not. I love you, and I'm done letting people I love slip away. We've been good for each other since we were children. I've never met a better match for me than you, even when you were calling me a butthead and trying to get me to do your homework for you."

His smile turned her heart over, then his impossibly blue eyes filled with tears.

"I didn't think there was any place in my life for love, either," he said. "After Lisa left me, I figured I was better off alone. Better off not wanting to feel anything, because that way it wouldn't hurt anymore. But you and Daniel came into my life, and you changed all that. And I want *you,* just as much as I want him, Amy. I want you shaking up my life for as long as I'm on this earth. I want to raise our kids together. I'll be lucky if I can learn to be half the parent you are. And I want all that fearlessness and fire inside of you for my very own. I can't live without you, Amy Loar. You're everything I need. Everything I'll never find again if you go away. Let me love you. Please, help me sweep away all the messes we've made and build something new."

"I . . . I don't know how to believe you." Amy shook her head. "I tried. But I don't know how to believe in any of this."

"Then I'll believe for you, how about that?"

Her breath caught on the familiar words. Words she'd used to encourage him not to give up on Daniel. And now Josh was asking her not to give up on him.

She felt the still-closed-off place inside her begin to crack open, just a tiny bit.

"And we . . ." Oh, how much she loved using that word. "We'd do this how?"

"One day at a time, sweetheart." Josh's earnest expression radiated the kind of love her dreams were made of. "Just like you told me to work things out with Daniel, we'll take it one day at a time."

The fact that Daniel was finally with his uncle for good was nothing short of a miracle, considering all the child and Josh had been through. It had seemed so hopeless not too long ago. Just as hopeless as making a happy family with Josh seemed for her now.

You're everything I need.

Everything.

Could she really believe in everything? The closest she'd come to it had been when Josh kissed her. Or cuddling Becky close at Gwen's. Or holding Daniel this morning as he'd cried away his fear.

Not when she was at work. Not when she'd shaken Hutchinson's hand. Not even when she'd all but closed the Kramer deal, and with it had won her promotion and her independence from Richard. None of that had come close to the rightness of coming back home to Sweetbrook, to the people she couldn't bear to be apart from.

She shivered deep inside, as the lonely place that had once protected her finally let go, freeing her of the doubt and the fear she'd clung to for so long.

She launched herself into Josh's waiting arms and held tight to her very own miracle.

"I love you, too," she said, still scared, but believing a little bit more by the second. Her breath mingled with his for another kiss. "I really do."

And somehow, as Josh tenderly pressed her head to the shoulder that had always been there for her, for the first time in a long time love felt safe.

From almost out of earshot came the sound of the kids playing below, near the pond Josh and Amy had fished in as children. Birds chirped on every side of them, and the wind played tag with the leaves of the ancient tree that housed the secret hideaway that had first been hers and Josh's, then had later comforted Daniel when he had nowhere else to turn.

And as Amy listened to the sounds of her home and hugged the man she loved closer, she realized that finally, after all this time, she was exactly where she belonged.

EPILOGUE

Amy flicked the remote to turn down her iPod in her home office so she could answer the phone. A quick glance at the clock told her she had fifteen minutes before the bus dropped the kids off from school. She picked up the receiver as she shut her computer down, straightening as she always did at the end of the day, when she took off her small-business owner's hat and turned back into her equally favorite role — that of mother and wife.

"Hello," she said, tucking the phone between her shoulder and ear so she could pack the contract she'd printed into an express envelope headed for her client in Raleigh, North Carolina.

"Ms. Loar . . . I mean, Mrs. White," said a voice from her not-so-distant past.

"Mr. Hutchinson." She sealed the postal envelope, her gaze skipping to the wedding photo of her and Josh that she kept beside her monitor. "What a surprise."

"I've heard good things about your new business venture in South Carolina," her former boss said.

Yet another surprise, that Hutchinson had been following her career since she'd left Enterprise Consulting at all.

She'd resigned six months ago, right after Hutchinson formally offered her the manager position she'd coveted. The Kramer Industries deal had closed without a hitch, despite her last-minute dash to Sweetbrook to help Daniel.

Doing it all on her own was no longer her goal, she'd found herself a new one. One where she would work for herself, but wouldn't be in it alone. Where she could be committed to the career she enjoyed, but happily entrenched in the family life she loved, as well. Her job would still be a priority, but never again would she let work become a day-in, day-out fight for survival.

All because Josh had found a way through her hurt and fear as he continued to show her what it was like to feel truly cherished by the man she loved.

And so it was that she'd found herself six months ago thanking a stunned Phillip Hutchinson for his confidence in her, then telling him she couldn't accept the promotion. And with a copy of her client database on a flash drive, she'd hugged a tearful Jacquie goodbye and had left her life in Atlanta behind.

"I have several steady clients," she was pleased to report to her former senior partner. "And my twelve-month business plan is on track."

"Do you think you have time for one more project?" Hutchinson asked.

"I'm sorry?" Amy stopped fiddling with the express packet. "I didn't quite hear you."

"I was asking if you had any time in your schedule to handle a job for Enterprise?"

She should be saying something. Something professional. But she couldn't, for fear that the only sound she could emit at the moment was a victory cry. Hutchinson had been less than supportive of her career change. He'd come right out and predicted she'd fail, sounding too much at that moment like her ex-husband. And now he was offering her business?

"I don't think that's going to be possible, Phillip," she responded, not even batting an eye before using his first name. "I have a very busy schedule right now, and I'm paying careful attention to how I balance my work hours with my family time."

"Yes, I imagined you would." The man

knew she was a newlywed. He'd sent her and Josh a wedding gift. "But I thought this one project might tempt you, and we could really use your help."

He needed her help?

"Ah." It dawned on her finally what they were talking about. "The Kramer project must be in a bind. What, did Thomas get in over his head?"

Jacquie kept her updated on Enterprise office gossip, particularly on how Thomas was trying to fill Amy's shoes since she left.

"No, actually . . ." Hutchinson cleared his throat. "He's taken a job with a firm out of New York. And all my other project managers are tied up with their own clients. I need a point person to work with Jed Westing on the implementation, and . . . well, you did such a fine job for us bringing Kramer Industries on board. I thought perhaps —"

"I'm going to have think about it," she said. It shouldn't have felt so satisfying to finally be in a position to make the man wait. "Why don't I give you a call on Monday?"

"All right," Hutchinson agreed. "Monday, then."

He didn't seem at all pleased at being put off, but it didn't sound as if he had much of a choice, either. Thomas's departure must have really left them in a pinch.

She and Hutchinson said their goodbyes, and Amy thoughtfully hung up the phone.

Something rankled at the idea of going back to do freelance work with Enterprise, after the way Hutchinson had dismissed her when she'd resigned. But she couldn't help but feel a professional responsibility toward the people she'd worked with at Kramer Industries. She'd talk with Josh and get his input before making a final decision. His support and insight had been hers for the asking every day of the last six months. It was second nature now to turn to him for his opinion, something she'd never have dared to do with Richard.

And thanks to her husband's help, she was having so much fun with her new company it should be against the law, considering that she did most of her work via phone and email. Of course, she made the occasional overnight trip to meet with a client in person, with Josh staying behind in Sweetbrook keeping their family running smoothly until she could hurry back to them.

Their family.

Becky and Daniel were thriving, though they still managed to get on each other's nerves without trying very hard. Just like a real brother and sister, which they would legally become in a few months when Josh and Amy's petitions for adoption were formally granted.

And her and Josh's love for each other grew stronger with each passing day, just as he'd promised. They had married four weeks after she'd moved back to Sweetbrook for good. In a private ceremony here at the White mansion. With just Gwen and a few close friends present, they'd pledged their love and their lives to one another. Becky had been Amy's maid of honor, and Daniel Josh's best man, completing the circle of family they were creating.

The sound of a school bus stopping outside pulled Amy from her memories. She usually met the kids at the bottom of the long driveway that stretched from the house to the street. Today, she was only halfway down when they came bounding toward her at a sprint.

"Mom," Becky called. "It's the coolest thing."

"We're studying Washington, D.C., in class," Daniel chimed in. "And when Mrs. Lathem started talking about the different monuments, she asked Becky and me about our trip this summer."

Once school had let out in June, Amy, Josh

and the kids had taken their first family vacation. Piling into the Range Rover, they'd driven up the coast to D.C., Philadelphia and New York. They'd stopped at every tourist site along the way, some of them even educational, at Josh's insistence. It had been a blast. But no matter how much fun they'd had, they each had been thrilled to return to Sweetbrook. Amy most of all.

Now, both kids were beaming in excitement about their latest school project. Josh had made sure they were placed in the same class again when school started up in September. They'd supported each other through so many rough times, it didn't seem right to separate them now that things were starting to settle down.

Becky's ADD was a daily challenge still, but she was making great strides. Daniel still fell into bouts of melancholy after all he'd endured, but he continued to meet with Dr. Rhodes twice a month. And Becky seemed to be the one most capable of helping him. She always found a way to tease Daniel, until he was too annoyed to be quite so moody anymore.

"Mrs. Lathem said we could bring whatever souvenirs we wanted to class, to show the rest of the kids," Becky said.

"That's great, you guys." Amy wrapped

an arm around their shoulders as they headed for the house. "Why don't you go look through the pile of things we brought back? Daniel, didn't you end up buying that fake replica of George Washington's wooden teeth?"

"Cool!" Daniel shouted as he sprinted away.

"Ew!" Becky said, trailing after him. "Boys are so gross."

Amy chuckled as she entered the house she'd been only a guest in for most of her life. She closed the front door and shut out the world beyond, and a sense of belonging filled her. This was her home now, hers and her husband's. Where she and Josh would raise their kids and one day baby-sit their grandchildren.

She retraced her steps to the office Josh had had custom-built for her, and lovingly caressed the mahogany desk he'd insisted she should have, even though it cost more than she would ever have spent on office furniture herself. He loved spoiling her, he'd said. To which she'd assured him that all the spoiling she'd ever need was waking up next to him each morning.

Gazing again at their smiling faces in the picture from their wedding, awed by the host of blessings filling her life, and the fact that she was finally starting to believe they were for real, Amy picked up the phone and dialed her husband's cell number.

"Hey, baby," he said warmly. "I'm just packing up to head home."

Home.

That's what this amazing man and their kids would always be for Amy. The home she'd been gifted with, just when she was convinced happiness was something she didn't dare reach for again. Her life was so full of love these days, she found herself fighting back tears at the oddest moments. Like now.

"Amy, you okay?" Josh asked, all teasing gone from his voice.

"I am now."

He'd been so patient as she worked through her memories of the past that had brought her to him. She liked to think of her first marriage that way now — because if it hadn't been for her desperation to be rid of Richard and to find help for Becky, she might never have returned to Sweetbrook and been reunited with her best friend.

"How was your day?" her husband asked. "Make enough money so I can retire and let you support me in the way in which I'd like to become accustomed?"

She laughed at their running joke. He'd encouraged her to keep working, if that's what she wanted to do. They'd talked for hours about how she could mesh the career she still wanted with her equally strong desire to be the wife and mother her husband and kids needed. Josh had wanted whatever she wanted, as always, as long as it made her happy. As long as they were together.

"As a matter of fact," she said, "I just received a very interesting call from a potentially lucrative client. You're never going to guess who it was."

And as her superlogical husband launched into deducing who she'd spoken with, Amy closed her eyes and lost herself in the sound of his voice. The sound of her future.

They were all due at her mother's later for dinner, something they did every Friday night now. Then an entire Sweetbrook weekend stretched ahead of them. And while Amy had some work she needed to get done before Monday, she'd be fitting it in around her family over the next few days, rather than the other way around.

And that had been Josh's greatest gift to her. He'd helped her believe that she really could follow her dreams, both the ones for their family and those for her career. Because she knew now without a doubt, no matter what happened, that he'd be there every step of the way. Dreaming with her. Loving her and their kids. And working through life, one day at a time, right alongside her.

ABOUT THE AUTHOR

Bestselling, award-winning author **Anna DeStefano** has volunteered in the fields of grief recovery and crisis care. Over the years, she felt privileged to walk alongside parents and children struggling to rebuild their lives after their family had come undone. She was inspired by the courageous single parents that she met, whose lives were filled with private battles, daily failures and victories that the outside world rarely saw. And yet they kept fighting, conquering one day at a time until they made a new life for themselves and the children they cherished. She hopes that with the characters in *A Sweetbrook Family,* she has done justice to the real single mothers and fathers out there who are fighting daily for the special kids in their lives.

For exciting news about her other titles and her paranormal romance suspense series, visit Anna at www.annawrites.com.